SHRAPNEL

ISSUE #1   **THE OFFICIAL BATTLETECH MAGAZINE**

SHR△PNEL

THE OFFICIAL BATTLETECH MAGAZINE

Loren L. Coleman, Publisher
John Helfers, Executive Editor
Philip A. Lee, Managing Editor
David A. Kerber, Layout and Graphic Design

Cover art by Ken Coleman
Interior art by David Kerber, Victor Moreno, Matt Plog, Tan Ho Sim, Franz Vohwinkel

Published by Pulse Publishing, under licensing by Catalyst Game Labs
7108 S. Pheasant Ridge Drive
Spokane, WA 99224

Shrapnel: The Official BattleTech Magazine is published four times a year, in Spring, Summer, Fall, and Winter.

Available through your favorite online store (Amazon.com, BN.com, Kobo, iBooks, GooglePlay, etc.).

ISBN: 978-1-947335-20-2

COMMANDER'S CALL
FROM THE EDITOR'S DESK

Attention, soldiers! Welcome to the inaugural issue of *Shrapnel*: The Official *BattleTech* Magazine! It's been a long journey to get here, but we hope the wait has been worthwhile.

Fiction set in the *BattleTech* universe has been a longstanding tradition of the line. I've lost count of how many times someone has said they first discovered *BattleTech* via the tabletop game but got hooked by the stories. Or, as many have said: "Come for the game, but stay for the fiction." And here at *Shrapnel*, story, much like the BattleMech on 31st-century battlefields, is king.

Short fiction in particular has an enduring legacy in *BattleTech*, especially when it comes to magazines and newsletters. The earliest magazine to feature short stories set in this vast, war-torn universe was *BattleTechnology*, which published its first issue in 1987 and was stewarded for most of its run by William H. Keith, author of the beloved Gray Death Legion trilogy (*Decision at Thunder Rift*, *Mercenary's Star*, and *The Price of Glory*). Within those pages, readers found short stories, articles, and game content chronicling the battles and intrigues in the Inner Sphere. Although *BattleTechnology* ended publication in 1995 after twenty-one issues, it set the standard for *BattleTech* short fiction, and is still held in high esteem by longtime fans.

Short stories also appeared in *Mech Magazine*, the quarterly newsletter of MechForce North America, an official *BattleTech* fan organization. This publication ran from 1990 to 1995, when it was renamed *MechForce Quarterly*, and its last issue published in 1999. Then in 2003, *Commando Quarterly* debuted, a digital magazine from the *BattleTech* demo team, which offered game-related articles and the occasional short story until it ceased publication in 2006.

However, in 2004, BattleCorps appeared, offering brand-new short fiction via a monthly digital-subscription service. Helmed by veteran *BattleTech* novelist Loren L. Coleman and later by prolific BattleCorps author Jason Schmetzer, it not only saw new stories by established *BattleTech* authors, it introduced fans to many new authors (some of whom appear in this first issue of *Shrapnel*). BattleCorps was the longest running venue for short *BattleTech* fiction; however, it shuttered at the end of 2016 due to unforeseen circumstances, and its closure left a noticeable void.

This is where *Shrapnel* comes in. As the assistant editor of BattleCorps from 2012 until its closure, I took its unfortunate end as a sign to move things into a new direction. Together, myself, John Helfers, the executive editor of both Catalyst Game Labs and Pulse Publishing, and Loren Coleman were able to bring back *BattleTech* short fiction in a new form—due in no small part to the wildly successful crowdfunding campaign on Kickstarter.com for the *BattleTech: Clan Invasion* box set. As a special thanks to everyone who backed the campaign, we packed this first issue of *Shrapnel* with several stories set during the Clan Invasion era, to give both longtime fans and newcomers a taste of what the Clan Invasion is all about.

"But why '*Shrapnel*' for the title?" you might ask. We chose this because it not only emphasizes the gritty destruction of 31st-century warfare, but it also has a more visceral and personal meaning. Explosions cause shrapnel, but when those fragments injure a soldier, that's when you're reminded that at the heart of each BattleMech, aerospace fighter, combat vehicle, spaceborne vessel, and suit of battle armor lies a flesh-and-blood person with hopes and dreams, with family and friends, with brothers- and sisters-in-arms. And this reminder of the human element in these war machines is vital because the best stories set in the *BattleTech* universe, though they might feature sprawling battles of giant war robots, are populated and driven by people—characters whose aspirations can either come to fruition or be cut tragically short in the space of milliseconds. In other words, *people* are the ones who fight wars in *BattleTech*, not 'Mechs or guns.

In the following pages you'll find a wealth of fiction, including short stories from longtime authors Blaine Lee Pardoe and Kevin Killiany, the first part of a four-part Kell Hounds serial story by the *New York Times*-bestselling author and celebrated *BattleTech* scribe Michael A. Stackpole, and a new recurring feature called "Tales from the Cracked Canopy," a spiritual successor to *BattleTechnology*'s "Tales of the Cobalt Coil." You'll also find several articles that run the gamut of conspiracy theories, newsworthy events, unit histories, in-depth looks at various weapons, and more—all of which can inspire a tabletop gaming session (using *Total Warfare* or *Alpha Strike* rules) or a role-playing adventure (using either *A Time of War* or the forthcoming rules-light RPG *MechWarrior: Destiny*).

Now, soldier, your mission is to strap on your coolant vest, calibrate your neurohelmet, and then sit back in your command couch to enjoy everything this first issue of *Shrapnel* has to offer. We're already hard at work on the next issue, so we hope you're ready to report for duty when the call comes to saddle up.

Thus shall it stand until we all fall.

Philip A. Lee, Managing Editor

GRIMM SENTENCE

CHRIS HUSSEY

**GRIMFORT
OBERON VI
CLAN WOLF OCCUPATION ZONE
29 SEPTEMBER 3049**

Hendrik Grimm tentatively and tenderly poked at the warm sensation on his bald pate. Something covered it. It felt slightly sticky to the touch and was warm. Unnaturally so. His entire head was warm. And sore. A dull pain throbbed back and forth across his skull. Grimm recognized the sensation and could tell, even in the haze of semi-consciousness, that it was muted. *Painkillers.*

Sounds seeped through his head fog and into his consciousness. They too were muted, but Grimm knew what they were. *Beep beep beep. I'm in a hospital.*

Everything was dark, but Grimm knew it was because his eyes were still closed. The sticky material covered one, but the ruler of the Oberon Confederation was reluctant to open his other eye.

Ruler? Memories coalesced in his mind. The radio comms, the questions about the strength of his forces. The invasion. Strange 'Mechs. The rapid series of defeats and retreats. The gorgeous view of Kennedy Beach from the cockpit of his *Atlas* as he raised his pistol to his head and—

Grimm bolted upright in his bed and shouted, his eye snapping open. Images flooded in with the memories. Guards, machines, tubes, a wolf's-head flag. He gasped for breath as his hands pulled at his clothes and the implements inserted in him. One of the guards approached with a calming hand, while the other's hand moved closer to his sidearm.

"Easy. Please stay calm."

"Where the hell am I?" Grimm shouted, spit flying from his mouth, the throbbing in his head rising. "Who the hell are you?"

The guard raised his gloved hand higher, his voice staying flat. "You are in a medical bay, currently healing from a self-inflicted gunshot wound to your head. I am warrior Abrams of Clan Wolf."

Grimm slapped the hand away. He saw the other guard grip his pistol but not pull it. The memories swirling in his mind slowed and sharpened. *Clan Wolf. The invaders. I tried to kill myself. I've been captured!*

"Get that hand away from me, you Spheroid scum. I don't know what new unit bonny Prince Half-wit Davion made for his bitch wife, but you'll end up paying just like all the others before who tried to put the Oberon Confederation under their heel! Get me your CO!"

The first guard lowered his hand and gave Hendrik a firm look. He said nothing.

Grimm nodded. "Oh, I've got it wrong then. You all belong to the Teddy Bear, is that it? It doesn't matter." He pointed a fat finger at both. "Wolves? Is that what you call yourselves?" He spat. "Wolves. Ghost Regiments. You're all Dragons. I've skinned you before, I'll skin you again. You made a big mistake saving my life."

"Oh, I disagree, Hendrik Grimm of the Oberon Confederation." A stern, confident voice spoke from beyond the doorway of the room.

The Confederation leader looked toward the doorway. In strode a tall, thin man. His dark hair was shaved close to his scalp. His olive-drab uniform with mottled gray speckling clung tight to his frame. He regarded Grimm with a curt smile. A woman followed behind. Dressed the same, she stood slightly shorter. She bore a much more fierce expression. Her auburn hair was shaved on the sides but draped past and behind her shoulders.

"Who the hell are you two?"

The man's pale blue eyes twinkled. "I am Star Colonel John Ward of the Eleventh Wolf Guard of Clan Wolf. This is Star Commander Niamh." Ward paused, letting a small smile cross his lips. "And you have the honor of being the first here in the Inner Sphere to be reunited under the banner of the Clans and the reformation of the Star League reborn."

Grimm blinked his lone, visible eye. "Am I supposed to be impressed?"

GRIMFORT
OBERON VI
CLAN WOLF OCCUPATION ZONE
17 OCTOBER 3049

Hendrik Grimm gasped desperately for breath as he stopped along the makeshift run track outside the Grimfort. The physical activity the

Wolves were putting him and the surviving Oberon Guards through the past few weeks proved brutal on his large, aging frame.

The upheaval in their physical lives mirrored nearly everything else. The entire structure of the Confederation had been torn down. Every aspect of Grimm's rule was vanishing day by day. It still wasn't clear what this Clan Wolf was or where exactly they came from. His sons, who were on Oberon VI when the attack occurred, had their theories. It was possible they were a special FedCom or Draconis Combine unit.

His son Johann thought differently. He was sure they were from beyond the Confederation, from deeper into the Periphery. How deep, he couldn't be sure. To Grimm, that option explained their odd 'Mech models. Grimm had witnessed plenty of cobbled together 'Mechs in his time. Hell, some served in his ranks. Even his new *Atlas* possessed some eccentricities.

These Wolf 'Mechs, though, didn't have that rough edge most hack jobs did. He'd also never seen the likes of their infantry before. The battle-armored troops were something completely alien to him, with the appearance of the men and women inside that armor even more alien, yet still human. He didn't know what these troopers ate, but they were big across the board. It was possible that some backwater state had found an old high-tech Star League cache and was using it, but Grimm wasn't buying that.

The third option, and the one his other son, Karl, bought into was these Wolves were some sort of ComStar force or experiment. Grimm played back all the conversations over the years with Precentor Rodrick, the administrator of the Oberon HPG station. Grimm had seduced him away from the order years ago, though the precentor still kept up appearances for the home office. If this proved true, the fact that Rodrick hadn't warned Grimm that something like this might happen filled him with rage over the betrayal, but Grimm would deal with that later. Right now he had other matters to attend to.

He felt the presence of another near him. It was Johann.

"Grimm, get moving. You can't stop again."

Hendrik heaved again. "I'm almost a hundred sixty kilos, Jo. And old. How much do you think I can run?" In a strange way, he respected the way his son refused to call him "Father" whether in public or private, choosing "Grimm" as many of his subordinates did. Hendrik never expected his son to use "sir." That would imply too much respect. *He wants to be a leader, and a Grimm in his own right. Ambition.*

The younger Grimm tried to move his father forward. "Enough to keep you alive, otherwise the plan won't work."

Hendrik waved his hand in dismissal. "Bah. If they'd wanted us dead, we'd be there already. Instead, we're in bondage."

"*Bondsmen.*" Johann corrected him.

"Whatever. Just another fancy name for 'prisoner.' But it won't be that way for long." Hendrik shot a sly grin at his son.

A sharp voice cut their conversation short. "Pathetic! If the two of you represent those who inhabit paradise, I will not be surprised if they welcome the Clans with open and begging arms."

Hendrik chuckled as he turned to Star Commander Niamh. She'd been the force behind the boot camp-like existence Hendrik, his sons, and the surviving Oberon Guards were dealing with. "I'm guessing delusion is a side effect of whatever brainwashing program they put you through."

The woman shot him a harsh look. "It is you who are deluded, Hendrik Grimm. Deluded to think that your way of life would continue. That your hedonistic ways here in the Inner Sphere would not come without cost. That you deserve the title of MechWarrior. Your fat, bloated shell barely fit inside the cockpit of your 'Mech. A 'Mech you did not earn, did not care for, did not cherish. I know many *sibkin* who would kill you without a second thought for the chance to pilot a BattleMech, yet you take it all with an arrogance that belies your devotion to honor and your skill in a 'Mech cockpit." She looked his body over in disgust, her lip curling. "And you delude yourself if you *ever* think you will pilot a 'Mech again. With luck, you may be able to someday have the honor of polishing a technician's boots."

Hendrik lurched at the woman, roaring, but his son held him firmly back.

"Grimm, no!"

Hendrik spat, his eyes locking with the Clan warrior. "We'll see about that."

Now it was her turn to chuckle. "Such fire to defend your honor. And to think you casually dismissed such honor by almost killing yourself."

Grimm renewed his struggle to free himself from his son.

"Save it for the track, Hendrik Grimm. You have just earned three more laps." Niamh paused, dropping her voice to a threat level. "Now go."

Father and son trudged slowly through the Grimfort to the prison cells that were their new home. While the Wolves insisted these were now simply barracks, Hendrik felt otherwise. Door after door of the long hallway shot memories through the bandit king. Memories of the countless opponents and criminals he'd sentenced here over the years. Were they still living, Grimm knew they'd be laughing. *But not for long*, he mused.

Johann's whisper shook Grimm from his thoughts. "Why'd you do it?"

Grimm turned his head slightly. "Do what?"

Johann paused. "Try to off yourself."

Grimm looked away. He didn't want to face the truth of that moment, and the capture and hard training from the Wolves had allowed him to avoid it. When Grimm noticed there might be a chance for a prison break and escape, he had another reason to not face his action.

"Dad, *why?*"

The harshness of Johann's question hit Grimm hard. He surprised himself with how his son's use of 'Dad' affected him. *Manipulation.*

Grimm swallowed and tried to answer. "I...I panicked. I was weak. I made...a mistake."

Johann scoffed. "I don't believe you."

Grimm smiled at his son seeing through his lies. *Shrewd as well.* He decided to hit his son with the full truth. "It was a moment of fear. I thought this was a FedCom or Drac unit. I did some bad things in the F-C a few years back. Figured it was revenge for the heist we pulled on Arluna. Thought I'd covered my tracks. Thought I'd been found out. Couldn't give them the satisfaction."

Johann looked confused. "I remember that raid. A simple smash-and-grab of some gold reserves."

Hendrik nodded. "That was the cover, yes." He paused as he weighed his words. "There were some Drac exiles on-planet. The Combine wanted them back home. They paid a hefty deposit for that job." He locked eyes with his son. "But I knew my underworld contacts in the Free Rasalhague Republic would offer more. So I took the gold, sold half the exiles to the Rasalhagians, and the other half back to the Combine. Then I framed King Morrison and his Extractors, claiming they had attacked, targeting the world at the same time. That's what I told the Dracs anyway, to keep the heat off."

Johann nodded but said nothing, so Hendrik continued. "To the F-C, I made it look like the Extractors attacked. Even fed a fake story through our beloved precentor not long after that I had died and Hendrik Grimm IV was now in command. With such internal upheaval, we could never have attacked. Deception is sometimes our greatest weapon."

Johann's only response was a muted huff. That was enough to convince Grimm he'd accepted the truth.

The pair passed by another cell, not unlike the others. Grimm saw Johann stealthily tap the door in sequence. *Time to talk, Karl.* Grimm's contact with Karl had been minimal since the Wolves took over, but had been enough to communicate and confirm that Karl was in on their plan of escape and counterattack. It was all just a matter of time.

Grimm and Johann entered their own cells in silence, positioned themselves on either side of the wall that divided them and quickly set to tapping. Grimm silently thanked his insistence that his sons learn the code he'd developed. It was one of the many contingencies he'd made to stay one step ahead of his enemies. And the Wolves were about to find out just how prepared Hendrik Grimm III was. *You don't* live this long with as many people wanting to kill you as I do, knowing that Hanse Davion or Teddy Kurita could come over your border any minute, without having a few tricks up your sleeve. These Wolves were tough, Grimm admitted, but he was confident they would fall just the same.

Hendrik tapped out a code to his son: *Meet with Ward?*

A response. Grimm decoded the sequence: *Yes. Believe he trusts. Wolves leave soon. Small garrison. Continue turning survivors.*

Grimm tapped again. *Tell Karl to look for opening. When Wolves leave, break for cache.*

Hendrik waited through the pause as his orders to Karl went down the cell line. Minutes passed, then the gentle tap of Johann's response: *Gamma cache?*

Grimm smiled. He'd stockpiled numerous hidden caches across Oberon VI. You never knew where your enemies might drive you. He tapped back. *Too far. Zeta cache.*

Johann's response was fast. Grimm knew he was nervous. *Don't know Zeta. Where?*

Grimm chastised him as best he could via the code. *Never told. Only I know. Will tell once free.*

Risky plan.

Keep me alive and success.

GRIMFORT
OBERON VI
CLAN WOLF OCCUPATION ZONE
12 NOVEMBER 3049

Star Colonel John Ward dismissed the concerns reaching his ears. "I appreciate your worry, but it is unfounded. This world will remain in the hands of the Wolves. If it is ever torn from our grip, it will not be from some aged, upstart, self-styled king." He turned toward the two people in the room, ignoring one and turning his focus to the other. "Unless, of course, Star Commander Niamh, you feel you are not up to the task."

"You have read the reports and heard the rumors. You know his history. He will never succeed as a bondsman. Use his information and then kill him. That is the only way."

Ward nodded as he moved about the office. " He will never succeed within the Clans. It is not his way. His life is nothing but deception after deception." The Clan commander paused as he reached a star map of the coreward section of the Inner Sphere. "What he has succeeded at is being honest about what we will face in the coming months. His belief that we are some secret unit of this ComStar organization makes him feel he is playing a game of sorts with us. He tells us what he thinks we already know."

Ward stroked a finger through the holomap, driving it straight down to Terra. "He has no motivation to lie. It will be his—" Ward jammed a finger through the blue dot that represented the cradle of humanity, "—and their undoing."

Niamh sighed. "If you have what you need, then eliminate him, or send him to the labor caste."

The third person in the room spoke. "It's dangerous to keep him near."

Ward shrugged. "You worry too much. And besides, if he does become a problem, just take care of it."

GRIMFORT
OBERON VI
CLAN WOLF OCCUPATION ZONE
26 NOVEMBER 3049

Hendrik Grimm III stood in the exercise yard of the Grimfort, a dozen rivers of sweat racing down his round frame under the hot November sun. He gazed up at the Clan Wolf DropShips burning away from the planet he once ruled. The warriors within, including Star Colonel Ward, were on their way to invade the Inner Sphere, or so Grimm and all the other captured Oberon Guardsmen were told.

Grimm smiled in satisfaction at their departure. *Just like everyone else. They come in, do some damage then leave, never finishing the job. Then they wonder why we keep coming back.* The bandit king acknowledged this time was different: a modest garrison remained. These 'Mechs were models that looked familiar, which gave more credence to his growing belief that this was indeed some advanced Com Guards force. The reports he'd heard about their advanced weaponry worried Grimm some, but he was more concerned about the larger-scale machinations ComStar might be planning. Surviving that scenario, whatever it might be, would take some thought.

First he had to survive this one.

The intel on the 'Mechs, garrison size, and other movements came from his sons. While Grimm cooperated and answered all the questions from the Clan commanders, it was clear he was failing in the testing they were putting him through. Both Karl and Johann were proving at least passable in the eyes of the Wolves, and this allowed them better access on the inside. The nightly reports via their code allowed Grimm to put all the pieces of his plan into action.

It would only be a matter of hours now.

Orange hues bathed the Oberon sky as the sun neared its arc towards the horizon's edge. Grimm stared out the window at the grounds of the Grimfort below as he walked the line back to his cell. The number of Oberon Guards with him continued to shrink. The testing process was separating the groups, and by all indications, Grimm was sure he was headed for the labor caste at some point. But as long as Johann and Karl were in their places, and their loyalists with them, that would be a distant memory. Grimm just needed to be patient.

Slowing his pace to buy his sons more time, Grimm signaled to the others to do the same. If all was going to plan, they would overpower their escorts soon. Thankfully, none of the Wolves' fearsome battle armor was left behind. He recalled the battle at Black Canyon, and the images of a 'Mech from his command lance swarmed by the things returned to the forefront. The armored troopers tearing and burning away armor plates like hungry scarabs ripping at flesh, the fear that gripped Grimm at that moment and entertaining the briefest of notions that it could all be over... If it hadn't been for the timely arrival of Karl's reinforcements, Grimm and the others might not have made it out alive. Hendrik did not want to deal with those troops again so soon.

Worry crept onto his brow. Something was wrong. Karl and Johann should have made their moves by now.

A shove hit Hendrik's shoulder. "Keep moving, *surat*. I do not care how tired you are."

"Easy, friend." Grimm's voice was low and rough.

"I am not your friend."

A loud *clunk* accompanied the darkness that suddenly filled the hallway. Grimm smiled.

A gasp escaped the warrior's lips at the shock of what happened. A grunt immediately followed as Grimm spun, his massive fist leading the way, connecting with the Wolf warrior's face, sending him spinning and sprawling to the floor.

"Now!" Grimm shouted as he leaped toward the Wolf desperately trying to scramble to his feet.

Shouts, the sharp reports of gunfire, and the occasional explosion filled the courtyard as Clan warriors scrambled to contain the growing breakout. The lights were still out, but the last glimmers of twilight provided enough to see and hide if needed.

Johann Grimm led his squad toward the motor pool, eyeing the APCs resting within. "Plow that road. We need those transports moving, fast!" He scanned the chaos, looking for two targets. He spotted one immediately as a silhouette lit against a chorus of muzzle flashes. That would be Karl and his men moving with purpose towards Johann's location. Continuing his scan, the second target eluded Johann. *C'mon, Grimm, this was your idea. Where the hell are you?*

One of the troopers shouted at Johann as they passed through the motor pool's gates. "Sir, if we're going to leave, we need to do it *yesterday*. Once their 'Mechs make it over here, we're done."

"Understood. Grimm said he had a plan for that."

The crew reached the first APC and hustled inside. "I get that, but what's *our* plan?"

Johann looked one last time. Karl's crew was close. They'd all be boarded soon. Seeing nothing but haze filled with shocked Clan soldiers trying to mount a counterattack, he shook his head. *Damn it. Now is not the time.* Looking back to his troops, he signaled all to move out. "Our plan is we get the hell out of here!"

The convoy of transports peeled out of their pen, top-mounted anti-personnel weaponry helping to clear the way. Johann saw first 'Mech approaching, backlit by the last rays of the setting sun, then a second 'Mech followed. *Great idea, Grimm.*

"Sir, I've got something. It's him!"

"What?" Johann braced himself as he navigated to the comm panel in the shaking transport. The image in the monitor was obvious. Hendrik Grimm, flanked by his own men, racing toward the transports.

"Of course." Johann spat in half disgust. "Let's get 'em." He keyed the comm to his brother's APC. "Karl, keep moving, we'll catch up!"

The trio of APCs slowed their roll, their bay doors sliding open. A handful of Oberon Guardsmen piled in, followed by Grimm himself.

Johann grabbed his father. "What the hell, Grimm? It should never have taken you that long to get down here. We'll be lucky to make it out alive. Where the hell did you go?"

Grimm shook himself free and looked down as the transport rocked back and forth. He patted a small satchel slung over his shoulder. "Without this, we won't make it anywhere. It was hidden in the throne room."

Johann gritted his teeth in frustration. His father had never said anything about this. He was tired of all his father's plans within plans. Too many secrets and none being shared. He wanted to punch him. Repeatedly.

"Oh, shit! We've got a problem!" The shout from the gunner's position on top of the transport changed Johann's focus. The full-auto staccato of the gun followed.

"What is it?" Johann pushed past his father to check the rear monitor. Through the smoke and tracer rounds, he spied the squat and big-shouldered shape of the Clan battle armor: An Elemental, the Wolves called them.

"I thought these bastards all left with the Wolves?" someone shouted.

"Apparently not," muttered Grimm.

The APC shuddered, and Grimm felt a wave of heat wash over him.

"Laser fire!" the gunmen shouted as his own weapon rattled its response.

Johann tightened the grip on his safety handle. "Don't stop moving! Radio the rest, tell 'em we make for the north gate. It's the fastest exit."

"No!" Hendrik shouted. "It has to be the west gate. It's our only chance."

Johann gave him an exasperated glare. "That goes through the marketplace. It's a maze of streets that way. We'll never make it with Elementals in pursuit." Johann pointed toward the rear of the transport. "And let's not forget those 'Mechs."

"SRM!" the gunman screamed again as he ducked inside the transport's cabin.

The passengers scrambled to secure themselves as the missile struck. The sharp *thrum* of the impact shook the vehicle violently. Johann's stomach lurched as the missile's impact spun the transport in a 360. The rear end fishtailed as the driver regained control and accelerated.

The gunner popped back into his position and resumed firing. Johann could tell by the sound of the APC that nothing important had been damaged.

"The west gate!" Grimm shouted as he fished through his satchel and produced a small transmitter. He presented it to his son. "Johann, trust me. We just need to get through the market."

Johann wasn't wrong. The path to the west gate was a twisting, winding labyrinth of streets. The transports ignored any semblance of order, careening and crashing through the Grimfort marketplace, destroying numerous storefronts, streetlights, and signs in their haste to escape. While the maze did its job slowing the 'Mech pursuit, the Elementals proved to be a different matter.

The jagged convoy emerged through the market, freedom through the west gate in sight. Johann kept his eyes locked on the transport's monitors. He stared in horror as a lagging APC fell prey to the Wolves' armored infantry.

The five troopers swarmed on top, tearing armor plating free as if they were unwrapping a birthday present. Their arm-mounted lasers did the rest, firing with abandon at the crew trapped inside. What the lasers didn't kill, the underslung anti-personnel machine guns on their opposite arm finished off.

Johann gritted his teeth in rage. He turned toward his father. "That one's on you!"

Grimm glared back at him. "If we didn't take this gate, we'd *all* be dead!"

"We would've been free and clear through the north gate and long gone by now!"

The APCs burst through the west gate, weapons blazing at the last bits of Clan resistance and small-arms fire pinged harmlessly off the transport's armor. "And easy pickings for those 'Mechs once we hit the open road," Hendrik shot back. "Their long-range weapons would have torn us apart, you fool. This way we keep them off our backs long enough to get where we need to go."

Johann checked a monitor. The 'Mechs were just on the edge of the market and about to pursue. "How, Grimm?"

Hendrik flashed a fiendish grin. "Like this." He held up the transmission box and keyed in a code. The boxed flashed to life and gave a few assuring pings. Grimm pointed toward the monitor near Johann. "Watch."

The Clan 'Mechs strode confidently into the open field and quickly picked up pace in pursuit. Johann saw their heads poke briefly over the Grimfort's walls.

Then bright flashes erupted behind the walls, with dull rumbles echoing inside the APC's bay a second later. Johann saw no sign of the 'Mechs continuing their pursuit. The Grimfort quickly faded in the distance as the transports raced away.

Mines. "I never knew..." Johann sputtered.

Grimm winked. "I never told."

BLACK JACKRABBIT HILLS
OBERON VI
CLAN WOLF OCCUPATION ZONE
27 NOVEMBER 3049

Johann Grimm didn't know if he should be angry or impressed as he stared at the 'Mechs tucked inside the cave complex of Zeta cache. Some of the models he recognized. Others didn't register, but they were obviously old. Despite that, Johann noticed they were mothballed properly. Oberon Guard MechWarriors were pouring over the company-sized cache, prepping and powering up systems, making sure everything was functional and combat ready.

Karl Grimm approached his brother. Johann gestured at all the 'Mechs. "Did you know about this?"

Karl chuckled. "Are you kidding? You're older, and Dad doesn't trust me any more than he does you. What makes you think I'd be privileged to this?"

Johann sighed. "Makes me wonder how many aces in his hole he really has." He knew Hendrik Grimm had stowed numerous 'Mech and weapons caches on nearly every world in the Oberon Confederation, and several other worlds beyond. Being the king's son meant he knew their locations and had access to many of them. It was a necessity when dealing with pirates, local warlords who held grudges, or even the occasional Inner Sphere force hell-bent on destroying you. Fleeing to a hidden cache to repair, refit, and counterattack was a tactic Johann had used many times to great effectiveness. And it appeared the time had come to use it again. His father wasn't messing around.

Karl pointed toward a section deeper in the caves. "Did you see the trucks?"

"Trucks?"

"Dad has about six trucks. They've all been modded with anti-'Mech weaponry. One even has a small laser. Another has an SRM two-pack."

Johann nodded, then chuckled. "That sounds like him."

The pair moved through the cavern to find the bandit king. It didn't take long. Grimm descended from a *Rifleman* with another warrior. Johann noticed that, despite his father's massive size, Grimm moved with determination. He couldn't be sure if the Clan training and testing had made an impact, or if his father was energized by the coming fight.

"I know it's not your *Victor*," Grimm said with a frown, "but it'll get the job done."

Johann returned the smile. "This one's mine?"

Grimm nodded. "Karl, you'll command your lance in the *Orion*. I'm taking the *Warhammer*."

Johann sighed. *This will probably be my only chance.* "Do you really think we can throw them off-world?"

"I don't plan to. I want to crush them all while they are here. We need to prevent any off-world communications."

"Are you planning on taking out the HPG station first?"

Grimm shook his head. "No."

"But they'll be abl—"

Grimm held up a hand. "The precentor owes me a favor. Besides, that station hasn't been able to transmit for four years. It can only receive."

Johann looked up. "Unless these Wolves really are ComStar and fixed it. Why can't we just flee off-world?"

Grimm smirked. "And go where? We have no JumpShip."

"There's the mining outpost in the rings around Oberon V." Johann gestured to take in all the cave. "With the size of force we have, there's more than enough supplies there to last six months. One of your merchants is bound to stop by eventually. We hook up with them, and we can go anywhere."

Grimm started to shake his head.

Johann pressed. "We have the rest of the Confederation. There's the abandoned base on Drask's Den, or Lackhove. We can also try Star's End."

"No."

"Or even Von Strang's World."

"NO!" Grimm shouted. "We're not doing any of that. Especially dealing with that criminal Von Strang. We're standing and fighting."

Johann laughed internally at his father's hypocrisy, steeled his resolve, and swallowed. "You sure you're not going to try to kill yourself this time?"

Lights exploded in Johann's vision as Grimm's fist connected with his face. Johann stumbled back, Karl catching him.

Grimm spat. "Let me guess. Next you're going to suggest we just stay in hiding and wait them out?"

Johann regained his footing. "Why not? You said it yourself. They'll just leave."

"But they haven't. And now they won't get the chance." Grimm stared his son up and down. "Maybe you got too close to them. Maybe they broke you."

Maybe I saw the writing on the wall. "If they broke me, why the hell am I here?"

"I'm asking myself the same thing." Hendrik's voice took a sinister tone.

Johann shot back. "What if they *aren't* ComStar? What if they're telling the truth? You ever think about that? What if they are invaders from beyond the Periphery and are hell-bent on conquering the Inner Sphere?"

Grimm stayed silent for a moment then looked back at his son. "If that's the case, they can have the Inner Sphere. If they wanted to keep this world, they would have stayed. If we were just a 'warm-up' for them, then they don't give two shits about us. That's been true of the Periphery for centuries. We get our freedom when we take it, which is exactly what we're about to do."

A low whistle caught Hendrik's attention as he circled around the feet of his "new" *Warhammer*. Grimm turned to see Karl approaching. He pointed at the markings along the thick legs of the 70-ton machine. "Is that...Rim Worlds Republic insignia?"

Hendrik looked up at the faded blue, looping shark on a field of red. "It is," he said smugly. "The merchant Kelly Hunt owed me a favor a few years back. Provided me with some supposedly old Rim Worlds records uncovered on Icar ten years prior. Turns out they were legit. Indicated a cache hidden on Lovinac. I hired Hunt and some old school *lostech* prospectors to find it." Grimm slapped the foot of the *'Hammer*. "They did."

Karl cocked his head. "These 'Mechs are pretty old, though. You really think they'll stand up against those Wolf 'Mechs?"

Hendrik eyed his son. "If the intel you and Johann provided is true. They only left behind five. A 'Star,' they call it. We'll outnumber them two to one. It's as good as won."

Grimm sat in the cockpit of his *Warhammer*. He slipped the small headset over his scalp, donned his neurohelmet, and punched several commands into the comm. He could hear the *tick-tick-tick* on the other end of the signal he was broadcasting. It was taking longer than usual to answer, but Grimm would be patient.

With a nervous breath, the ticking stopped and a voice on the other end spoke in a whisper. "You're not dead."

"Neither are you," Grimm answered.

"Heard you'd escaped. Where are you?"

"Oh no, Precentor Rodrick. You don't need to know that." Grimm's tone turned dark. "How come you didn't tell me about this invading force?"

"How could I? I didn't know," Rodrick continued to whisper.

"Don't play me for a fool. I have more than enough on you to defrock you to your masters. And I know your station still receives transmissions. Perhaps it can even still send. Perhaps you've been deceiving me for years. Taking my gifts and then being disloyal. I'm very displeased."

"I'm not playing you, Grimm. That force was not Com Guards. I swear." A pause fell between the men. "And it is neither Combine nor F-C. I do not know where they are from."

Grimm furrowed his brow. "Are you sure?"

"I have no reason to lie. Especially to you. What would I gain from it?"

Grimm clenched his jaws, doubt creeping into his mind. "What have they done to your station?"

"Nothing. They hooked up some additional equipment I've never seen before. By all accounts, it appears they did fix our transmission problem, but we've been restricted from access. There is only a token garrison here now."

"I'm going to crush them, Rodrick. Whoever they are. They won't have ownership of this world much longer. When I do, whatever troops there will likely be distracted. Plus, I'll be sending some help your way. I'm also sending you a data packet. I want a message sent someplace special."

"I'll do what I can, of course," Rodrick reassured.

"Good. See that you do. And let me make this crystal clear. This is to be the only transmission you make. Do not tell your masters what happened here. Even now you have proven your loyalty. I would hate to see that streak broken."

There was a pause before the whispered response came. "Of course."

Grimm killed the connection and looked out into the dimness of the cave through the *Warhammer's* viewport. After pulling a holo-

recorder from his satchel, he placed it atop the command console and turned it on.

"Hello. It's your father. I have something I want to tell you."

BLACK JACKRABBIT HILLS
OBERON VI
CLAN WOLF OCCUPATION ZONE
28 NOVEMBER 3049

The twin, jagged, azure beams from Grimm's *Warhammer* sparked toward the Clan 'Mech angling across his path. Both beams went wide, and Grimm felt the heat levels in the cockpit jump into the yellow.

The Clan machine couldn't be fully identified, looking like some sort of mash-up of a *Phoenix Hawk* and possibly a *Crusader*, but it sure as hell wasn't behaving like either. It was slower than a *'Hawk*, but not by much, and the data coming back indicated it was almost twice as heavy. It made no sense.

The strange *'Hawk* returned fire. Grimm watched as muzzle flashes erupted from the paired autocannons mounted on the 'Mech's chest. It shuddered as the excessive hail of fire raced from both barrels. Grimm braced for impact.

The shells flew straight by, instead hitting the *Scorpion* ninety meters behind and to Grimm's left. The assault seemed to never end. Autocannon fire shredded armor plating down to the *Scorpion*'s internal skeleton, where the shells continued to tear through the myomer muscle fibers and bones of the quad 'Mech's forelegs. Grimm screamed in rage as he watched Bently's *Scorpion* collapse face-first into the chewed up earth of the Black Jackrabbit Hills.

Another 'Mech down.

The assault was not going according to plan. The gunnery trucks had set out first, half toward the HPG station, the other half to create a diversion toward the Grimfort. To Hendrik's surprise, the Clan warriors were already on patrol, searching for them. He'd rushed his 'Mechs forward at that point, hoping to catch these Wolves off guard.

Hendrik Grimm had started with a company of 'Mechs spread out in a wide net he had planned to pull tight. True to intel, Grimm had seen only a Star of Wolf 'Mechs. His hopes had further lifted when it looked as if their defending force was much lighter than expected. A pair of the odd *Phoenix Hawk* variants and a *Locust* were three-fifths of what the Clans fielded. But Grimm had quickly realized his error when the *Phoenix Hawk*s proved deadly, and the *Locust*'s speed was giving his unit targeting fits.

The second surprise to dampen his spirits was the Clan battle armor. There were five times more Elementals than those who had chased them from the Grimfort, and they'd come out of nowhere, making quick work of Antar's *Wasp* and Kenyatta's *Javelin*. Now with the *Scorpion* out of the fight, only nine 'Mechs remained on his side.

The Wolves were not unbloodied, however. Thanks to the concentrated efforts of Karl's lance, the second Clan *Phoenix Hawk* was down, leaving them with four 'Mechs.

And for garrison troops, they were fighting like front line warriors. Hendrik suspected it was fueled by the anger of Star Commander Niamh, bent on avenging her honor. Her reaction to the 'Mechs being old Rim Worlds machines seemed oddly out of place.

"I do not know where you obtained these 'Mechs from, Hendrik Grimm," Niamh spoke over a broadband signal when they first came in contact. "But you bear the insignia of the realm of the Usurper. That is a dishonor we cannot abide. You have signed your death warrant."

Even almost three hundred years after the fact, anything in regards to the Rim Worlds Republic and Stefan Amaris wasn't looked at fondly.

Grimm pushed his *Warhammer* forward and to the right. A few quick keystrokes reconfigured his medium-range target interlock circuit, then he swung the targeting reticule in line with the Clan *Phoenix Hawk*. The crosshairs pulsed red, and Grimm pressed the firing stud.

Smoke and flame filled his viewport as the sextet of missiles speared toward the Clanner. Twin beams from the *Warhammer's* medium lasers cut through the smoke. Grimm smiled as the sensors recorded 50 percent effectiveness with the missiles, which blasted a line from the *'Hawk*'s left side down to its leg, with the two lasers scratching solid lines across the Clan 'Mech's chest.

Hendrik felt a new blanket of sweat break across his skin as the heat bumped slightly, the 'Mech's heat sinks still working to cycle out the spike from the twin PPC fire. "Johann, status," he spoke hard as he keyed his comm.

"Holding their *Griffin* and *Locust*, but not for long. They're too fast for us. Plus the damned *Griffin* is staying at long range and can hit us from well outside of ours."

Useless. "Karl, bring your *Orion* and that *Phoenix* around to my left. We need to tighten the circle. Their *Hunchback* is moving in and out of those woods, and Trent and Hu are trying to flush it out. Last thing we need is that 'Mech surprising us. Scheslinger, your *Phoenix* is with me on this *'Hawk*."

Grimm was afraid of that strange Clan *Hunchback*. How the Wolves had figured out how to arm not one, but *two* Class-20 autocannons that could double-fire—something it seemed all their autocannons could do—was disconcerting, to say the least. Its presence somewhere in those woods was forcing Grimm to steer clear and engage the weird *Phoenix Hawk* out in the open. A fight he knew was going to eventually lose.

Not again. Grimm backed his 'Mech away from his opponent, angling toward a nearby hill. "Jacoby, I hope you're in position. I could use your help real quick."

His comm crackled as she responded. "I see you, sire. Need you another ninety meters closer if I want to get a good grouping. This *Archer*'s targeting system is showing its age."

Jacoby was doing her best to get the *Archer* to a high point where she could rain fire from above on the Clan 'Mechs as needed, but their mobility had forced her to relocate twice, limiting her effectiveness. Just one more frustration.

"Almost there, Grimm," Scheslinger reported over the comm. The Rim Worlds-manufactured *Phoenix* wasn't a spectacular model, but the PPC it carried and the fact it was an extra target would be enough.

The enemy *Phoenix Hawk* turned toward Grimm, marching forward, tearing up earth and snapping small trees as it closed the gap. Grimm's focus narrowed as he saw the twin autocannons adjust their positioning slightly. The weapons tone in his cockpit pinged in the affirmative that both PPCs were recharged and ready to go.

"Just a little more," Jacoby spoke as Grimm watched muzzle flashes erupt from the *Phoenix Hawk* toward him. A split second later, Grimm keyed his firing stud.

The autocannon rounds kicked up dirt plumes as they traced a path toward the *Warhammer*, then tore up the machine's legs. Both bolts from the *Warhammer*'s PPCs lashed across the chest of the Clan 'Mech, blasting and warping armor plates until they snapped free or simply melted off.

Grimm's *Warhammer* shuddered violently and tipped forward as if both legs had been swept out from underneath it. Moving with the motion, he stumbled slightly, but kept one leg secure beneath him, then the other.

Another cerulean bolt crackled just to the *Phoenix Hawk*'s right as Scheslinger made his presence known. *Good. You're pinched now.*

Looking at the sensor readings on the Clan 'Mech, Grimm smiled, realizing both particle projection cannons had caused enough damage to expose the *Phoenix Hawk* to danger. Then flames erupted around the enemy machine as missiles rained down from Jacoby's *Archer*. The *Phoenix Hawk* stumbled out from the flaming wreath created by the two score of warheads, stumbled to the left, then collapsed in on itself, its central armor and skeleton damaged beyond use. *Check that. You're DRT.*

Grimm cackled and opened the comm. "The second 'Hawk is down. We've got 'em now." He urged the *Warhammer* toward the tree line. "Jacoby, stay where you are. Johann, pull back and draw their *Griffin* and *Locust* toward her position."

Johann answered back. "Looks like both are breaking, Grimm. They're angling for Jacoby's position. In pursuit."

The bandit king was getting frustrated. "Do not let them get to Jacoby!"

"Roger that," Johann answered back. "We've lost track of the Elementals. Anyone got a read on them?"

Grimm felt his stomach start to burn.

Jacoby was the one to answer. "I've got a read. About three hundred meters from my position."

That was not what Grimm wanted to hear. "Jacoby, get out of there. Coordinate with Johann, but do not—"

An emergency alert cut Grimm off. It was Trent in one of the *Griffins* chasing the Clan *Hunchback*. "I'm done, sir." There was pain in the MechWarrior's voice. "Thought we had it pinned, but it turned and came at us. Big guns ripped one of my legs clear off in one volley. Hu got spooked and is running."

Karl's voice came over the comm. "Hu, cut to your left. I'm almost there. I can see you. Just circle back and I can get a shot!"

Damn it! Grimm kicked his *Warhammer* toward Jacoby's position, hoping to intercept the Wolf *Locust* and *Griffin* while Jacoby avoided the armored troopers. He called up a larger view of the region. They were going to need an escape path; he just had to find it.

"Taking laser fire." It was Jacoby. "Damn, that *Griffin* can shoot far. That's beyond the range of my LRMs! No hit, but that *Locust* will be on me before I know it. They've got angles on me, Grimm!"

Before Hendrik could answer, Karl cut in. "It's coming toward your position, Grimm. I hit it hard, and it's moving away. Hu, get back here *now!* We've got this."

Hendrik looked toward Jacoby's position. He might make it there in time to help her, but then the *Hunchback* would be behind him. He was sure Niamh was in that 'Mech. It fit her personality. "Scheslinger, get moving and assist Johann's lance. Do not let me down."

"Of course not, Grimm." The *Phoenix* vaulted into the air on jets of plasma and toward the high hills where Jacoby was fleeing for her life.

Grimm wheeled the *Warhammer* around and made for the tree line. Zooming his visual sensors, he saw the path of shaking and shattering trees. *There you are.* He slowed his pace and took aim where he expected the 'Mech to emerge.

Missile fire arced briefly above the treetops as Karl's *Orion* took a risky shot. The aftermath of the attack made itself quickly known as limbs as deciduous shrapnel exploded in multiple directions. Hendrik massaged the control stick in his 'Mech and waited.

"She's almost out!" Karl screamed as Grimm squinted.

As if summoned, the *Hunchback* roared above the leafy head of the forest, flames from the jets in its legs lifting it high. Hendrik hadn't expected this and quickly adjusted his aim. The *Hunchback* arced downward, with Hendrik clear in its sights.

An affirmative targeting pulse, and Grimm hit the stud. Heat washed over him like a blast furnace as the dual particle beams lashed out at the dropping Clan 'Mech. The first went high, passing right through the space where the *Hunchback* was a moment before. The second ripped a line straight up the 'Mech's left side as it landed. Grimm could see the *Hunchback*'s exposed internals. He knew the 'Mech was not long for the world.

Before the Clan *Hunchback* had even steadied itself, one of its massive autocannons opened fire. Shells hammered into the left side of Hendrik's *Warhammer* with such force that the 'Mech spun slightly and Grimm felt his teeth rattle. Warning alarms sounded in the cockpit, and when the assault was finished, Hendrik saw the left arm and a good chunk of his 'Mech's left side were no more.

Another tone pinged in the cockpit, and Grimm saw Johann's *Rifleman* and the *Gladiator* and *Phoenix* from his lance were now in visual. While Hendrik was pleased to see their arrival, they weren't where they were supposed to be.

"I don't know what the hell you're doing here, Johann, but let's cut the head off this snake!" Grimm stepped back, set his weapons—or what remained of them—to an alpha strike and targeted on the fly. The reticule pulsed affirmative.

The *Warhammer* shuddered as laser and autocannon fire cut across the legs of his 'Mech. Hendrik spat when he saw the source.

Johann.

The other two traitors held their positions, and Niamh hesitated.

Here it is. Grimm reached for his satchel with one hand, and with the other activated the private channel between him and his sons. "So, this is where you're throwing your lot, then?"

He could hear the pleading in Johann's voice. "It's over, Grimm. Lay down now and you might find mercy."

Grimm laughed. "Mercy? I staged a prison break and a counterattack. Are you that foolish to think mercy will be given?" He found what he sought in his satchel and placed it in his lap. His fingers moved across the keys. "Tell me, son. At what point did you finally embrace the betrayal?"

"Grimm, stop this. The *Hunchback* pilot is Star Commander Niamh. She's going to hunt down Karl and kill him."

"Not if I kill her first!" Karl shot back. "I'm on this comm channel too, traitor!"

Hendrik looked past Niamh's *Hunchback* as Karl's *Orion* emerged from the trees. Plumes of smoke and fire announced a volley of missiles. It paired with the heat shimmer from the 'Mech's Class 10 autocannon. The *Hunchback* reeled from Karl's strike, and Grimm could tell he'd shredded the weak rear armor of the 'Mech and destroyed one of its deadly autocannons.

Despite the hit, Grimm knew his time was done—but maybe not Karl's. "Karl, get out of here. Rendezvous with the trucks. Retreat to that place I took you hunting a couple years ago. Hopefully you kept your word and never told your brother. Otherwise he'll find you."

The Clan *Hunchback* turned toward Karl's position.

Johann shouted. "Karl, don't! They will find you. I can help you!"

The bandit king switched back to the company channel. "Jacoby, I hope you are on the move. It's over. Johann betrayed us."

Silence answered Grimm. He responded with a sigh.

Switching back over, Grimm hovered a finger over the execute key on the transmitter resting in his lap. He saw Karl turn and fade back into the trees. "Son, I just want you to know I expected this, and planned for it."

He hit the key and looked at Johann's *Rifleman* and the two remaining 'Mechs from his lance. They were marching toward Hendrik's position, then suddenly froze, dead in their tracks. Grimm centered the targeting reticule on the *Rifleman*'s cockpit. From the corner of his eye, he saw the *Hunchback* had turned back toward him.

Hendrik depressed the firing stud just as the thrumming impact of multiple autocannon rounds slammed into the legs of his *Warhammer*, knocking him off balance and crashing his 'Mech to the ground.

Grimm shook like a rag doll held by an angry child as the 'Mech impacted. Blackness overtook him.

GRIMFORT
OBERON VI
CLAN WOLF OCCUPATION ZONE
6 DECEMBER 3049

The pain in Hendrik Grimm III's lower back was burning. He'd been on his knees, leaning forward for the past twenty minutes. He was only half-listening to the charges read against him by Star Commander Niamh. Grimm didn't care about them. Right or wrong, it wasn't going to change the outcome. After Niamh was done, Grimm would be executed. He knew that for certain. He would be made an example of.

Wincing, Grimm adjusted his posture, raising his head and locking eyes with Johann. His son stared back. Grimm thought he saw a hint of regret in Johann's eyes, but he couldn't be sure. Again, he didn't care. This betrayal was as expected. Johann had given himself to these Wolves.

The Wolf Clan. Grimm knew if there was one thing he didn't fully consider, it was who they truly were. Granted, he still didn't know that, but it was obvious now they were not from the Inner Sphere. Not FedCom, not Dracs, and certainly not ComStar. A near-alien force from beyond the Periphery with highly advanced tech—tech decades beyond even the Star League relics he'd seen. He didn't know who could possess such technological marvels, but if what Johann claimed was their ultimate plan might be proven even half true, the House lords were about to experience a pain and fear they hadn't in ages.

Grimm chuckled at that thought. *Welcome to my world, fools.*

"—to be executed for these crimes immediately." Niamh handed the noteputer to her attendant and faced the defeated bandit king. "Hendrik Grimm III, do you have anything to say?"

"Making an example of me will mean nothing to these people. They hate me anyway."

A curious smile came across the Star Commander's lips. "An example? You think we are making an example of you? To put fear into the hearts of the people you ruled? To make them afraid to challenge the supremacy of Clan Wolf?"

Grimm remained silent as Niamh opened her arms, taking in the crowd gathered in the courtyard of the Grimfort to witness the execution.

"No, Hendrik Grimm. Your offspring Karl will be made an example of, to show the folly of resisting Clan rule."

Hendrik scowled. He'd tried to buy Karl time, but the Wolves had caught him a day later.

Niamh continued. "You, Hendrik Grimm, are not going to be an example. You are going to be a monument. Your people will not mourn you. They will witness a prosperity under the Wolf banner. They will look to your head on the spike it will soon grace and see it as a monument to a failed society. A people left to live in paradise and squandered all the gifts they were given while those who fled so long ago were reforged by the most unforgiving fires to become the ones to restore the glory of the Star League."

Grimm could not contain his laughter. Spit shot from his mouth as he cackled at Niamh's speech. As he coughed out the last of his chuckles, he stared at her. "Whatever you want to tell yourself. In the end, odds are you'll find yourself right where I am. All the arrogant do."

Grimm looked again to Johann. "I had hoped you wouldn't betray me, but then again, you are a Grimm. For better or worse, the name lives on in you now."

Star Commander Niamh cut off any chance at a reply with a wave of her hand. "*Neg.* That will not happen. If bondsman Johann is deemed worthy through his testing, he may earn the title of warrior, but Grimm is not a Bloodname of the Wolves, nor of any Clan. It will be stripped from him, and fade from memory. No, Hendrik. The Grimm name dies with you." Niamh unsheathed the sword at her side, stepped to Hendrik's side, and raised the blade in a practiced stroke.

Grimm looked at Johann and gestured his head toward Niamh, smiling. "That's what she thinks."

Hendrik's vision narrowed, his son the only thing framed in his sights. He expected to see his life flash before him, but all that greeted him was Johann and the pack of Wolves who surrounded his betrayal.

The bandit king felt a hot pinprick somewhere on the back of his neck, then all was empty.

LOCATION UNKNOWN
INNER SPHERE
6 DECEMBER 3049

Ella Grimm's noteputer beeped. The transmission complete, she hoped whatever came in for her from ComStar was good news. Things hadn't been well lately. She'd caught her boyfriend Zander in an affair, and the local constabulary was breathing down her neck a bit too closely of late. She feared that they might be poking holes through her fake identity of Ella Grimes.

She keyed the noteputer and sorted through the data. Much of it was nothing of note, but a holomessage from someone listed as "H" stood out. It was verified as safe, so Ella opened the message.

She stumbled back into her chair as the image of her father appeared before her.

"Hello. It's your father. I have something I want to tell you."

SECRETS OF THE SPHERE: THE CAMERON QUESTION

MICHAEL CIARAVELLA

—Recorded at an undisclosed location, 10 June 3150

Good evening, ladies and gentlemen! Welcome back to *Secrets of the Sphere*, your source for the *true* story on all that occurs in the Inner Sphere. As always, I am your host, Kyle DiNoto, the Questioner.

Tonight's topic: the Cameron Question.

I believe it's safe to say that all of our discerning listeners know the history of House Cameron, the grand dynasty that saw the Inner Sphere through the Golden Age of the First Star League. Betrayed by the usurper Stephan Amaris, all seventy-nine members of First Lord Richard Cameron's family were murdered in a single act of barbarism whose repercussions would last for centuries...

Or so they would have us think.

As some of you might not know, there were actually *eighty* members of the First Lord's royal family. Amanda Cameron, the eleven-month-old daughter of Robert Cameron, was actually a twin, and she and her brother Ian were secreted off-planet in the final hours of Amaris's strike on Terra. I will not rehash the evidence of their clandestine escape from the Terran Hegemony—my esteemed colleague Sandra Raines has more than proven the truth to the story already—but many had always suspected that the Cameron line did not die that night.

I know what you are asking yourselves: Why bring this up now? The downfall of the House of Cameron has been lost into the annals of history. What more needs to be said?

Except, dear listeners, the *Secrets of the Sphere* team has recently come into possession of new evidence that Daniel Cameron, a direct-line descendant of Ian Cameron and the Star League throne, *might still be alive.*

Yes, you heard it here first, folks! There is a chance a descendant of House Cameron still lives!

While working on an exclusive piece on the current whereabouts of the mysterious Knights of St. Cameron, I recently happened on a former member of the Cult of St. Cameron, the semi-mystical order that still worships the Cameron family, who provided the information that led this stunning revelation!

Our informant—who has requested to remain nameless to protect their identity—has informed us that the modern descendants of the Cult have long suspected that a descendant of one of the Cameron twins might still be alive. They based their beliefs on a set of "lost prophecies" that allegedly came from the lost journals of Mother Jocasta Cameron herself, which foretold of a child that would bring House Cameron back to the stars.

With that as a starting point, we returned to the Taurian world of New Vandenberg, the closest major planet to where the SLS *Tripitz* was lost. (This WarShip, rumored to have secreted the twins away from Terra, was later found adrift in a system not far from New Vandenberg.) Using this new information, we located a pair of twins of approximately the correct age that had traveled toward Horsham, a former Star League shipyard and a habitable colony only one jump from the holdings of the Stewart-Cameron family of the Federated Suns!

Through tireless searches, our team was able to find one Daniel Cameron on Mendham, a planet just one jump from Horsham! Daniel, a computer programmer, graduated at the top of his class at the University of Mendam–Doran City, and was also rumored to be the illegitimate child of Johnathan Stewart-Cameron, one of the members of the distaff Stewart-Cameron line. Further evidence was destroyed, however, as Daniel's birth records were lost in a suspicious server failure three years ago.

The clincher for Yours Truly is that Mendham *just happens* to host the largest remaining population of the Cult of St. Cameron left in the Inner Sphere, an obvious connection when you think of how they would wish to keep an eye on the young heir until he can come into his true destiny.

Could this all be coincidence? Perhaps. Or perhaps this is just a part of far larger conspiracy...

Three days after we uncovered Daniel's potential lineage, our suspected Cameron heir decided to take a sudden, unplanned business trip to Addicks in the Draconis Combine, the same day that our informant left their home, never to return.

Does all this portend a return to power for the Cameron lineage? While House Cameron is currently landless, the merging of the Kurita royal family with the historic House Cameron line could provide legitimacy for the next heir to the Dragon's throne, not to mention a formidable claim to the legacy of the Star League itself. I don't think that it's too much to say that not since the wedding of Hanse Davion and Melissa Steiner has there been a better chance for a massive matrimonial upheaval to rock the very core of the Inner Sphere.

I'm sure I don't have to tell our politically savvy listeners what sort of a game-changer this is! A direct descendant of the Cameron line, despite having no major political power of their own, would be a powerful marriage prospect even now, giving the beleaguered nations of the Inner Sphere someone to rally behind.

Unfortunately, all of our subsequent attempts to learn more about Daniel Cameron and his current whereabouts have been for naught. Requests for information from both Daniel's employer and the passenger liner he supposedly boarded have been refused, citing "privacy concerns." Inquiries to an MIIO agent, speaking anonymously to protect their position, informs us that Daniel Cameron is not a person of interest to the Davion intelligence apparatus. My team finds themselves stymied at every turn, a clear sign that there is nothing more to find...or that someone desperately wants us to believe that!

Furthermore, we cannot ignore the potential opportunity before us: with three Clans currently bearing down on the birthworld of humanity itself, we cannot underscore the potential effect the return of House Cameron would have upon the various Clans. While Nicholas Kerensky is the Founder of the Clans, it was his father, the fabled visionary and SLDF Commanding General Aleksandr Kerensky who took the remaining Star League Defense Force beyond the Periphery. After the massacre of the Cameron family, Aleksandr believed that no one who truly deserved to be the custodians of the Star League's vaunted ideals was left.

Many of the Clans still revere the family that ushered their ancestors through some of the best times the Inner Sphere has ever seen, and they remember all too well the horrors of what came later when the House Cameron was betrayed. Warden or Crusader, if a Clan was given the opportunity to serve a true descendant of the First Lord of the Star League, what sort of effect would that have on the galaxy as a whole?

This begs several questions. What does the existence of a living descendant of House Cameron mean to the Inner Sphere as a whole? Where are the Knights of St. Cameron, and will they return? Are there more lost prophecies from Mother Jocasta, and are the Cult of St. Cameron keeping them from us? And will the Cameron family once again become a major player in the epic history of the Inner Sphere, or will they remain only a haunting reminder of all we have lost in the last great betrayal of human history?

As always, I leave it to each of my listeners to decide their own answers.

Tune in next week for another broadcast of *Secrets of the Sphere*! This is your host, Kyle DiNoto, reminding you to remain ever vigilant and *keep questioning!*

THE FLAMES OF IDLEWIND

BLAINE LEE PARDOE

DROPSHIP *BLOOD OF HUNTRESS*
IDLEWIND
DRACONIS COMBINE
10 MARCH 3050

Star Colonel Paul Moon glared at Idlewind on the viewscreen of the *Blood of Huntress* as if it were a rotting piece of meat, foul and disgusting. His officers of the Third Cavaliers Assault Trinary were assembled around him. He could feel their gaze split between the planet and him. *They are anxious, which means they will be aggressive.* It made him proud. Aggression was core to the Smoke Jaguar psyche—that, and ruthlessness. The Star Colonel embraced those feelings wantonly. *Our ruthlessness will pave the road to Terra, and ultimate victory.*

"This," he said, flicking his hand dismissively at the image of Idlewind as he turned to face them, "is Idlewind. It is a planet hardly worthy of our attention, other than it lies in our invasion corridor and stands in defiance to our Clan.

"We reached out to the defenders of this world, only to find disappointment. They have a battalion of heavy armor and a regiment of mechanized infantry. We were surprised they had the audacity to call themselves the 'Idlewind Stormtroopers.' As if calling themselves something as proud as stormtroopers has the power to make it so." Contempt rolled off his tongue as he spoke.

"I would ignore this world. It is beneath our attention as warriors. Freebirth scum in tanks and inferior tactical gear...hardly worth an orbital bombardment, let alone an honorable fight. Then again, what do we expect from the Inner Sphere but such feeble defenses? It is as our Khan said—these Houses are mere shadows of the warriors we are." He chose his words deliberately, to compel his Star Commanders to bid low. Several of them nodded as he spoke, mumbling agreement under their breaths.

"We will take this world because our Khan deems it so. I have been given this honor, but I share that honor with you. I cannot see us committing the entire Trinary against such weak foes. So I put it to you, my Star Commanders. Who would like the honor of quickly destroying these 'stormtroopers' so that we can move on to more worthy targets?"

Star Commander Matthew Wimmer spoke up first. "Star Colonel, armor, even inferior armor, requires armor as a response. I bid a Star of our Clan's finest OmniMechs. Best to do this quickly and effectively."

Star Commander Ferrin of Sweep Star stepped up. The female Elemental Star Commander was even taller than Paul Moon and, in some ways, more muscular. "A Star of OmniMechs against a mere battalion of ground armor? That bid is unworthy of the Smoke Jaguar. My Elementals are more than a match for these so-called Idlewind Stormtroopers. Where Matthew would seek quick victory, I prefer a challenge for my warriors. As such, I bid four Points of Elementals for the honor of taking this planet." Her bravado was met by murmurs of agreement and respect.

Star Commander Joal stepped forward. Shorter than most Elementals, he made up for his lack of height with sheer muscles. They called him the "Jungle Jaguar" for his remarkable bulk. "Star Colonel, you have heard from two of your commanders. One would use a sledgehammer to swat a fly. One goes in to give her warriors exercise. I came to the Inner Sphere to fight, as did my warriors. I do not seek just victories, but victories worthy of the Smoke Jaguar. I bid two Points of my best warriors to take on the Idlewind Stormtroopers."

There were nods from the other officers, and Paul Moon crossed his arms and stared down at Star Commander Joal with a stern expression that was a mix of respect and honor. *Joal has been chafing for an opportunity to prove himself, and his bid reflects it.* "Very well, are there any others who would challenge Star Commander Joal's bid?"

Star Commander Wimmer shook his head. Star Commander Ferrin crossed her arms and said nothing.

Moon gathered himself. "Very well then. Star Commander Joal, Idlewind is yours to take. Let us contact these stormtroopers and see where they desire to die."

IDLEWIND STORMTROOPERS HEADQUARTERS
BREEZEMONT, IDLEWIND
DRACONIS COMBINE
TWO HOURS LATER

Tai-sa Marc Lutz of the Idlewind Stormtroopers stared at the viewscreen with a look of puzzlement on his face. Years before, he had been a young *tai-i* fighting in the War of 3039, leading this tank lance to victory after victory. He had been posted to Idlewind because one does what the Dragon demands. They had promoted him and given him a posting along the Periphery, commanding a militia unit. Some officers would have seen it as a just reward, a soft posting where no action was likely. Others would have seen it as punishment...being sent out to the middle of nowhere to defend a backwater world against threats that would likely never arise.

Marc Lutz saw his posting more simply: a duty. He had long ago pledged himself to serve the Dragon. If this was where the Coordinator deemed he was needed, he would be pleased to serve here. He had not rested on his laurels either. Lutz had turned a ragtag pair of companies into a well-trained armor battalion. His regiment of infantry was mostly volunteer militia, but he had ensured that they were trained to fight the kind of wars that came to the Periphery—raiders and pirates. Their equipment was not new-production tanks and transports, but he had made certain that they were in the best operating condition. Lutz was prepared for a battle that might never come...until a few days ago.

Now he faced something different. Clan Smoke Jaguar. They had showed up in-system ten days ago at the nadir jump point and leisurely burned into planetary orbit. When they did reach out to him, they demanded to know what forces he would defend Idlewind with. "With all the Dragon can muster," he'd replied. "My battalion of armor and regiment of mechanized infantry." The Jaguars' language was precise, very military—with no contractions. The question of defending forces was a warning, and he saw it as such. *These are not Periphery raiders. Raiders do not ask such questions. They demand surrender and submission. Tai-sa* Lutz had immediately put his troops on alert.

Now the image flickered before him, and he saw a massive figure, larger than any human he had seen before, judging by the officers standing beside him. He was not dressed as a raider, but in a perfectly pristine gray uniform, devoid of medals.

"I am Star Colonel Paul Moon of Clan Smoke Jaguar. You are the commander of these Stormtroopers, *quiaff*?"

The last word puzzled Lutz, so he ignored it. "I am *Tai-sa* Marc Lutz, the commanding officer of the militia forces on Idlewind. I serve at the behest of the Coordinator, Takashi Kurita."

"Very well then. You still intend to defend this world with all the forces you have, *quiaff*?"

"I do not know what '*quiaff*' means, but yes, it is my intent to fight you with all we have." *Who would do otherwise? Why would an attacker pose such a question?*

"Very well. The warriors of the Third Cavaliers Assault Trinary will honor you by bidding two Points of Elementals under Star Commander Joal to take this world."

Lutz winced. "You have me at a disadvantage. I do not know what an 'Elemental' is, nor what a 'Point' represents."

Moon nodded, seeming to understand. "I forget how ignorant you Spherers are to our ways. I am an Elemental warrior, genetically bred for battle. We wear suits of battle armor. A Point is five warriors."

The *tai-sa* was staggered by the proposition. "You are sending ten armored troopers to take on my militia?"

"*Aff*," Moon said. "It is an aggressive bid, but Star Commander Joal is an exceptional warrior, as are those under his command."

They send their troops to their death. "And if I defeat this Star Commander?"

"Assuming you fight honorably, you may yet win this world. Joal may bring in the rest of the Trinary that was bid in the fight, but he does so at great risk to his own honor."

"Your ways are new and strange to me."

"You will learn them, if you survive. The Smoke Jaguar invasion will teach your Combine a great deal about our people. So, *Tai-sa* Marc 'Lutz' of the Draconis Combine, as the challenged, the right to choose the field of battle goes to you."

This Paul Moon wanted me to tell him my forces, and now he wants me to pick where we fight. He mentioned an invasion... This is not some Periphery scum or an arrogant Federated Commonwealth commander. He is massive...one of these 'Elementals.'

"There is a forested region some two kilometers outside of Breezemont, the capital of this world. If you are intent on fighting, that is where I choose to face you."

"We shall arrive tomorrow at midday, *Tai-sa*."

Lutz nodded. *If you wish to fight there, we will be prepared. This will be a quick battle for you, Paul Moon.* "We shall face you there."

"Well bargained and done," Paul Moon said, then his image flickered off in the viewscreen.

Tai-i Benjamin Kondo, who commanded the Stormtroopers' armor, had been standing off camera to the side, silently taking in the conversation. "Speak," Lutz said to his junior officer.

"We must be prepared. There is much about these Smoke Jaguars we do not know or understand. Their language is different. You saw that—what did they call it?—Elemental. They are giants. These are not invaders. They are aliens in many respects."

"I agree. They send ten warriors to take us all on—which means they very well may have superior technology. Their size suggests they are performing abhorrent genetic manipulation. We must assume the worst."

Tai-i Kondo nodded. "We must tip the fight to our advantage. We have had a drought for the last month. The forest you have chosen for this fight is dry. I suggest we drench it with napalm. When these Smoke Jaguars land, we ignite the forest and burn them."

The thought of burning warriors to death was unappealing, but so was the prospect of losing Idlewind to these invaders. *I will not be the one to disappoint the Coordinator.* "I approve of your plan. Do so quickly and discreetly.

"*Hai!* These Jaguars will rue the day they came here."

DROPSHIP *BLOOD OF HUNTRESS*
OUTSIDE OF BREEZEMONT
IDLEWIND
DRACONIS COMBINE
12 MARCH 3050

Star Commander Joal looked across the bay of the DropShip at the other nine Smoke Jaguar warriors who would accompany him. Their dark gray Elemental suits bore the stenciled name of their Trinary, the Stormriders, on their left chests. Three yellow stripes on the right shoulder marked them as warriors under his command. While he could barely see faces through the armored ferroglass viewports, he knew they were as excited as he to get into battle.

Since the arrival of ComStar's JumpShip *Outbound Light* at the Smoke Jaguar capital world of Huntress, the talk of war had changed to preparation. The weaker Clans, those of the Warden decay, favored not striking before a new Star League was formed. In the great rallies, he had heard from his Khans of the threat that would propose. The thought of the Star League re-forming without a place for Kerensky's chosen in its ranks tore at warriors like him. *These House lords are pretenders to a throne–a throne we shall reside on.*

Clicking his tongue twice quickly, he activated the tactical channel. "Stormriders, in two minutes we are landing on this world—one of the first the Smoke Jaguar will conquer on the road to Terra. We have traveled far along the Exodus Road. Now we stand at the threshold of destiny."

He paused and waited as the DropShip doors opened. "I want a good, tight dispersal. We fight as we trained, as a unit. I want good fields of fire. These Stormtroopers have chosen to face us in the forest, not knowing of the trials we faced during our training in the jungles of Lootera. Let us show them the fury of the Smoke Jaguars!"

From the open hatches he saw the dense growth, and wondered why a tank commander would choose such a place to fight. As the ship hovered over a clearing, kicking up leaves and dust, the green light over the doors came on, and Joal found himself grinning. "All right, Stormriders—deploy!"

He jumped down, not even bothering to light up his jump jets. He landed next to Lenov, both of them sweeping the dense growth of trees and brush for potential targets. Above him, the *Blood of Huntress* roared, the thrust pushing him as it departed.

"Battle Arc B formation," he barked.

The Elementals moved out, all prepared for battle against targets that thus far were unseen.

"Where are they, Star Commander?" Lenov asked. "I have no IR signatures or targets to destroy." Frustration and disappointment laced his voice.

For a moment, Joal did not reply as the forest drew to a strange calm with the departure of the DropShip. "I do not know," he finally said. "We will move east, toward the city."

He headed into the brush, the weight of his suit crushing the dead tree limbs he stepped on. It was tempting to sweep ahead fast, but he knew he had bid low and did not want to face the dishonor of being forced to call in the rest of the Trinary to finish his work.

They had moved some fifty meters forward when Lenov signaled him. "Star Commander, over here."

Joal approached Lenov, who pointed his left mechanical claw at a tree. A pinkish fluid ran down the side of its trunk. Pools of it lay all around where Lenov stood. It did not appear to be natural...its consistency was that of snot, though in far larger quantities. *What is that?*

Suddenly there was a loud *whomp!* It shook Joal hard. Everything around him erupted in flames. Napalm, a crude form of the payload in inferno missiles! The fluid burst into brilliant orange fire, and in two milliseconds, his entire formation was engulfed in flame. The brilliant fire momentarily overloaded his Elemental suit's sensors, but they quickly compensated.

They have trapped us, and are trying to burn us alive...

BREEZEMONT
IDLEWIND
DRACONIS COMBINE

From the top hatch of his Pegasus hovertank, *Tai-sa* Marc Lutz heard a great *whoosh*, followed with a powerful wind as the forest containing the Smoke Jaguars erupted in a massive ball of flame. The plume rose skyward, like a boiling black-and-orange balloon of heat that was so intense, he could feel it here, nearly half a kilometer from the tree line. A sudden stiff wind drew air toward the fire, whipping at him hard. The ball of smoke and heat rose, then broke wide open in the sky, billowing in the winds.

The forest itself was a vision of *gouka*, pure hellfire. The napalm-soaked trees stabbed skyward like blackened sentinels standing over the deaths of his enemies. The ground looked like a volcano, seared and glowing crimson.

Lutz lowered his enhanced binoculars for a moment...there was no point. Nothing could survive that inferno. *I have not fought with honor, but instead fought to win this day.* The Smoke Jaguars might employ more force in response, but he was prepared for it. *The only true honor is in victory.* The mental image of the large warriors burning alive would haunt him, he was sure of that.

Tai-i Benjamin Kondo's Maxim transport, filled with infantry, moved alongside Lutz's Pegasus, and he rose from his top hatch as well, his eyes fixed on the inferno. "We have taught these Smoke Jaguars the price of their arrogance, *Tai-sa*," he called over.

"Do not relish such victories," Lutz warned him. "They all come with a price."

Some of the burning trees collapsed, so intense was the flames. A tiny snow of gray ash rained down around Lutz, all that would remain of the forest he had destroyed. *When the fire has died, we will need to examine these Jaguars, and perhaps learn their true origins...*

Then he spotted something in the fire... Movement. It looked at first like a shadow or a trick of the flames, but he saw more shifting in the furnace he had created. They were humanoid, walking through the fire, toward his position.

This cannot be. No one could survive those flames.

Raising his binoculars, he zoomed in on the figures. Boxy projections on their heads resembled the hood of a cobra. Their armored suits were massive, with a protruding torso. They emerged from the fires, their paint charred black, wisps of gray smoke rising from their heated armor...but they walked, still very much alive.

"Look," *Tai-i* Kondo called out. "It cannot be!"

Five of them rose on plumes of fire from their legs—jump jets—arcing through the air toward Lutz's forces, their massive armored suits framed against the roaring flames in the forest. As they came down, the boxy projections behind their heads flared, and short-range missiles rained down on Lutz's line of vehicles. One missile hit behind him, the concussion throwing him hard into the hatch edge and knocking the wind out of him. A blast went off to his right where Kondo's Maxim was; another two blasts tore into the hover APC transport next to him.

Lutz struggled for a moment to regain his breath, and from the ache he felt, he had either bruised or broken one of his lower ribs. Looking over at the Maxim next to him, he saw the decapitated body of *Tai-i* Kondo slumped to one side. Blood ran down the left flank armor, dripping on the grass below. *He never stood a chance.*

The *tai-sa* struggled for his binoculars and realized they were no longer around his neck, no doubt lost in the blast. He dropped down, fumbling with the hatch, but eventually closing it and throwing the latch to lock it into place.

"Driver, take us south, flank speed," he sputtered as the Elemental warriors rose again on their jets, closing the distance quickly. Lutz's lip hurt and he realized it was cut and starting to swell. *I was lucky. That missile could have killed me.*

"Stormtroopers armor, I am taking direct command," he said into the throat mike he wore. "Follow me to the south. These Smoke Jaguars are armed with missiles."

Those barbarians tried to kill me with fire...and now they will pay. Star Commander Joal knew all too well what his suit was capable of. To an Elemental warrior, the suit was like part of their body, an extra layer of skin. The Elemental armor was well insulated from such hazards for short durations. He was hot, soaking in sweat, but not frying like his foe had hoped. *These Combine troops did not know their enemy, but now they will learn.*

"Lenov," he commanded as he broke through the flames, "target those troop transports. Alpha Point, form up on me and target their largest vehicles." He blinked his eyes to activate his jump jets and rose from the inferno of the forest, firing down at the vehicles with his short-range missiles.

One missile slammed into the top-rear of a Pegasus hovertank, leaving a hole near the ventilation system for the engine. His second missile slammed into the turret of a Schrek PPC carrier. That missile had hit where the particle projection cannon barrels were attached to the turret, leaving a caved-in piece of armor in its wake.

As he dropped to the ground, Alpha Point formed up around him, their missiles hitting the Schrek and an old Manticore tank. Having disgorged their missiles, they switched to their arm-mounted lasers or machine guns and fired at their targets. The Manticore bolted, heading full speed to the city in the distance.

The Schrek started to turn south, exposing its flanks to three lasers, including Joal's. He hit near the front bogie wheel, leaving a hot, glowing scar on the track. The others tore into the turret, which was attempting to adjust and return fire.

Bravo Point fired their jump jets again, landing on top of the Maxim. Enraged by the deceitful attack against them, the Elementals blasted at the thin top armor of the vehicle. One pulled a decapitated body out of the top hatch and poured a burst of machine gun fire into the interior. The rear and side doors popped open, and infantry poured out, firing at the Smoke Jaguars with small-arms fire. Another Elemental jumped down, sweeping the infantry at point-blank range with his small laser, swinging it like a scythe mowing down grain in a field. Arms, legs, and heads dropped, followed by the bodies they had been attached to. Sickly white smoke rolled off the dead, mingling with the raining ash.

The Star Commander aimed another laser strike at the Schrek as the Pegasus accelerated and made a break for the open hills to the south. The Schrek turned and fired its PPCs at the far end of his Point. As an anti-Mech weapon, a PPC was devastating. Against highly mobile, armored Elementals, the blasts were ineffective. The brilliant bursts of white-tinged blue beams missed their marks, burning the grass around his warriors. The static-discharging arcs from the bursts danced off the Elementals' armor, leaving little black furrows on their already charred paint. *Battle scars...*

Joal lit his own jump jets again, coming down just behind the Schrek as it finished its slow turn. He aimed perfectly at the rear of the tank, his laser humming in his ears as he fired. The brilliant crimson beam stabbed through the thin rear armor and seared deep into the vehicle.

Another warrior in his Point, Juan, landed haphazardly on the top of the PPC carrier. He smashed his left-hand claw into the tank top and pulled up enough armor to grip on. With his right-hand machine gun, he fired sustained bursts into the top armor near the engine compartment. There was a dull *poof* from the bowels of the vehicle, and billows of white-gray smoke poured out of every port on the Schrek, proof of the fires within.

The hatched popped open, and the crew started climbing out as the vehicle ground to an agonizing halt. Juan and two other Elementals helped them out, grabbing the driver and gunner and tossing them high in the air. They landed with thumps so hard that Joal swore he heard bones cracking.

The Maxim burst into flames, and Bravo point jumped immediately to the hover APC that was attempting to break for open ground. They rained down laser and machine gun fire on the thin top armor, savaging it so badly that the vehicle suddenly swerved and plowed into the sod, tearing a long trench as it groaned to a stop. It disgorged infantry who fired and threw grenades as the Elementals landed.

Joal was amazed at their gall and audacity. Bullets ricocheted in every direction, and the Elementals walked toward the infantry casually, unafraid. Their own machine guns tore into the dismounted infantry, and in less than five seconds, they were all dead, lying in a collective bloody heap as the APC belched gray smoke from the open doors.

One of the Elementals atop the APC suddenly exploded, his arms and legs flailing in the air over Joal. He bit his lower lip at the sight. He had seen warriors die before; that was part of being raised in a *sibko*. This was different. *We have traveled back to the Inner Sphere, and now one of us is dead...so close to Terra.*

Anger swelled over him. He saw the Pegasus that had fired the deadly blast. "Alpha Point, I want that vehicle destroyed!" Activating his own jets, he roared into the air straight at the Combine vehicle.

Tai-sa Lutz's Pegasus banked around hard and unleashed a wave of short-range missiles at the giant armored infantry. Two missiles caught one of the warriors in the chest and blew them apart. He saw one arm spinning wildly in the air before thudding into the grassy hills.

"*Banzai!*" he cheered for a moment. *They can be killed!* "Swing us wide, line up for another wave of SRMs," he commanded. The hovertank swung around tightly, almost lining up in the direction it had been coming from.

Then he saw it: four of the Smoke Jaguars, rising in the air like avenging angels, arcing straight at him. From the viewport, he lost them as they rose, but he knew he had kicked open a beehive of vengeance.

"Back off, back off!" he barked to the driver, and he felt the Pegasus lunge backward hard. He almost hit the padded ring near the viewport as he glanced back out. Then he heard it, a crunching bump above him. Then came a sound of moaning metal, and the rattle of machine gun fire as the Smoke Jaguar tore into the hovertank.

"They are on top of us!" he called out. "Full speed, tight turns! Shake them off!"

The vehicle lurched in the opposite direction, and he heard the scraping of metal above him. Glancing out of his viewport, he saw a Saladin hovertank ablaze with several of the blackened armored warriors literally ripping armor plating off of it while three others were firing away at a Scimitar scout.

The sounds above him drew his immediate attention. They sounded like punches, or pile drivers, hitting the top armor with deafening blows. *Those claws of theirs are strong. They will tear us apart.*

"*Tai-sa*, they are over the engine compartment," the gunner called as the turret whirred around. "I cannot get a shot!"

For the Dragon... Tai-sa Lutz reached down and pulled out his service pistol. *Against these armored monstrosities, this is a peashooter. We all have our duty and I will not shirk from mine.* Biting his swollen lip, he threw the latch on the hatch and pushed it open.

The hatch opened at almost the same moment the engine was disabled. The Pegasus was moving fast, and the loss of power made the front skirt furrow into the hillside, throwing off two Elementals. Star Commander Joal held on, though he was tossed hard over the side. His left arm ached as he flexed it, pulling himself back up.

He saw a man half out of the hatch, his face bloody from a cut on his lip, aiming a pistol at him. The gun blazed, and the shots glanced off of Joal's viewport harmlessly as the shooter emptied his magazine. When he moved to reload, Joal reached over and pulled him out of the turret with his claw. He heard the man's arm *crack* as he clamped onto him, and saw the grimace of pain.

Joal was going to toss him hard to the ground and finish him off, but the face...he recognized it. Activating his external speaker with a click of his tongue, he pulled the officer before him. "*Tai-sa* Marc. Order your troops to stand down."

"Never," the man said in anguish. "I answer only to the Coordinator. We will fight on, block by block if we have to. You will never take this world."

The Star Commander paused for a moment—his expression a mix of appreciation and duty. *Even in defeat he is defiant. Such a waste.* He studied the bruised and bloodied face and thought back to the rallies on Huntress, before the Grand Crusade. *We were told that these were inferior troops, unworthy of us. While his ambush and fire attack on us was dishonorable, he does not shirk from duty. Perhaps there is more to these Spherers than we know.*

"Very well," he said and tossed the *tai-sa* to the ground. The man moaned loudly, his broken forearm jutting through his uniform sleeve. The Star Commander raised his laser at him and fired. The weapon throbbed and hummed as it ended the Combine officer's life.

Such a waste...

BREEZEMONT
IDLEWIND
DRACONIS COMBINE
12 MARCH 3050

Star Colonel Paul Moon watched his Elemental troops destroy another building the Stormtroopers' infantry had been using as a base of operations. Flames poured out of it as the Elementals smashed through the exterior walls to fire at the enemies within.

This victory was slow in coming, ponderously so. *This militia, these Idlewind Stormtroopers, they have behaved without honor. They deserve little more than death.*

Star Commander Joal stepped up before him and saluted. Moon, in his Elemental armor did the same. "Report."

"The surviving tanks and infantry have dug in at the center of Breezemont. I have lost three warriors thus far, but we are more than able to finish the job. Some of their infantry have run out of ammunition, and are throwing stones at us. It will take time, and in the end, we will have to raze this city to ensure that they are all dead."

Paul Moon shook his head. "Star Commander, I agree with your results, but not the means. You have done enough, but we are on a timetable. It will take too long with the forces you have."

"I will not be denied the honor of a complete victory, Star Colonel," Joal replied.

"And I will not be responsible for holding up Delta Galaxy's schedule for this invasion. These Combine troops tried to slaughter your warriors in a fire trap. If they had known anything about us, they would have known it was doomed to fail. Our superior technology enabled our victory. Still, they violated your honor first—so there is no dishonor for you to bear."

"Star Colonel—" Joal pushed.

"*Neg.* It is done. I am bringing in the entire Trinary. We will level this city by tomorrow morning. These Idlewind Stormtroopers will be a fading memory, and the Jaguar can return to prowling the stars."

"I have failed you," Joal said.

Moon shook his head. "*Neg.* You have taught me an important lesson about these Spherers going forward. Now we will teach them the price of dishonor." With those words, he used his communicator to signal for the rest of the Stormriders to debark.

Moon watched Star Commander Matthew Wimmer's OmniMechs fan out from the DropShips and form their line of battle. He did not enjoy the moment, nor did it make him cringe.

There are many steps before I stand on Terra, this is merely one of them.

"Stormriders...open fire!"

FORGOTTEN HEROES, SLANDERED HONOR

PATRICK WYNNE

—Terran Legion newsletter, 3096

"Old soldiers never die, they just fade away." At least, that seems to be the hope of many within the Republic of the Sphere, regarding those of us who served in the Protectorate Militia or Terran Security during the Jihad.

For over a decade now, we have undeservedly endured discrimination and social mistreatment from those who claim to be more enlightened and just than the powers who have come before. Despite legislation explicitly prohibiting such treatment, such as the General Amnesty Act of 3082, many of us continue to be shunned by our neighbors for no greater crime than simply doing our duty.

The halls of the Terran Legion are filled with such veterans. Here are some of their stories.

Pippel Ximenez, Procyon: Yeah, I served with the Militia until the end. I was attached to Colonel Janocek's personal staff. After the war, I tried to join up with the Republic Armed Forces, figured it didn't matter whose flag I fought under as long as I was defending Procyon. But the recruiter sure didn't see it that way. Took one look at my service record, and that was it. Oh, he smiled and nodded and made excuses, but I could see the hate in his eyes. I've been slaving away making doughnuts ever since. My woman left me because I couldn't support her. The Terran Legion's all I got.

Helen Ocampo, Basalt: Most people think that because I fought alongside the Word, I'm some kind of Blakie nutcase or something. Nothing could be further from the truth. I don't go for religions or ideologies at all. Most of us don't care about that mumbo jumbo, but try telling your average civvy that. I've lost friendships once they found out I served.

John Harper Kennil, Terra: I know it's not politic to say in this day and age, but we really did believe the Word had our best interests at heart. Certainly more than the Houses did, and forget about the Clans. Maybe Stone can make us feel that way again, but so far I haven't really seen it. All my neighbors here in Port Askaig though, they just worship the ground that man walks on. I nearly came to blows over it with old Boyd Somhairle down the road a ways. Nowadays I just keep my mouth shut.

"Perceval Cromwell," Caph: I quit my job. Couldn't take all the "rah-rah Stone" shit all the time. Me and the boys are heading up country. Gonna set us up a place where we can believe what we wanna believe, drink with whoever we wanna drink with, hunt some dinos, and to hell with everybody else. And if the Stoners don't like it, well, we'll teach them a thing or two. Between all of us, we got nearly 200 years of service time, and most of that was in the thickest fighting of the Jihad. So, Militia, Blakist, or if you just can't stand that Stone prick and all his smug cultists, come join us at Camp Cameron.

AIRS ABOVE THE GROUND

JASON HANSA

BLED
VIPAAVA
GHOST BEAR INVASION CORRIDOR
24 SEPTEMBER 3050

Point Commander Lauren grimaced in pain as her injured leg slid over loose rubble. Catching herself, she continued toward the small group conferring near the gate of the Clan Ghost Bear compound. Previously a planetary militia position inside the capital city, it had been declared the headquarters of the occupying Clan forces due to its convenient location to transportation networks, maintenance bays, and the spaceport.

It was a decision she was beginning to reconsider, due to the daily mortar attacks from Rasalhagian rebels. Stepping over a fire hose and sidestepping to avoid a pair of firefighters, she approached the front gate, where she could see Captain Jošt Koren of the Bled Police Department waiting alongside his horse.

"This crap's starting to piss me off," a voice said beside her. "No casualties, thank God, the secretaries were out to lunch."

"Language," Lauren said, correcting her bondswoman's use of contractions. The local militia, the Twenty-Second Rasalhagian Free Company, had fought honorably and well when the Ghost Bears had taken the planet. Her bondswoman, Zala, had managed to knock Lauren's *Adder* down a slope, but had tumbled down after it in her *Wyvern* due to gyro damage. Lauren had returned to consciousness with her left leg broken in two spots and Zala standing in her cockpit aiming a pistol at her head. Luckily, they could both hear Elementals approaching, and Lauren convinced her to surrender before the armored infantrymen arrived.

"Hmmph. This *stuff's* starting to *annoy* me—better, oh wise Point Commander?" Zala quietly replied, tongue firmly in cheek.

Lauren sighed and ignored it. Though many Clan warriors would have beaten Zala for the impudence—maybe even killed her—Lauren allowed her cheekiness to continue in private because overall it was a small price to pay for her other talents. Zala spoke the local languages, seemed to know everyone worth knowing on Bled, and was an efficient and orderly aide. Best of all, unlike many other Rasalhagian bondsmen she had heard of, Zala was actively trying to conform to the Way of the Clans. Because of that, Lauren had decided a softer touch would work better on her than an iron fist.

"Funny. The office is a loss then, *quiaff*?" Lauren asked.

"*Aff*, Point Commander," Zala replied formally to the rhetorical question, now that they were within earshot of the local police. "Two rounds hit the parade field, but the third, currently estimated to be a one-oh-eight-millimeter round from the damage, landed straight on the admin building."

"Three rounds, Detective. Please tell me you have *something*," Lauren said, turning her attention to the police captain.

The tall man swung his hard gaze onto her, and she returned it unflinchingly. The policeman was straight-backed, with dark hair going gray at the temples, but maintained a bearing that showed he still found time to work out. His face relented somewhat, and Lauren saw some weariness in the corners of his eyes. She had initially believed his lack of openness demonstrated his resistance to Clan Ghost Bear's control of the world, but her bondswoman had informed her that he held no political concerns as such. He was a law enforcement officer, charged with maintaining order, and considered the Ghost Bear compound to be just another neighborhood to study, watch, and protect.

"We have reports of rounds fired from the north side, Point Commander. One of my officers could hear the mortar echoing down an alley, but by the time he got on-scene, he saw nothing."

"Was he mounted?" Zala asked, stroking the neck of Koren's mount. He nodded.

"How long does it take a horse to cover a block?" Lauren asked.

Zala snorted. "If the sidewalk was clear? Thirty seconds, maybe a little longer. These horses are big *and* fast."

"The officer said he was on-scene in under two minutes," Koren answered. "He had to go up two blocks and over one."

Lauren nodded as she saw three people, two men and a woman, approaching from the garrison barracks. Seeing the scowl on the woman's face, she decided to wrap things up.

"Zala, finish debriefing Police Captain Jošt, and then meet me in the conference room."

Ten minutes later, Zala entered the conference room, slipping into her chair in the midst of a heated discussion.

"Three mortar rounds this morning makes fifteen over the past two weeks—and we all know we will receive at least one round tonight," said Star Commander Antoinette, one of the Steel Viper MechWarriors, scowling. Still clad in her skintight blue-and-yellow cooling suit, the athletic woman had returned from patrol just after the rounds landed. The route had taken her through the city's south side, the opposite direction of the mortar's point of origin, a fact no one believed to be a coincidence. She had pulled her hood off, her ink-black hair streaming behind her and gleaming in the fluorescent light. Her dark eyes flashed as she continued, "Or does your captain have some reason to believe this attack has depleted them of ammunition?"

Zala flared for a second. but quickly brought her temper under control, for which Lauren was thankful. Had her bondswoman publicly disrespected Antoinette, the Steel Viper would have immediately corrected her, probably with lethal consequences.

Zala looked at her datapad, reviewing her notes. "Ammo for the calibers targeting us come twelve and eight to a case. Since we have received fourteen seventy-five millimeters and three big ones this morning, Captain Koren estimates we can expect at least ten more small ones and five more one-oh-eights." Silence dominated the table for a moment as her words sank in.

"Captain Koren is...honest and reliable, according to my reports," interjected the thin man sitting across the table from the MechWarrior. Clad in a business suit, and with a white robe carefully folded across the back of his chair, ComStar Precentor Alvarez looked comfortable even surrounded by Clan warriors. "No, Star Commander, the problem is the rebels have infiltrated his force, as they have every organization on-planet. They haven't taken to attacking their own countrymen—yet—but their so-called resistance finds it no trouble at all to avoid those either trying to help us or simply carrying on their duty."

He leaned back, interlacing his fingers, thinking as Lauren studied him. Like the police captain, Precentor Alvarez did not seem to particularly like or dislike the Clans; his superiors had ordered him to help administer the world for the Ghost Bears, and he was doing his best to execute those orders.

"We could burn the city to the ground," the Steel Viper said, menace in her voice. "On your behalf, of course, Point Commander," she added, turning to Lauren with a wicked smile.

Lauren's eyes narrowed in irritation.

Since beginning their invasion of the Inner Sphere, Clan Ghost Bear had been leaving minimal garrisons behind on the conquered worlds. In the invasion's early stages, they had left behind only their wounded, giving them time to heal while executing the "light duty" of bringing an entire world into submission. Unfortunately for the Clan, this had resulted in numerous worlds overthrowing their garrisons and forcing the Ghost Bears to slow their forward assault to secure their lines. Clan

Ghost Bear had swallowed its pride and asked for help, striking a deal with Clan Steel Viper for warriors to assist in garrisoning Ghost Bear worlds. Steel Viper frontline units, nominally under the command of the highest-ranking Bear on-planet, soon arrived, eager to fight any opponent and prove their value among the invading Clans.

Lauren, as the only ambulatory Ghost Bear MechWarrior, was left in command of an ad hoc Point of injured Elementals when the rest of her Cluster departed Vipaava for the Clan's next target. Antoinette's attitude constantly irritated Lauren, but as none of her wounded Elementals could wear their armor and she could barely pilot a BattleMech with her injured leg, she was very happy to have the Vipers on world with her. Even though Antoinette commanded a reinforced Star—five OmniMechs and five Points of Elementals, a Star variant the Vipers called a "Rattler"—her Vipers were stretched thin across the city, and she was also getting frustrated by the rebels and their ability to consistently elude her patrols.

"I would prefer to keep 'razing the capital' as plan B for now," Lauren replied dryly. "Do you have any further notes, Zala?"

"Point Commander, the police captain did have one more item of interest," Zala began hesitantly. "He is hearing rumors that the rebels have found the *Ronin*."

Lauren cocked her head, confused, but Precentor Alvarez slowly sat back in his chair and whistled quietly.

"That's not good," he said, and then turned to Lauren. "About twenty years ago, several Draconis Combine units went rogue, trying to keep what would become the Free Rasalhague Republic in the Combine. The Coordinator declared these units *ronin*, that is, warriors without honor or a lawful master, an incredibly shameful designation in their culture. Here on Vipaava, the ten surviving *Ronin* MechWarriors conducted *seppuku*, the ritualistic suicide of the disgraced. But their BattleMechs were never found. Until now, apparently?" he asked, turning back toward Zala.

"Ten ancient BattleMechs?" the Steel Viper interjected, a vicious smile on her face. "I hope this rumor is true. If my Clan is not moved from reserve status to active status in this invasion, this may be my Star's only opportunity for glory."

Lauren looked at her bondswoman, who seemed uncharacteristically embarrassed. "This is unconfirmed, *quiaff*? The detective is still investigating these rumors?"

"*Aff*, Point Commander. Captain Koren has someone he wants to talk to...a, ah, person with experience in this sort of guerrilla campaign, someone who might know about the *Ronin*," Zala said, her cheeks red in embarrassment.

Lauren quirked an eyebrow, looking around the table at the others, first at Alvarez, then Antoinette, and finally Benjamin, the Ghost Bear Elemental Point Commander who had been sitting quietly at the far end of the table. He shook his head; he had been spending almost as much time with Zala as Lauren had, teaching the bondswoman Ghost Bear customs and working on her hand-to-hand combat skills. Now curious, especially since the precentor seemed to know who this person was, Lauren turned back toward Zala.

"Who, Bondswoman?"

Zala studied the floor, hooked some of her hair over her ear as she shuffled, and replied without looking up. "My father."

As casually as she could, Lauren reached up and grabbed the handle on the ceiling of the police cruiser as Captain Koren took a curve at what she thought was near-impossible speed. Somehow, though, the tires maintained their grip on the mountain road, and the cruiser kept from plummeting hundreds of meters down a sheer cliff.

"The view is worth it, trust me," Koren promised.

Lauren glanced over, unsure if he was teasing her or not. Then, as the car completed the curve and cleared the mountain blocking her view, she could see what Koren was talking about.

"Great Kerensky," she whispered, and then glanced into the back seat.

Benjamin sat next to Zala, and Lauren could see he was in as much awe as she was. Bled, the capital of Vipaava, curved around the shore of a large bay. The curves of the bay consisted of rolling, forested hills that bled into another large semicircle around the city, the mountain ridge they were traveling on. The apex of the mountain curve was about fifty kilometers outside town; the land between them was fields of cropland. From her vantage point, Lauren could see over the entire bay.

Koren pulled off into a designated scenic view, and the four of them exited the car. Below them, the bay was a deep, luxurious sapphire; small triangles of sail marked pleasure craft, and Lauren spotted small dots of fishing boats returning through the narrow bay entrance with their late catches.

"There is...nothing like this at home. I always knew the Inner Sphere would look beautiful, but I could never have imagined anything like this," she quietly said to Koren. She noticed Benjamin and Zala also having a similar subdued conversation off to her right.

"Sometimes," Koren began, before pausing. "Sometimes, after a particularly rough case, after seeing the worst of what humanity can do to itself...I like to come up here. Just to reflect, to remember that life is worth fighting the dark for."

She nodded and smiled at his openness, thinking that maybe she would not mind spending an evening alone with him. As she made a mental note to ask Zala about Spheroid mating customs later, Koren cleared his throat.

"Of course, this terrain is also your problem, tactically and philosophically, you understand," he went on, all business.

His sudden shift jarred her thoughts, and he saw the confusion on her face.

"The north and south sides of Bled merge into the ridge lines that run out to sea and form the arms of the bay, so it is child's play for the rebels to run in and out of the mountains." He pointed to two small figures moving west out of the city. "Additionally, from anywhere along the ridge, rebels can see any movements out of the city you might make—that appears to be Antoinette in her *Battle Cobra* and one of her *Summoner*s. And as for the philosophical point..." He looked at her. "This is land worth fighting for."

She nodded. "Point taken." She turned again toward the view. "A land worth fighting for, indeed."

Fifteen minutes of driving brought them to the small town of Železniki, an alpine village nestled between two mountains. As they passed through, Lauren noticed the lack of motorized vehicles. Though there were some, it seemed that most of the people in town rode horses singly or hitched to wagons.

"Is this common in the mountains? More horses than cars?" she asked.

"Yes, Point Commander," Zala replied. "Our people have been raising and breeding horses since we left Terra. It is a point of pride among us. Many of those living in cities have at least one horse stabled in a small town somewhere. We are 'born in the saddle,' as they say. My family..." She trailed off, watching the last of town pass by. "My family is well known for our breeding techniques."

"I think 'well known' is a bit of an understatement, Zala," Koren said. "But they can explain for themselves." He pulled through a wrought iron gate into a rolling, well-manicured field. In the distance, a herd of mottled gray horses slowly moved and grazed. Heading up a long, gravel road, the cruiser passed a series of buildings Zala identified in turn, several of them stables. As they pulled up in front of a large mansion, Lauren saw a round, cheerful woman with long gray hair standing next to a bent old man leaning heavily on a polished wooden cane.

They stopped, and Zala jumped out. "Mom! Dad!" She hugged them in turn as the other three exited. "You both know Captain Koren," she said, and he stepped forward to present them both with a bottle of wine—a local custom when visiting, he had explained to Lauren in the car.

"This is Benjamin," Zala went on. "I mean, Point Commander Benjamin." Lauren saw both Koren and Zala's mother narrow their eyes, and knew she had missed something important. She made another mental note as Zala went on, saying, "This is Point Commander Lauren, the Ghost Bear administrator of Vipaava and my, uh..." She trailed off.

"Zala is my bondswoman," Lauren put simply. "It is very nice to meet you."

"Slave?" the man asked darkly.

"No, Dad, more an...'indentured aide-de-camp.' It is complicated," Zala finished, flustered.

"Your daughter fought bravely and honorably in defense of your world. We have adopted her into our Clan, and in time she will finish her probationary period and become a full warrior among the Ghost Bears," Benjamin said, more words than Lauren could remember him ever saying.

The man nodded, accepting the answer. "You have the data?" he asked Koren, and then accepted a data disk from the policeman. "Very well. Please, make yourselves at home. Zala can show you around."

Zala turned. "I guess I should start by showing you the airs."

Fifteen minutes later, they entered a large, oval-shaped building that smelled of horses and manure. In the center, ten gray horses with riders were performing intricate maneuvers.

"More horses?" Lauren asked.

Zala looked appalled, and then shook her head. "Point Commander, these are not just horses, these are *Lipizzans*!"

Seeing the lack of comprehension on Lauren and Benjamin's face, she took a deep breath. "Okay. Lipizzans are one of the most regulated and controlled breed of horse in existence. The recognized beginning can be traced to a single stud back in 1580—thirty years from now will be the fifteen-hundredth anniversary of this breed." She looked at the horses, and then back. "As of now, there are only thirty-seven recognized mare lines and twelve stud lines. We have the only recognized stud line from Terra itself! Our ancestors received permission to take frozen genetic material with them when they departed to colonize this planet. Watching these horses perform is like seeing a living piece of Terran history."

Lauren looked at Benjamin, and then back at the horses. "Great Kerensky," she whispered.

It took Zala the rest of the afternoon to show them her family's estate. The family, apparently, was extremely wealthy and, up until the Ghost Bears landed, held minor nobility status. They had just under a hundred retainers, employees, and workers of every kind on the land, most working or caring for the horses, and several guest and employee houses on the premises. Zala explained that her family had raised and bred the Lipizzans since before the fall of the Star League, and were known across the Inner Sphere, "at least in circles that give a crap about horses, pun intended," as she put it.

They were back in the practice facility, watching handlers lead the horses through their maneuvers, and Lauren had laughed at Zala's joke.

Her jaw then fell, though, when Zala nonchalantly discussed her visit to Terra. Zala was proud of the one time she had visited when she was nine, and was hoping she would be allowed to visit again as a Ghost Bear. Her father, she explained, had traveled to Terra about twice a decade for almost his entire adult life transporting genetic material to trade with other Lipizzaner breeders.

"Do you think that ComStar and the Clan will allow me to accompany him, once I become a warrior? His traveling is necessary for the stability of the line, you understand."

Lauren threw a look to Benjamin—they had been very careful to not tell the populace that Terra was the eventual target of the Clan invasion—and now her head spun, trying to calculate how valuable Zala and her family had just became to the Clan. As far as she knew, no one else in the Ghost Bear Occupation Zone had been to Terra recently; firsthand accounts of their destination could be of invaluable assistance to her Clan when they moved to conquer it and win the title of ilClan.

"Zala, I believe your father—because of his knowledge of genetics, breeding techniques, and wealth—is eligible for adoption into either the scientist or merchant caste of our Clan," she finally said. "And as ComStar is working with our Clan in a neutral capacity, I am sure he will get to travel there again."

"Of this I am certain," Benjamin grunted in response, and Lauren smiled slightly at his dry humor. Even if officially designated a scientist or a merchant, she was positive Mr. Kotnik would be accompanying them on their final push toward Terra. She frowned upon remembering that they had not come up to discuss Terra with him, and asked Zala and Koren why they had brought data to her father to study.

Before answering, Zala waved them all toward the door. Catching the hint, Lauren led the way back out into the setting sunlight, the sky quickly darkening as the local sun started to shrink behind a mountain.

Zala started talking over her shoulder as she led them up the path to the house. "My father was involved in the Rasalhague resistance for decades. He was a member as a teen, and then helped finance and lead it as he got older. He personally attacked the Draconis Combine dozens of times and planned dozens of further attacks. They never suspected him, and he was recognized as a hero of the nation on our tenth founding anniversary. Sorry, not 'ours,' anymore, since I am a Ghost Bear now. You know what I mean," she said, flustered. "Anyways, Captain Koren figured he might have some ideas about them."

The tall captain, walking behind Lauren and Zala, shrugged. "It might be a long shot, but I figured, why not? But I have hope Mr. Kotnik will see something I missed."

"But what if he is funding these guerrillas?" Benjamin asked.

Lauren frowned as she thought about it, and Zala shot Benjamin a dark look.

Koren shrugged again. "I think he left that life behind after the Ronin War, but I believe what he discovers will show us if he is clean."

"*Mojoře*—my father," Zala clarified to Lauren and Ben, "retired from that life, Captain. You will see."

"I think so too, Zala," Koren said. "But investigating suspects with experience and talent is what they pay me to do."

The large wooden door swung open before them, and a well-dressed servant stepped forward. Koren and Zala nodded to the servant, but the two Bears ignored him as they entered the foyer of the large home. A large wooden staircase led to the upstairs directly in front of them and corridors to either direction. Zala led Benjamin to the left, toward the kitchen as Lauren put a hand on Koren's arm.

"A moment, please. I have a lot of questions for you," she said, letting what he had said about Zala's father run through her head again. She frowned, then thought for a second. "But first, have you not used any contractions all day?"

He glanced down at her hand, still on his arm, and smiled. "I had hoped you might notice." He smiled again as she flushed, but her hand remained on his arm. "What was your next question?"

Before she could answer, however, a cane rapped hard against the floor in the right-hand corridor. Zala's father leaned heavily on his cane in the hallway, with a serious but positive look on his face. "Sorry to interrupt, but I found something."

A few minutes later, the four of them stood behind Zala's father as he fast-forwarded surveillance footage on the data disk. Pausing it, he transferred the image to his wide wall-mounted monitor. He spun in his luxurious office chair, his cane leaning against his desk as he raised a laser pointer.

"There," he said, drawing a circle on the screen. "Dump truck." He rotated to face them. "Jošt, I looked through all the footage you gave me, and before or after every attack, you have a dump truck in the vicinity of the projected launch site. No footage of firing, but you already knew that." Koren nodded affirmatively, and waved for him to continue. "What caught my eye is that this is a full dump truck heading *toward* a construction site up the block. I thought that was odd enough to watch for them. Once I started looking, there they were. It's the common thread."

Benjamin leaned toward the screen to study the image. "As an Elemental, I am familiar with infantry support weapons. As you said, this truck is full of dirt, and I do not see the mortar. Do they quickly assemble it on site? Is the dirt a loose cover over a tarp?"

Lauren had been about to ask this herself but had paused in her embarrassment, thinking she was the only one who had missed the weapon.

The old man shook his head. "No. This is both simpler *and* devilishly more clever than that." He paused, considering. "You all know that mortar fire, like artillery, is trigonometry. You fire on an upward arc to come down on the target. Years ago, we operated in a cell system against the Dracs. We would have an innocent bystander dig a hole where we wanted it, at a very specific distance from the Combine base. Later, a fire team would lay in a mortar, on the specific bearing and elevation we specified, before filling in the hole up to the muzzle. Finally, much later, the third team would come by, and move the branch, rock, whatever was protecting the upper centimeters of the muzzle from the elements, and drop two or three rounds down the barrel before putting the cover back over it."

He moved his hands to demonstrate. "Only the second team might have known the target if they knew enough about ballistics. This resistance cell clearly knows where the blind spots in coverage are. That gives them predetermined distances—akin to the holes we would dig. They adjust the mortar to the azimuth required so it will arc into the compound once they park the truck in the blind spot. They probably have another team fill in the bed, the dirt keeping the tube in place, before someone—probably a third team—drives there. A member of team three hops up into the bed, drops the round down the tube, and then they drive off, no one the wiser."

There was silence in the room for a moment, and then the old man went on. "I double-checked the impact reports against the known firing positions as a way to validate my theory. The rounds show some left-right drifts from the presumed targets, but the distances are spot on—exactly what you'd expect from a mortar laid to the proper angle but with the driver unable to get a perfect azimuth on the street."

"How many people knew the triple-team mortar trick, Sergei?" Koren asked, all business.

"The teams, of course. The Dracs' Internal Security Force eventually figured it out, and Mimir learned it once we became the Free Rasalhague Republic. A few historians wrote some books about that time period, but even though I mentioned it to them when they conducted interviews, they never actually included the technique in their writings."

"I need their names, and anyone still alive from the firing teams."

The old man's face fell, and his look grew distant as he spun back toward his desk. "The authors are easy. Zala, can you grab those four books on the second shelf to your right?" As his daughter nodded, he looked at Koren. "The others? I mentioned the ISF discovered our trick, right?" He looked away, and quietly said, "The Dracs caught the firing team back in '32. Their interrogations led to them hunting down and eliminating a lot of our lower-level cells. There's a list of survivors, but it's a short one."

The group had moved from Sergei's office to a library, datadisks and books filling the many shelves of the richly appointed room. Lauren had slowly walked around and studied it, noticing dozens of disks on bioengineering and genetics, while the books ran the gamut from ancient classics to local histories.

The five sat in separate chairs, skimming the books Zala had grabbed, plus several others her father had mentioned that might be pertinent. They discussed facts and personalities as they perused, Koren taking notes on the discussion, focusing on those possibly still alive.

After mentioning one name, Sergei nodded. "If he's still alive, he'll be involved. He is a diehard Rasalhagian patriot, and a stone-cold killer. He would never pass up the chance to attack any invader, and assuming he hasn't mellowed in his old age, he's probably champing at the bit to do something up close and personal instead of attacking at a distance."

Jošt nodded and took notes, and Lauren leaned forward in her chair. "The detective mentioned you may have information about the *Ronin*?"

The old man looked surprised. "After all this time? Is it possible?"

"We are hearing rumors they have found them and they are fully operational."

The old man shook his head and looked at Lauren. "I don't have much to add from what Jošt has probably already told you. I was in a command post in Bled when we got a report passed to us. A team was deep in the mountains to the north, almost a hundred kilometers away. One of our distant cells. They came across the *Ronin* MechWarriors, still lying on their mats, facing the sunrise, but they'd been dead for at least a day. The team put them in an unmarked mass grave and then departed, because they had a Draconis Combine Mustered Soldiery counter-guerrilla team hot on their heels. They said they would send in the coordinates of the grave on their next check-in, which they never made. We found out later they'd been killed less than two hours after they talked to us." He shrugged and took a sip of whiskey. "We always assumed the Dracs pulled those 'Mechs out—you can't possibly understand how much a 'Mech was worth in the Inner Sphere back then. Someone could sell a 'Mech and provide for their family for a century. Ten 'Mechs could buy them the title to a world. People have spent their lives, their fortunes, and their sanity trying to discover whether the *Ronin* 'Mechs were still somewhere on this world." He finished his glass. "And you say the resistance has found them?" he asked Jošt.

"Rumor has it." Jošt shrugged. "Do you have any ideas where the grave might be, or who the rebels might go through for parts or ammo if they did find them?"

Sergei stood and walked toward a large, framed map of Vipaava prominently displayed between two bookshelves. "Well, let me start by giving you an idea where our team was operating."

"You too, Father?" Standing in the doorway, body language screaming anger and tenseness, was a middle-aged man Lauren could easily tell was part of Zala's family. "I expected better from the 'Butcher of Bled.'"

"That was a long time ago, Matevž," Sergei replied. "My war ended when our nation was founded."

The newcomer scoffed as Zala stood. "Point Commanders, this is my older brother Matevž. Mattie, these are Point Commanders Lauren and Benjamin. Point Commander Lauren is the Ghost Bear administrator of our world."

Matevž sneered. "I expected this from you, *ljube⬚a sestra*, leaving the family to shovel horse shit while you live in the lap of luxury. But convincing o⬚e to help them? Even for *you*, this is a new low!"

Zala rolled her eyes in frustration. "*This* fight again? With company?"

Lauren opened her mouth to say something, but she felt a hand on her arm. Thinking it was Koren, she was surprised to see it was Zala's father.

Also catching Benjamin's eye, he shook his head. "Families fight. Let them go, they'll burn out soon enough." Glancing at each other, they both nodded once and leaned back in their chairs. Lauren understood—Clan Ghost Bear was founded by a married couple; warriors considered everyone in the Clan as part of their family, a word unknown to other Clans, but rich in meaning among the Ghost Bears.

"I am working my *ass* off to keep this family together, Matevž," said Zala, her voice rising in anger. "Do you think that just anyone gets to manage estates this large in the Clans? That Mom and Dad will get to stay here just because our family always has? Only by becoming a warrior can I hope to protect you."

Lauren gave a start. She had never stopped to question the reason behind Zala's wholehearted adoption of the Clan's ways.

"A responsibility that should have been mine. If you'd stayed here like you should have—"

"You got hurt!"

"Instead of singing about kitty-cat heaven..."

Lauren quirked an eyebrow at Sergei, and he quietly whispered, "She took theater as an academy elective."

"*This* again?" Zala shouted as she paced.

"I would've been the one piloting Dad's 'Mech when they landed!"

"They would have *killed* you, Mattie. You have never wanted to admit the reason you got hurt. The reason *you* run the horses and *I* got the *Wyvern* is because I am a much better MechWarrior than you ever were."

The room went deathly silent with her announcement.

Zala waved an arm toward Lauren while Matevž seethed. "She nearly killed me, and she *would* have killed you. In your heart, you know this."

"You don't know that," he whispered, anger and frustration heavy in his voice. "You never sparred against me."

"I do know that. But perhaps you will come to the compound and spend some time in the simulators with me?" she asked, hope in her voice. "For old time's sake, to let you pilot a 'Mech one more time?"

"*Jebi se, sestra*. I don't need your charity," he said roughly before turning on his heels and walking out.

Benjamin's face tightened, and Lauren guessed that he had picked up enough of the local language to understand Matevž's curse.

An awkward silence filled the room before Zala looked at Lauren, her cheeks red with embarrassment. "I am sorry you witnessed all of that, Point Commander."

Lauren waved it off. Glancing at Sergei, she said, "A wise man once said, 'families fight.'"

Zala looked away and took a deep breath. "Still, I apologize on his behalf. If you do not need me, I will take a walk and get some fresh air. Ben, would you like to see the south lagoon?"

The Elemental nodded, and as they started to head out the door together, Lauren saw Zala's hand slip into his.

Her jaw dropped, and she turned to Koren. "I think they are coupling!"

He was distracted, looking at Sergei's bookshelves, and just gave her a simple shrug.

Her eyes narrowed. "You knew."

At that, he did turn slightly. "I suspected," he corrected her. "I was not positive until we arrived earlier today. I think her mother put it together too."

Sergei nodded. "She did, and told me. That's why Ana had the maids prepare Zala a room in the guesthouse with you three, instead of her bedroom here. Let me get back to talking about the northern cell and their area. Dinner will be ready soon."

Sergei and Koren talked through dinner, discussing possible rebel remnants that had fought the Draconis Combine and could now be fighting the Clans. Over lamb, braised potatoes, and homemade pie, they rehashed everything they had known about the *Ronin* and possible guerrilla cell leaders or members.

Zala's father gave them a stack of references to peruse for notes on the *Ronin*; after dinner they said their farewells and headed to the guesthouse. Koren opened a bottle of wine and spread the books out across the coffee table. Ben and Zala, however, only lasted about an hour before saying goodnight and slipping off to a bedroom.

For another hour, Koren and Lauren continued their research, reviewing the various attempts to hunt down the *Ronin*, slowly getting closer on the couch. Finally Lauren shook her head.

"It is hard to concentrate with them coupling in the other room."

Koren chuckled. "I think this is their idea of being discreet. I must say I am impressed with his stamina."

Lauren shrugged. "He is an Elemental. I am more impressed with her durability."

Koren leaned back in the couch and laughed.

She smiled, then stood and said, "I am done reading. I do not know Spheroid customs on such things, so I will be direct in the Clan manner. I consider you a friend, and would like to couple with you tonight. Are you interested?" She extended him her hand.

"Yes," he replied before standing and taking her hand. He smiled as they headed to the second floor and her bedroom. "Thank you for asking. There is a lot to admire about your Clan customs of honesty and candor."

She quirked an eyebrow at him as she opened her bedroom door. "Believe me, there is a lot to admire in everything we do."

BLED
VIPAAVA
GHOST BEAR INVASION CORRIDOR
29 SEPTEMBER 3050

Lauren stepped back in the giant airship hangar the Clans had repurposed into a BattleMech repair bay. She smiled, and nodded at her technician.

"Excellent work, Michael. Giving it the Cluster's paint scheme and insignia is a nice touch."

The older, freeborn caste member nodded deeply. "Your words are unneeded but welcome, Point Commander. I will pass them onto the team."

Noticing Koren approaching, she nodded once in dismissal and walked toward the detective.

"Police Captain Jošt, how nice to see you. Good news, I hope?" She almost smiled as he clearly kept his hands to his sides. Koren had spent every night in her bed since returning from the ranch, and she knew he was getting attached to her. Love, as it was normally defined, was an unnatural emotion to the Clans. Lauren was honest enough with herself to know she had no intentions to follow the Spheroid path into overly complex emotional entanglements, even though her Clan had been founded by a married couple. As much as she loved the beauty of Vipaava and enjoyed Jošt's company at night, she ached at the chance to rejoin her unit and return to action as a warrior of Clan Ghost Bear.

He opened his mouth to speak, then looked past her and frowned. "Is that Zala's *Wyvern*?"

She *tsk*ed him theatrically. "Detective, I *won* that 'Mech as *isorla* in honorable combat." She smiled as she waved toward the BattleMech. "My technicians have performed a field refit on it, replacing the Inner Sphere weapons with Clan upgrades. They also installed extended-range medium lasers and anti-infantry weapons on it, almost perfectly replicating our *Wyvern IIC* model. It has less ammo than our *Wyvern*s, but with a third medium laser, it will make a most serviceable garrison BattleMech for one of our second-line units one day. For now, however, since it is currently the only functioning Ghost Bear 'Mech on planet, I have spent hours in the simulator familiarizing myself on it."

"And your leg?" he asked quietly, so none could overhear.

She glanced around once to ensure no one was close; among the Clans, admitting a weakness was to invite challenges to one's leadership position. "It hurts if I go too long. I cut today's sim a little short to ensure I did not push myself. I have already eaten and taken a shower—though I could be convinced to take another..." She smiled mischievously and raised an eyebrow in invitation.

He chuckled, but the smile quickly slipped away. "I am tempted, but let me complete my duty first." He stepped back a little, outside of her personal space, and straightened his shoulders. Recognizing the shift in his bearing, she did the same, standing at parade rest to receive his report.

"The good news is we finally broke one of the guerrillas we caught. Once he started talking this morning, we were able to play them off each other, and got them all confessing in the hopes of lighter sentences."

"Which will not happen," she said forcefully.

He quirked an eyebrow. "Point Commander, your Clan legal system is a mishmash of local precedence and 'might makes right.' Clan Ghost Bear has not yet identified its legal proxy, but Bled's prosecuting attorney and your interim defense advocates have approved these deals."

She frowned. "I would not, but the ends justify the means, I suppose. Continue."

He looked her straight in the eyes. "The guerrillas confirmed that they did in fact locate the *Ronin* BattleMechs almost three weeks ago. Ten of them. I did not want to tell you until we located the cavern with the BattleMechs. One of the prisoners guided us there, but it was empty."

"Empty? How can that be possible?"

He grunted. "Unfortunately, the cell system is effective, Point Commander."

She walked away toward the *Wyvern*. "*Stravag!*" she said, slamming her hand on the foot of the medium BattleMech. "I thought by waiting we would scoop them all up."

"It was a well-established network, Lauren," he said quietly, moving behind her while still maintaining a professional distance. "We should have expected it." She shook her head in irritation.

After Sergei had explained that the targets were moving in dump trucks, Jošt had immediately instituted a surveillance program. Using police VTOLs and plainclothes officers, the police had spent three days tracking the trucks' movement from their firing locations and back to their hiding spots. His officers had then trailed the drivers and mortar teams, and they had finally seized them just after midnight on the twenty-eighth. It had taken over a day of interrogation and threats about Clan-style justice to provide Koren with actionable intelligence—but it had come too late.

"Where do we go from here, Detective?" she asked in frustration.

Before he could answer, however, his handset chirped. Frowning, he pulled it off his belt and answered it.

"Three One Charlie, Dispatch. We have a request for you and military liaison at the Starlight Motel, located at nine-five-three North Chapman, triple homicide. One female, two male victims, suspect still at large, over."

"Dispatch, copy triple homicide. I know the Starlight. Why do you need me and a Bear, over?"

"Three One Charlie, officer on the scene reports one of the male victims fits the description of a Clan Elemental and is wearing a Clan-style metal bracelet, over."

Lauren frowned as she overheard the conversation, and then was startled as the blood ran from Jošt's face. He looked around quickly, and then asked her, "Where are Zala and Ben?"

"I gave them the night off." Understanding of his question hit suddenly, and she felt like someone had punched her in the stomach. She took a deep breath, leaning on the *Wyvern* for support.

"Dispatch, good copy. Three One Charlie en route." He gently grabbed Lauran by the arm. "My cruiser is outside. Try to reach Zala."

The drive across town took less than ten minutes. Lauren tried to raise Zala and Ben on the official frequencies three times, each with increasing desperation until Jošt had reached across the front seat and put his hand over hers. They rode on in silence, lights flashing on dark streets until they pulled up to the motel, an impressive establishment resembling a wooden cabin, with a commanding view of the bay. However, the multiple police cars parked with flashing lights and the large van with forensics stenciled on the side destroyed the tranquility of the location.

"Captain, over here," a uniformed officer waved. He introduced himself and walked them toward an open door on the ground floor. "We received the call from the manager of shots fired at approximately twenty-eighteen. I was onsite about five minutes later and identified myself. The manager led me to this hallway, and the door was already open."

Lauren could see multiple personnel in white one-piece outfits taking holos from the covered walkway and entering and exiting a motel room, walking to and from the van.

"Show me the scene," said Jošt.

The three entered the hotel room, and Lauren's breath caught. Just inside the entrance, there was a blond, middle-aged man lying on his stomach with his head facing the door—spun a complete 180 degrees backwards on the neck. To the left, next to the bed, was Benjamin, naked and nearly cut in half from bloody gunshot wounds, his entrails spread in a heap around him. On the bed was what seemed to be the corpse of Zala, but she was so bloody and cut up it was hard to tell. Bile rose in Lauren's throat, and she turned away, trying to keep her composure.

Jošt whispered a prayer, and then he said, "The one on the left is a Clan Ghost Bear Elemental, which now makes this a governor-level investigation, not local. The other male is a suspected guerrilla. We had an alert out to bring him in for questioning."

Lauren heard Jošt pause and then walk toward the bed. She turned back into the room and watched him, keeping her eyes off her bondwoman's form.

"From description of the noise and the initial forensic evidence, we believe the Elemental was hit with at least one shotgun blast. He managed to snap the shooter's neck before going down, though," the officer said, pointing at the guerrilla. "We think the second victim was shot once by a second assailant with a small-caliber weapon, possibly a laser, and then fell onto the bed."

Jošt shook his head. "I believe this is Zala Kotnik, of the Železniki Kotniks, but I cannot be positive because of..." He shook his head mournfully. "Was it postmortem?" he asked as he walked back to the open doorway.

"Forensics estimates she was stabbed in excess of twenty times. They don't have an exact count yet or cause of death yet."

"Twenty?" Lauren whispered. Her voice solidified. "Who would do this? What *monster* would attack her so viciously for joining our Clan?"

"This doesn't fit that pattern, begging your pardon, ma'am," the officer said.

She tilted her head questioningly.

"No, he is right, Point Commander," Jošt said. "When attacking in person, the rebels always kill with precision. Assassinations are traditionally a surgical strike to reduce the chance of apprehension. An attack like this—vicious, personal—it indicates a deep-seated rage against the victim. Odds are we are looking for someone Zala knows, someone..." He trailed off for a second before loudly swearing. "Lord, curse me as a damn fool." He snatched her hand and led them out the door.

He grabbed his handset as they jogged to his cruiser. "Dispatch, Three One Charlie, Alpha Traffic, over."

"Three One, Dispatch, copy Alpha Traffic, go ahead."

"Dispatch, I need an immediate planetwide warrant issued for the arrest of Matevž Kotnik. He is a suspect in the murders of two Ghost Bear warriors, over." As he talked, he popped the trunk on his patrol car.

"Three One, warrants like that need the approval of the military governor's office, over."

Jošt flipped the communicator toward Lauren, who easily snatched it out of the air. "Are you sure?"

He nodded. "He's listened to his father's stories for decades, and not just the ones about horses. He took up *all* of his father's trades."

She keyed the handset. "Dispatch, this is Point Commander Lauren, Ghost Bear governor of Vipaava. Any and all instructions from Captain Koren are approved on my authority."

"Point Commander, Dispatch, good copy."

Jošt was shrugging into a bulletproof vest. As soon as his hands were free, Lauren tossed back the radio. He caught it and walked a spare vest over to her. "Dispatch, get a car up to the Kotnik estate just west of Železniki, take Mr. and Mrs. Kotnik into protective custody until we catch Matevž, over."

"Understood," replied the dispatch officer.

Lauren put the vest over her sky-blue jumpsuit, feeling the comforting weight settle into place as she tightened the straps. Jošt reached into the trunk and passed her a holstered pistol. She accepted it without a word and strapped it to her waist.

"Dispatch, I also need a planetary alert posted. Intelligence reports the rebels have up to ten working BattleMechs, and sightings should be reported to the Ghost Bears immediately. Tell the Watch commander to send someone over and *personally* notify Star Commander Antoinette. They can probably find her in the 'Mech bay or the barracks. Give her my cruiser's frequency in case she wants to reach me or Point Commander Lauren." He slammed the trunk and carried a pump shotgun to the driver's side.

"Understood."

"Three One Charlie en route to the Kotnik estate." He slid into the driver's seat, and with a serious nod toward Lauren, started the cruiser. Tires squealing, he whipped out of the parking lot, heading west down the half-empty streets, green and blue emergency lights reflecting off the skyscrapers as he raced through Bled toward the distant mountains.

They drove for forty-five terrifying minutes at a speed far above their first trip up to Zala's estate. Lauren tried to remain calm as the car threatened to slide off the road and plummet down the mountain on every hairpin turn, and she was thankful it was too dark for her to see the terrain clearly.

Star Commander Antoinette had contacted them during the trip, and agreed there was trouble in the air. She was alerting her MechWarriors and putting them on standby in the 'Mech bay, able to quickly respond if the resistance attacked.

They were still outside Železniki when the dispatcher broke the silent drive, reporting that uniformed officers had reached the Kotnik estate, but the couple was found shot down in the driveway. They entered Železniki, their police car's lights reflecting off the white-washed timber houses.

"'Shot down,' as in killed by firing squad?" Koren asked the dispatcher as they exited the small town.

"Yes, they were found with their hands bound, but according to the officer, it appears they were machine-gunned down from above."

Lauren had only a moment to think about that before a shadow detached from the alpine woods surrounding Železniki and entered their path.

"Jošt!" she screamed as their headlights illuminated a white *Warhammer* ahead of them, its PPCs leveled.

He yanked the wheel, swerving them off the road and into a ditch, where they crashed, then slid through mud to a stop as a blue bolt of charged particles ripped through the air where they had been. The driver's side faced away from the *Warhammer*, and Lauren slid across the seat and followed Jošt out. She ran for the woods behind him as the *Warhammer* fired its torso-mounted medium lasers. The car exploded behind them. She was flung forward as the shock wave hit her. Her armored vest absorbed most of the blow, but her left hip slammed down, a sharp rock slicing across her cheek. Lauren turned toward the BattleMech, panting hard to catch her breath, and reached for her pistol.

A useless gesture, she knew, wiping blood off her cheek with one hand and drawing her sidearm with her other. *I may die here*, she thought, *but I will not die unarmed*. The burning car stood between her and the BattleMech, its broad feet planted on the road, its waist twisted to aim its torso-mounted weaponry toward her. She saw the machine guns twitch, which told her he was using a thumb trigger to aim them independently of the PPC arms.

"I almost don't know who I hate more, Clanner," Matevž spoke over the BattleMech's loudspeakers. "You, with your arrogance and condescension toward my world and my nation, or my traitorous *kurba* of a sister, abandoning us and spreading her legs for the first troll that wanted to mount her." He paused for a moment. "No, it's Zala. She turned her back on our people, while you were just doing your duty. Goodbye, Ghost Bear."

Lauren clenched her teeth as she saw the machine guns steady on her. But before any rounds hit, Jošt knocked her to the ground. They crashed backward together into the ditch, the armor hitting her spine hard. She heard a series of sonic booms from near-misses crack by her head, and then the sickening sounds of bullets slapping into Jošt's back, the armor-piercing rounds ripping through the vest and into him as he lay on top of her.

"White with jade stripes," he whispered, looking at her. "*Ronin*," he said, his voice trailing off. His eyes rolled back and his head collapsed onto her chest.

"Jošt?" she cried out, wrapping her arms around him and looking up at the *Warhammer* that was moving clear of the flaming wreckage to get a clear shot at her. From above, though, came the heavy whipping noise of a VTOL on approach.

The BattleMech paused, and looking toward the sky, fired its lasers at a target she could not see from the ground. Tracer fire streaked in and hit the *Warhammer* as a VTOL quickly flew by overhead. Flames illuminated the belly for a second, and she could tell it was a Bled police helicopter, armed with only one chain gun. But the BattleMech was turning away from her to track it; in that moment, she dropped her pistol and grabbed Jošt.

With adrenaline racing through her system, she heaved him partially onto her shoulder and took off running for the woods. She heard the BattleMech fire its PPCs into the sky; with Jošt's feet dragging as she carried him, she ran desperately, weaving around smaller trees before finally ducking behind a meter-wide pine reaching upward into the darkened sky. She peeked around the tree and saw the *Warhammer* firing, PPCs again blasting at an unseen target. It paused, and then moved away from her and into the woods on the other side of the road.

She looked to Jošt's wounds. Seeing three deep holes that made it through the solid armor plating, she undid it and opened the medkit attached to the front of the vest.

She lost track of time as she bandaged him, his breathing shallow, his pulse erratic, and was surprised when a voice called to her from behind.

"Ma'am! Miss Lauren!"

She spun in place and reached for Jošt's holstered pistol. She saw a uniformed officer there, his hands up.

"Don't shoot, I'm Železniki PD."

"The captain is seriously hurt," she said.

The officer nodded. Turning, he waved forward a pair of medics wearing bright-red jumpsuits. "We were on the way up to the estate to pronounce the time of death so forensics can open the case," he said as the medics began tending to Jošt's wounds. "We were still in town when we saw the 'Hammer ambush you."

She kissed Jošt gently on his forehead, then stood to face the officer. "Can you reach the VTOL on your communicator?"

He nodded.

"Good. Tell it to land. I need to reach Bled before that murderer does."

Within minutes, the orbiting police helicopter landed in a nearby small clearing barely wider than its blades, and the medics loaded the stabilized Jošt into the VTOL's cramped confines. As soon as Lauren climbed on board, the pilot shot them skyward, accelerating to full speed within seconds. The trip that had taken forty-five winding minutes only took fifteen by air, but in that time, the city of Bled had seemed to explode.

Riots were forming in several separate neighborhoods; Antoinette notified Lauren, as governor of Bled, that she was sending her Elementals and infantry out across the city in support of the Bled police. As soon as Lauren had approved of her actions, police dispatch calmly announced across the frequency that ten BattleMechs had been spotted clearing the mountains.

"At their current speed, they will enter the city in twenty minutes," Antoinette told her a moment later. "They may pick up speed now that they are in the open fields, however. I am moving my Star to intercept."

"Understood, Star Commander. I will join you shortly. Contact me before you engage," Lauren replied over the borrowed VTOL headset, watching the ground approach quickly. She unhooked the holster and passed it to a crewman, then shed her vest. The VTOL flared for a landing in the courtyard of the Ghost Bear compound, and she grabbed Jošt's unconscious hand and squeezed it. The crew chief flung open the door and, glancing once to ensure the area was secure, flashed her a thumbs-up.

As the ground crew swarmed to unload Jošt, Lauren jumped out and sprinted for the open doors of the 'Mech bay. As she ran for the *Wyvern*, she instantly saw that the five Viper BattleMechs had already departed. Just as she reached her BattleMech, her grizzled technician came around its foot, placing a coolant suit and neurohelmet on the *Wyvern*'s toe.

"Are you hurt, Point Commander?" Michael asked, pointing at the blood on her clothes.

She shook her head while sitting on the 'Mech's foot and quickly pulled off her boots. "Captain Jošt's," she replied, stripping off her jumpsuit. Michael said nothing and ignored her nakedness, simply passing her the coolant suit when she reached for it. He picked up her neurohelmet as she fastened and zipped.

"The lift is ready to take you up, Point Commander. Also, we heard what happened to your bondswoman." Lauren paused for a second and looked at Michael. His face was hard and full of anger. "She was well liked by the support staff. Anything we can do to avenge her, you need but ask."

Lauren took the neurohelmet from his hands and considered his words as she led them to the gantry that would elevate her to the cockpit. As per Clan law and custom, she could demand anything she needed from the lower castes, but she understood the technician's sentiment. She turned toward him, clasped his shoulder, and said, "Tell everyone thank you from me, Michael. She meant a lot to us all." She let him go and stepped on the gantry. "Take me up."

Lauren quickly settled into the cockpit and connected her coolant vest and neurohelmet to the *Wyvern*. Michael, she saw, had activated the BattleMech as she had flown in; the fusion engine was already at full power, and all her weapons were hot. She reached for the joysticks and walked the *Wyvern* out of the hangar. Glancing once at her monitors, she double-checked her frequencies and activated her radio.

"Star Commander Antoinette, this is Point Commander Lauren. I am in my *Wyvern*, and I should be at your position in less than five minutes."

"Point Commander, may I remind you of the agreement between our Clans?" Antoinette broadcast formally. "As military governor of this world, we answer to you in all situations except in active combat. Then I, as the senior onsite commander, assume tactical control. You may request a course of action, which I may or may not approve, as the situation warrants."

"I remember," Lauren said, guiding the *Wyvern* down the empty city streets by instinct as she considered exactly what she wanted to say. "Star Commander, a lot has happened recently. Let me ensure you understand our opponents and the situation. The BattleMechs originally belonged to a regiment that rebelled against their liege lord and were declared honorless over twenty years ago. This world issued and fought an honorable challenge, and these guerrillas are acting independently of their world's choice. Their leader, in the *Warhammer*, murdered two Ghost Bears tonight and attempted to murder me. Per the agreement between our Clans, I concede the others for you to handle as you see fit. But as governor I *formally request* to fight the *Warhammer* and avenge my Clan."

Antoinette fell silent for a moment. "The *Warhammer* is yours, Governor Lauren. None of my warriors will deny you this honor, and we will not interfere."

Lauren smiled slightly. By acknowledging her as the Ghost Bear governor, Antoinette was able to honorably agree to her without appearing deferential to a junior warrior.

There was a pause, and Lauren saw that Antoinette had switched to a private frequency between them. "For what it is worth, Zala was *terrible* at hiding the fact she was a sassy little runt. But I liked that about her. We will help you execute these *dezgra surats*."

Lauren exited Bled and joined the Steel Viper Star in the open fields a minute later. At a five-to-nine ratio, the Steel Vipers would have had a slight technological advantage against their opponents, and presumably an edge in training.

"This is not an honorable challenge," Lauren reminded them. "These are bandits and murderers, no more than rabid dogs to be put down. Your honor arises from your speed and efficiency tonight."

"I fully support the Ghost Bear governor," said Antoinette. "You will destroy the targets I designate, or you will face me in a circle of equals, *quiaff*?"

Her Star chorused their understanding while Lauren slowly moved past the Vipers, watching the approaching rebel BattleMechs, now just a kilometer away.

"Matevž," she said on an unencrypted frequency as the five Vipers automatically spread into a wedge behind her. "I am in your sister's *Wyvern*, and I challenge you to single combat. I do not extend this challenge because you are worthy, but to ensure that your death comes at my hands."

"Ghost Bear," he replied after a moment. "I'm almost glad you survived, though I can't believe you're in my grandfather's ancient wreck. The 'Mech my sister took from me, the one that was rightfully mine! Killing you in it will be gratifying on a *number* of levels."

"Then come and get me," she replied, watching the distance decrease as the two lines slowly converged. At just under four hundred meters, she squeezed her main trigger, tied to her extended-range large laser, and then triggered her long-range missile rack. As the ten missiles left their tubes, streaking away on long gray trails of smoke, the Steel Vipers flanking her fired on their designated targets.

Her laser struck the *Warhammer* just under its right-torso-mounted six-pack of short-range missiles, with six of her ten LRMs scattering along the *Warhammer*'s right arm. The heavy 'Mech swiveled its PPCs toward her, and she realized that the four BattleMechs flanking him— two *Dragon*s, a *Crusader*, and an *Ostsol*—were also aiming at her.

Lauren whispered a curse and came to a halt, planting the 'Mech's feet as forty missiles flew at her. Just over half ripped across the *Wyvern*'s chest and arms; she fought to keep her balance as more than a ton of armor was blasted off her BattleMech. The hammerblow of a *Dragon*'s autocannon rapped against her left leg, threating to knock her over. She was forced to take a step back with her right leg to remain upright as the *Ostsol* melted sheets of armor off her torso with its lasers. Her *Wyvern* swayed, smoking, and she saw the *Warhammer* taking careful aim at her.

She whispered another swear and tried to move forward, but her world lit up in blue lightning as a PPC struck her 'Mech's exposed head, dead center. Neural feedback sent shocks of pain through her neurohelmet directly into her temple, and the *Wyvern* fell forward, crashing onto its left side.

Lauren fought to stay awake as her vision tunneled. She shook her head and tried to move, and screamed. Looking down, she saw a large shard of transparisteel from her blasted cockpit windshield embedded in her left leg. It was five centimeters wide, and over thirty centimeters of it protruded from her thigh. She tried to shift her leg and grimaced as she felt bone scrape against the unyielding spear.

I am pinned to the seat, she thought as another explosion sounded nearby. Shaking off the last of her disorientation, she watched a *Dragon* fall to the ground about two hundred meters away and explode, the ground shaking from the 'Mech's destruction.

Lauren tasted bile as the shockwave shook her immobilized leg. She realized she was exposed to the elements, the wind coming across the fields and mixing the sweet smell of sorghum into the burning insulation and ozone of her damaged cockpit. The *Warhammer*, she could see, was aiming at someone else, though the Steel Vipers were ignoring it and focusing on other targets, abiding by her demand until they were sure of her incapacitation. She shakily grabbed the controls and, raising her *Wyvern* to one knee, fired all three medium lasers and the large laser at the *Warhammer*. She was about to ripple-fire both racks of missiles, but paused as a rush of heat, far more than usual, flooded her cockpit. Lauren gasped in the furnace as the *Warhammer* staggered from her strike, the lasers slashing across both legs.

Life support is out, she thought, confirming it a second later with a glance toward a row of red indicators on a secondary panel. She gritted her teeth against the pain she knew would come from her thigh as she brought the *Wyvern* fully to its feet.

"Ghost Bear!" Matevž said over an open frequency. "You're still alive? Well, I'll be damned." He turned his *Warhammer* toward her and closed, less than two hundred meters away.

"Not yet damned," she replied, "but soon." She carefully lined up her shot and fired, her large laser and one of the mediums burning deep into the *Warhammer*'s right torso. The white-and-jade heavy 'Mech came to a halt. She saw a quick explosion, then another, and then the top hatch of the BattleMech blasted off, Matevž ejecting into the chilly air as the exploding ammunition ripped the *Warhammer* apart from within. She calculated where he would land, and started trudging toward him. She looked at her left leg—throbbing with pain, her coolant suit soaked through with dark violet blood—and she felt woozy.

"Just a little longer," she whispered.

She slowed as her 'Mech stood above him, Matevž trying to undo his seat restraints with only one good arm. His chute flapped gently behind his command couch as he finally sat back, cradling a broken arm and glaring at her.

"This isn't over, Ghost Bear!" he shouted, loud enough that she could hear him through her cockpit breach. "The people of this world will never give in! They will never stop until you've left forever!"

She stayed silent, checking her monitors. As expected, the other nine enemy BattleMechs were down with no casualties among the Vipers.

"Well?" he shouted. "No smart comebacks, no propaganda about how the Ghost Bears will rule triumphant, or how you've avenged my sister? No pithy statement to send me to my grave thinking about?"

Lauren stared at him, seeing only the torn-up body of her bondswoman. She activated the *Wyvern*'s speakers and replied with a single word.

"Burn."

His eyes widened in fear as she triggered her flamer. His screams and the popping of his flesh as it cooked were clearly audible through her breached cockpit. Her vision began to gray, so she ceased fire and locked her BattleMech into an upright position. She keyed her microphone as the darkness flooded in.

"Antoinette, I am injured. You are in command until relieved," she said, and passed out before she heard a response.

"Lauren. Point Commander Lauren, can you hear me?"

Lauren's awareness came creeping back as a familiar voice called her. She slowly opened her eyes. "Star Captain Tseng?" she quietly asked, confused.

Tseng nodded and began talking to a nurse as Lauren frowned and looked around. The room was a cream color, with plush furniture, wooden dressers, and blue curtains, not the antiseptic look of a hospital.

"Where am I? How are you here?" She wiggled, trying to sit up, and her left leg throbbed underneath the fleece blanket.

"Easy, Lauren," the Star Captain said as she reached over and pushed the controls, raising the back half of Lauren's bed. "You have been in a medically induced coma for three weeks. As soon as I heard of the battle, I brought reinforcements from the front. We arrived yesterday, but the world has remained quiet since you killed the guerrilla commander."

"Three weeks?" Lauren whispered.

Tseng nodded.

"The rebels were defeated? The uprisings in town?"

Tseng nodded again. "*Aff*, Point Commander. Once the BattleMechs were destroyed, the spirit of the rioters broke. Ringleaders were imprisoned or shot, and no further uprisings have occurred. Police Captain Jošt and Star Commander Antoinette have kept the world secure while you recovered."

Lauren sighed and closed her eyes. "Jošt is okay, then?"

The Star Captain laughed. "Better than okay. He is a fine addition to the Clan, and is the reason you are here, in fact."

"Where am I?" Lauren asked again.

"At your estate." At her confused look, Star Captain Tseng continued, "According to the police captain, as your bondswoman Zala had no immediate surviving heirs, you are the executor of her family's land and assets. He said you would consider it a point of honor to continue their work." She paused for a moment. "I have inspected the grounds and the horses, and I know of their value to the Clan. I agree that a Clan warrior should supervise the scientists that will undoubtedly flock here once word of these Terran trophies spreads."

Lauren shook her head, a motion that triggered a wave of nausea and fresh pain from her leg. She winced and shook her head, trying to clear it. "Star Captain, I *am* honored, but I cannot supervise the estate and resume my place in the invasion force at the same time. My leg was injured in the battle, but once I am healed again, I wish to rejoin your Trinary."

Tseng shook her head. "Lauren, I am sorry, but you will not rejoin us. Perhaps, with years of therapy, you could achieve a spot in a garrison Star, but for all practical purposes, your time as a MechWarrior is over. The injury to your leg, so soon after your previous injury, prohibited standard treatments or regeneration. And then our scientists discovered you have an incredibly rare myomer allergy that prohibits a bionic replacement. I am sorry, Lauren. What you are feeling right now is phantom pain."

"Phantom pain? That is...a term they use on amputees," Lauren whispered, realization setting in.

Tears unwillingly flooded her eyes, and she looked away to hide her shame. A Clan amputee, unable to receive a regenerated limb or a full bionic replacement, could never fight as well using a mere prosthetic. If she had not done so already, Star Captain Tseng would request a MechWarrior from the Homeworlds to replace her and fill the Trinary's hole. The arrival of that MechWarrior would automatically dismiss Lauren from the unit and relegate her to a service caste. A tear rolled down her cheek.

"Then, I am no longer a warrior?" she whispered.

"Well..." Tseng said, drawing the word out.

Lauren blinked twice, rubbing the tears out of her eyes. She turned back toward the Star Captain.

"Your police captain has a suggestion."

ŽELEZNIKI, VIPAAVA
GHOST BEAR INVASION CORRIDOR
2 DECEMBER 3050

Closing her noteputer, Lauren slid it into the cargo pocket of her uniform top. She thanked the chef for breakfast, then quirked an eyebrow upon noticing that Jošt had left half a cup of coffee on the table. Whispering "Waste not, want not," she smiled and quickly drank it in one throw before leaving the kitchen and heading toward the mansion's foyer.

It had been six weeks since Star Captain Tseng had talked to her. The doctors had already fitted her for a prosthetic before Tseng touched down, so once Lauren had regained her wits, the doctors taught her how to wear her new leg and pushed her into rehab.

Jošt had recovered far quicker than she: since he had been treated at a Clan hospital and gunshot wounds were one of their specialties, he was mobile and released within seventy-two hours. He had then assumed her role as interim governor—possibly violating several Clan laws in the process, but it had met with Tseng's approval upon her arrival—and worked with Star Commander Antoinette to bring peace to the world. He had also argued for Lauren to gain the Kotnik estate, another semi-legal move the Star Captain retroactively approved.

He had visited every day, spending more and more time with her until finally, a week after she had awoken, they carefully and slowly made love again, taking care to not hurt her "stub," as she called it. She was not sure she would have absorbed so many changes so quickly without him: she had always identified herself as a Ghost Bear warrior, but her amputation had made her take a step back and reconsider what it meant to be Clan, a warrior, and a Ghost Bear. Jošt had moved into the mansion with her two days later; while she still felt uncomfortable with the realization that she was probably falling in love with him, whenever she thought of their unknown future together, she took comfort by remembering her Clan was, in fact, the only one founded by a married couple.

She reached the foyer, then strapped on the police body armor and pistol that hung on sturdy hooks near the door. After ensuring her communicator was fully charged, she slipped it into its carrier and picked up her badge.

Clan police forces existed as a generally disparaged subcaste of the warrior caste. Usually more efficient at imposing order than enforcing Clan law, their primary function in Clan space was to employ extreme punishments to deter crimes from happening. In the Homeworlds, the police forces consisted mostly of warrior-caste test-downs and freebirths, and were despised by nearly everyone. In the occupation zones, the invading Clans had found it simpler and more practical to elevate the local police forces out of the service castes.

The investigative arm of the Clans' police forces, however, was looked on with favor, as it was normally performed by a designated active-duty warrior. Usually an additional task assigned to warriors stationed with the garrison force, "Inquisitors" received additional training and schooling to fulfill the dual purpose of detective and prosecuting attorney.

Jošt had proposed to Star Captain Tseng that designating Lauren the Vipaavan Inquisitor would be an efficient use of limited assets: Lauren was no longer capable of piloting a BattleMech, but keeping her on Vipaava would eliminate the need to divert a fully qualified warrior from the front in the middle of the invasion.

It might also placate the populace, he pointed out, knowing the assigned Inquisitor had longevity and a homestead. The people of Vipaava would respect and listen to a warrior with a vested interest in peace and justice instead of the passing dalliances of garrison units. Star Captain Tseng had agreed it was a method worth pursuing, especially if it would help stabilize the Clan's rear areas.

Lauren's rehabilitation had been a continuous grind of physical therapy, legal lessons, and training on criminology, an exhausting daily routine that left her to collapse in bed next to Jošt each night only to wake up the next morning and repeat the process. But, finally, she was declared trained, healed, and fit for duty.

Lauren smiled as she looked at the badge, and hooked it onto her armor. After double-checking her appearance in the full-length mirror next to the heavy wooden door, she went outside and saw Jošt standing next to his new cruiser. She took a second to stand on the steps, looking over her land, with the town of Železniki in the distance, the herd of Lipizzans that had caused so much strife in Zala's family grazing about a kilometer away. She closed her eyes and enjoyed the scent of fresh mountain air.

Nothing like this at home, indeed, she thought.

She opened her eyes, looked at Jošt, and smiled slightly. "Detective," she said formally, even though they had made love, then eaten breakfast together that morning.

"Inquisitor," he replied in the same tone. "Officially, this is your first day. Where to?"

She tilted her head, and said, "I think we should see where the day takes us, *quiaff*?"

The corner of his mouth quirked into a smile, and he nodded. Reaching through the open window of the cruiser, he grabbed the handset.

"Dispatch, this is Three One Charlie with Iota One. Please log us as on-shift. Where do you need us, over?"

The radio came back immediately. "Three One Charlie, Iota One, this is Dispatch. We have an Elemental in the tank on a drunk and disorderly, and a double homicide on Seventh and Autumn, perps unknown at this time, over."

He looked at her.

"The Elemental automatically falls under my jurisdiction," Lauren said.

He did not reply, just inclined his head toward her communicator.

She pulled it off her hip and keyed it. "Dispatch, this is Point Commander Lauren," she said automatically, then checked herself. "Correction, this is Inquisitor Lauren. Let the Elemental know we are on our way to collect his statement."

"Iota One, good copy—and welcome back."

SNIPER RIFLES: DEATH FROM A DISTANCE

CRAIG A. REED, JR.

The sniper has been a part of the battlefield for over a thousand years. No matter the technology, the basic concept is still the same: to eliminate the enemy from a long distance with a single bullet. This article examines a number of sniper rifles seen on thirty-second-century battlefields and several notable examples from recent history. Most of these weapons are semiautomatic, but a couple are bolt-action, being little different from rifles from ten centuries ago.

The Clans consider snipers *dezgra*, and manufacture no sniper rifles of their own, though Star League–era sniper rifles can be found among the Bandit Caste.

Note: All stats in this article are for *A Time of War* (*AToW*).

LANCELOT MK V (FEDERATED SUNS)

The Lancelot series has been employed by the AFFS for the last 150 years. The current model, the Mk V, is reliable weapon with an integrated scope. Used mostly by AFFS scout/sniper detachments, the Mk V was built to be the Federated Suns's main ballistic sniper rifle.

Equipment Rating: C/C-C-C/C
AP/BD: 4B/4
Range: 125/250/500/1000
Shots: 10
Cost/Reload: 400/4
Mass/Reload: 6kg/50g
Notes: +3 to Attack Roll Modifier at M/L/E Ranges

BARTON AMR (FEDERATED SUNS)

The Barton Anti-Materiel Rifle was originally designed to destroy equipment rather than personnel. One of the heaviest sniper rifles in the Inner Sphere, the AMR came into its own during the Jihad when AFFS and Allied Coalition forces used the weapon against the Word of Blake's Manei Domini troopers, gaining the nickname "Can Opener" for its effectiveness against the armored cybernetic soldiers. The anti-armor round developed for the AMR is particularly effective, but is manufactured in limited quantities.

STANDARD ROUNDS
Equipment Rating: D/X-D-D/D
AP/BD: 5B/7
Range: 200/400/800/1600
Shots: 8
Cost/Reload: 700/9
Mass/Reload: 14kg/110g
Notes: Encumbering, +2 when rolling on Location Effects Table (*AToW*, p. 191)

ANTI-ARMOR ROUNDS
Equipment Rating: D/X-E-E/D
AP/BD: 6B/7
Range: 200/400/800/1600
Shots: 8
Cost/Reload: 700/12
Mass/Reload: 14kg/120g
Notes: Encumbering, +2 when rolling on Location Effects Table (*AToW*, p. 191)

SAIRENTOSUTOMU (DRACONIS COMBINE)

Used by the Combine's DEST teams and the DCMS's top snipers, the Sairentosutomu (Silent Storm) is designed to be almost impossible to detect when fired. With a built-in sound-and-flash suppressor, it is equally effective in both urban and wilderness battlefields. Rarely seen outside the Combine, the Sairentosutomu is considered an assassin's weapon by most other states. Few, if any, exist in private hands.

Equipment Rating: D/X-D-D/E
AP/BD: 4B/4
Range: 150/300/600/900
Shots: 8
Cost/Reload: 900/7
Mass/Reload: 7kg/50g
Notes: –3 to Perception Check (Sound/Vision)

YUÀN LÍNG (CAPELLAN CONFEDERATION)

Designed to be used by Capellan Special Forces, the Yuàn Líng ("Wrath" in Mandarin) is a favorite among Confederation snipers. Built to be accurate at longer ranges and containing a built-in night-vision scope, this rifle gives the sniper a decided advantage over most opponents. There is a rumor that a Death Commando once assassinated an AFFS colonel from more than a kilometer and a half away using a Yuàn Líng.

Equipment Rating: D/X-D-D/E
AP/BD: 4B/4
Range: 205/410/820/1600
Shots: 10
Cost/Reload: 1000/10
Mass/Reload: 6kg/60g
Notes: +2 to Attack Roll Modifier at M/L/E Ranges; Negates Darkness Mods up to 1000m

HAMMEL MARKSMAN (FREE WORLDS LEAGUE)

This Free Worlds League rifle is unique among the rifles listed here, as it is an offshoot of the popular Hammel Hunting Rifle. With the exception of a slightly longer barrel and military-grade scope, the two are identical. The rifle also comes with its own repair kit built into the stock, allowing the shooter to make repairs and technical adjustments in the field. It is one of the few weapons that can be found evenly distributed across the state, and most of the individual provinces have a Hammel factory located within their borders.

Equipment Rating: C/C-C-B/B
AP/BD: 4B/4
Range: 130/260/520/780
Shots: 12
Cost/Reload: 500/6
Mass/Reload: 5kg/50g
Notes: +2 to all repair rolls, +1 to Attack Roll Modifier at M/L/E Ranges

THORSHAMMER (LYRAN COMMONWEALTH)

Rumored to be a payoff to a certain weapons manufactory, this rifle is solid and robust, but not outstanding in any particular area. It has been noted that the Thorshammer has a tendency to overshoot targets at short range while being accurate at more distant targets. There aren't any plans to correct the problem at the factory, so a sniper using this weapon must either take extra care with short-range targets or make the necessary adjustments themselves.

Equipment Rating: D/X-C-C/D
AP/BD: 4B/4
Range: 175/350/700/1050
Shots: 10
Cost/Reload: 750/12
Mass/Reload: 7kg/60g
Notes: -1 on Attack Roll at Short Range, +1 on Attack Roll at Extreme Range, -1 to any modification/repair rolls

SR-17 SUNS KILLER
(TAURIAN CONCORDAT/CALDERON PROTECTORATE)

This sturdy Concordat model has been around for more than 300 years. A bolt-action rifle, the Suns Killer can be found at all levels of the Concordat and Protectorate militaries, from the TDF down to planetary militias. Thousands of retired Suns Killers are sold to the Taurian public, making it the most common rifle in the Concordat. In some cases, militias carry the same rifle their great-grandparents carried.

Equipment Rating: C/C-C-C/B
AP/BD: 4B/5
Range: 150/300/600/900
Shots: 15
Cost/Reload: 600/10
Mass/Reload: 6kg/70g
Notes: Simple action to chamber next round, +2 to Attack Roll Modifier at M/L/E Ranges

PRAETORIAN S-3 AND S-5 (MARIAN HEGEMONY)

The S-3 was common in Marian Hegemony Legions a century ago, before being phased out for the more modern S-5. Both rifles are designed to withstand heavy abuse and still operate. The S-3 is still manufactured and shipped to the Lyran Commonwealth, where it is sold as a hunting rifle. Both rifles' built-in scopes can calculate range, wind, and air pressure to assist the sniper in hitting their target, though the S-5's scope is superior to the S-3's. The S-5 is almost never seen outside of the Legions.

PRAETORIAN S-3
Equipment Rating: C/X-C-B/C
AP/BD: 5B/5
Range: 145/290/580/870
Shots: 10
Cost/Reload: 400/10
Mass/Reload: 8kg/80g
Notes: Encumbering, +1 to all repair rolls. +2 to Attack Roll Modifier at M/L/E Ranges

PRAETORIAN S-5
Equipment Rating: C/X-C-C/D
AP/BD: 5B/6
Range: 150/300/600/900
Shots: 10
Cost/Reload: 600/12
Mass/Reload: 7kg/70g
Notes: Encumbering, +1 to all repair rolls. +3 to Attack Roll Modifier at M/L/E Ranges

LRS-53 SNIPER RIFLE (MAGISTRACY OF CANOPUS)

The Magistracy's most common sniper rifle is the LRS-53. A bolt-action, the LRS is designed to be accurate at all ranges, and can hit target as far out as a kilometer. Its bullpup design allows the rifle to have a longer barrel without making it unwieldy. Sales of these rifles to the public are strictly controlled, and military access is limited only to serving MAF military or close allies.

Equipment Rating: C/X-E-D/C
AP/BD: 4B/4
Range: 140/290/650/1000
Shots: 9
Cost/Reload: 1000/20
Mass/Reload: 6kg/60g
Notes: Simple Action to chamber next round, +2 to Attack Roll Modifier at all Ranges

WILIMTON RS-14 (COMSTAR/WORD OF BLAKE)

ComStar's dedicated sniper rifle, the RS-14 takes advantage of the Order's superior technological edge to produce what most experts consider the finest sniper rifle in production. It boasts superior range and accuracy, and was designed to be maintained and repaired in the field by the snipers themselves. When the Word of Blake broke away from ComStar, they inherited many of these rifles, and when they took Terra, they controlled the main factory. During the liberation of Terra, the factory was badly damaged and has only recently returned to full production. The RS-14 is now the Republic of the Sphere's most common sniper rifle.

Equipment Rating: E/X-D-D/E
AP/BD: 4B/5
Range: 160/320/640/960
Shots: 10
Cost/Reload: 1500/25
Mass/Reload: 7kg/75g
Notes: -1 to all repair rolls. +3 to Attack Roll Modifier at L/E Ranges

WILIMTON RS-17 (WORD OF BLAKE)

The RS-17 is infamous because of its exclusive use by the Word's Manei Domini shock troopers. Superior to the all other sniper rifles, the weapon integrated with the sniper's own cybernetics, making it a deadly combination on the battlefield. A built-in flash hider and sound suppressor made it a nightmare for Coalition troops to locate an active sniper. Very few of these weapons were recovered after the Jihad, and those found were deemed useless for non-cybernetic troops, as the weapon was heavily dependent on integration with the sniper's own cybernetics. There has been some success with a stripped-down model, but its reputation makes it rarely used.

RS-17 (MANEI DOMINI)
Equipment Rating: E/X-X-E/F
AP/BD: 5B/6
Range: 175/350/700/1050
Shots: 10
Cost/Reload: 2500/50
Mass/Reload: 9kg/85g
Notes: Usable by Manei Domini only, +4 to Attack Roll Modifier at M/L/E Ranges, –4 to Perception Check (Sound/Vision). Non-Manei Domini who attempt to use an unaltered RS-17 suffer the following penalties: Encumbering, –1/–2/–3/–4 on attack roll at S/M/L/E Ranges.

RS-17 (STRIPPED)
Equipment Rating: E/X-X-E/F
AP/BD: 5B/6
Range: 170/340/680/1020
Shots: 10
Cost/Reload: 2000/50
Mass/Reload: 9kg/85g
Notes: +2 to Attack Roll Modifier at M/L/E Ranges, –4 to Perception Check (Sound/Vision)

FNF-J12 (STAR LEAGUE/DARK CASTE)

Originally manufactured in the Federated Suns before the fall of the Star League, the FNF-J12 saw limited use before the Amaris Civil War, but was in heavy use during the war, as the SDLF needed weapons that the Federated Suns willingly supplied. A number of the rifles were taken with the Exodus, but with the rise of Clan society, the FNFs were either left in looted caches or destroyed. Those that exist nowadays are exclusively in the hands of the Clans' Dark Caste, who use them as hunting weapons or for personal defense.

FNF-J12 (DARK CASTE)
Equipment Rating: E/X-X-E/F
AP/BD: 4B/6
Range: 150/300/600/950
Shots: 8
Cost/Reload: 3500/70
Mass/Reload: 6kg/80g
Notes: +1 to Attack Roll Modifier at S/M Ranges, +2 to Attack Roll Modifier at L/E Ranges, –2 to Perception Check (Sound/Vision)

FNF-J12 (PRISTINE/RESTORED)
Equipment Rating: E/X-X-E/F
AP/BD: 4B/6
Range: 175/325/600/950
Shots: 8
Cost/Reload: 3500/70
Mass/Reload: 6kg/80g
Notes: +2 to Attack Roll Modifier at S/M Ranges, +3 to Attack Roll Modifier at L/E Ranges, –2 to Perception Check (Sound/Vision)

YESTERDAY'S ENEMY

LANCE SCARINCI

WASEDA HILLS
LUTHIEN, PESHT MILITARY DISTRICT
DRACONIS COMBINE
5 JANUARY 3052

I am not a wolf.

He had come in the company of wolves, but he was not one of them. He'd always been more of a cat person, but today he'd come with Wolf and Hound to punish many Cats. "Hawks, keep right and stay in spitting distance of a Hound or Dragoon. Be the eyes, not the targets. That means you, Grange. Pull your lance in tighter."

"Cap'n," came that Outback drawl as Grange's *Valkyrie* stepped into formation.

Contrails streaked the sky over the Waseda Hills, a white crisscross dotted with puffs of flak like some demented god's tic-tac-toe board. The Khan of the Nova Cats was up there somewhere; maybe that was him, streaking by in a black *Visigoth*. A good pilot could take him on, disrupt the Cats by taking off their head. Jason was man enough to admit he was not that pilot. His *Phoenix Hawk* might fly, but he was a MechWarrior by nature, better suited to stay on the ground. Let Hosni or Darian take him in their *Lucifers*. If they were still alive.

"Incoming!" shouted Stacy Drumm, coordinating with the Kell Hounds from her *Griffin*. "A big wedge of Nova Cats trying to punch through."

Blips flashed on Jason's tactical map, a blob of red icons pressing towards the Kado-Guchi Valley. A full Galaxy on the hunt. Strategies based on the terrain and allied troop positions coalesced in his mind, but not even a Galaxy of Nova Cats could capture his full attention, not here. The Cats were strong, as were the Jaguars, the Wolves, and the Hounds. But this was Black Luthien, home to something more dangerous than any of them.

A Dragon.

And Jason Youngblood was born to be a dragon slayer.

Jason had been meeting with Morgan Kell when a verigraphed message from Hanse Davion himself had arrived. The First Prince could send orders any way he liked, even under ComStar interdiction, but only the most critical came as an unforgeable verigraph. Fidgeting and nervous glances shot around the room as Morgan read. Orders like this meant combat, and in 3052 that meant the Clans, an enemy the entire Inner Sphere had learned to respect—and to fear.

The Kell Hounds' high command held their collective breath; Akira Brahe stoic, Christian Kell unreadable, Dan Allard calm but with a worried twinge around his eyes as Morgan looked up. It would be war, but not even Cat Wilson, with his innate ability to know things he shouldn't, could have guessed where the Prince of the Federated Suns would ask them to go.

Morgan had immediately offered Jason a subcontract at five times the Crescent Hawks' usual rate. Jason had just spent a year behind Clan lines; he knew them, knew their spirit. Some of his people piloted captured Clan machines. Training Morgan's Kell Hounds in anti-Clan tactics was the reason he was on Arc-Royal. The Hounds weren't going alone. Davion had sent the same missive to Wolf's Dragoons, and Morgan said that Jaime Wolf would accept it, because Wolf understood the idea of the greater enemy. If Jaime Wolf could set aside his feud with House Kurita—and had there ever been a greater feud in the history of the Inner Sphere?—then could not Jason Youngblood? *What would my father do?* Jason thought as he nodded. Jeremiah, who had spent years recovering after his stint in a Kurita prison...

The Crescent Hawks would come. They would come to kill the Clans, they would train the Hounds to kill the Clans, but there were other deaths to be had on Luthien, the Black Pearl of the Draconis Combine.

The wedge of Nova Cats tore through the first line of Kell Hound defenses and flowed in waves around Jason's Hawks, black 'Mechs striped with a blue field of stars. They might have been beautiful. One oddball Trinary had opted for a rocky sort of camo, perhaps a leftover from their previous conquest. Jason employed camo, as he did every conceivable tactical tool, but he always felt a twinge of disappointment when it worked. One didn't simply paint over sixty-five tons of steel powered by a miniature star and strut through a battlefield untouched, but that's what the *Loki* at the head of this Trinary was doing. Strutting like a peacock with his Trinary trailing behind like helpless chicks, confident in their painted invisibility.

"Hello, Star Captain Target of Bloodhouse Acquired." Jason flipped to IR. The magnificently camouflaged *Loki* and its fellows lit up like a nova. "Oops, I see you." He toggled his comm to his Striker Lance. "Sonja. That Trinary of rocky Cats look a little too reliant on their leader."

"The *Loki?*"

"That's the one. Bring it down and the rest will scatter. Falcon Fool them. No heroics."

Early in their year of raiding, the Hawks had perfected the art of Falcon Foolin', as it was known in the Federated Commonwealth, until they'd learned how bad the consequences could be. Treat a Clansman with honor and they'd return that honor to you. Accept their challenge to single combat and then run, or lure one into an ambush, and their comrades will seek fiery revenge, denying you the chance to demean them ever again. The Crescent Hawks had long since burned the bridge of honorable combat with the Jade Falcons, but the Nova Cats were new in the Inner Sphere.

"Commencing Foolin'." Sonja stepped her *Thunderbolt* out of cover and pointed at the *Loki*.

The Loki drew up short, then raised its arms. "I am Star Captain Branden—"

"Yeah, okay," Jason muttered as he muted the comm. He'd heard enough Clan prattle to last a lifetime.

The *Loki* rushed in while the rest of his unit spread out. Sonja waited, enduring a hail of autocannon and long-range-missile fire before unleashing her secret weapon—a Clan PPC, grafted onto the spot where a large laser usually sat. Coupled with her own LRMs, the blast brought the *Loki* to a staggering halt, grinding down onto one knee. Jason had to admire this Branden's ability to stay upright. Before he could catch his bearings, Sonja ducked her *Thunderbolt* behind a rockfall.

The rest of the Nova Cat Trinary formed a line on their side of the duel, but did not try to root out the other Hawks yet. They preferred to watch their captain fight, and that was fine. They also collectively fielded enough firepower to obliterate Jason's entire command, so he let them take their time. Time was *his* ally.

A quick glance at his tactical map gave Jason his out. He smiled and punched his comm. "Colonel Parella, this is Captain Yougblood. Can you do a man a favor?"

The duel continued, but not as the Nova Cats might have liked. Sonja's *Thunderbolt* maneuvered in and out of cover, taking potshots at the *Loki*, but never standing up to fight. The Nova Cat 'Mech may have been fast enough to run her down on open ground, but it stepped carefully on the loose rock of the Waseda Hills, lest it die on its back. The *Loki's* wild shots gave away its pilot's frustration as Sonja lured him farther and farther from his own troops. The Cats and Hawks had arrayed themselves in two lines, squaring off at maximum range.

Jason checked his map again and smiled. "Things are almost in position, Sonja. Thirty more seconds, then we move on your mark."

Sonja didn't answer. She was giving good, but her 'Mech limped, smoke coiling from a crack in its torso and coolant bleeding down one leg in green stripes. The *Loki* had yet to show any serious damage. *Damn Clan technology.*

A brutal strike brought her *Thunderbolt* to one knee. Sweat beaded on Jason's lip. He could see the next round chambering in the *Loki's* autocannon, but Sonja had lured it close to the Hawks' line. "Striker Lance, strike!"

Lasers and missiles converged on the *Loki* from three points, lighting it up like a bonfire on harvest night as the rest of Sonja's lance broke ranks. The 'Mech's auto-eject blew, launching an angry Star Captain Branden skyward. His *Loki* crumpled, and after a shocked pause, the Nova Cats opened fire. Outraged by this breach of honor, they sought revenge without thought for cohesion or basic caution. Theirs was a clumsy charge, rudderless and futile, and too late.

From the west, two companies from Wolf's Dragoons' Gamma Regiment tore into them. Caught between the Hawks and the wolves, the Cats crumbled. Only a pair of gangly *Dasher*s and a *Shadow Cat* broke away to retreat.

"One favor, as agreed." Colonel Parella waved from his bulbous, ugly *Imp.* "Put it in your ledger, Youngblood."

Jason saluted back, and the flow of battle carried the Dragoons away.

Explosions rang to the left and right, but the Crescent Hawks existed in a moment of calm. One skirmish at a time; even the largest battles broke down into a series of little fights, and in those moments victory could be found. A Crescent Hawk always found a way.

Jason called his people to him. Most had only superficial damage, but for one. "Sonja, how bad are you?"

"Busted up pretty good, but I'm still in the fight, Captain."

Jason scanned her 'Mech. "No, you're not. Your armor is Swiss cheese and your reactor shielding took a hit. Get to a field gantry and see what they can do. If you're not in danger of melting, stay and guard the techs. You're done on the field, Lieutenant."

"Yes, sir." Disappointment filled her voice, but Jason didn't care. As her *Thunderbolt* limped away, he knew there was one less life he had to worry about.

"Grange, take the company closer to the Hounds. I'm going airborne."

"Show-off," Grange said as Jason converted his *Phoenix Hawk* to AirMech mode, then to full aerospace fighter.

There was something liberating about blasting into the air and leaving behind the ground-bound world. Even after two decades and endless glitches in the conversion gears of his centuries-old Land-Air 'Mech, Jason felt the rush every single time.

From on high, the battle looked like little more than a contest of toy soldiers, mobile models connected by missile trails and deadly rays of light. Blackened hulks dotted the Waseda Hills, sending up columns of smoke that called in the vultures. Kurita salvage crews already worked the field, watched over by platoons of infantry as they hauled spotted Smoke Jaguar OmniMechs off to depots, or perhaps directly to Luthien Armor Works for reverse engineering. *Just like a Kuritan to act like a snake, stealing salvage that could rebuild the mercenaries who came to save their hides.*

He eyed the position of the Nova Cats relative to his Hawks, trying to read the ebb and flow for a pattern he could exploit. The Cats tested every front at once, washing against the Kell Hounds and various Dragoons elements like waves on a sea of black death. Some of the Hounds companies were clearly employing tactics he had taught them on the month-long trip to Luthien, and were faring better for it than their brethren who relied on traditional methods. On a rise, he spied Morgan Kell's red-and-black *Archer,* utterly unscathed. *How does he do that?*

In the east, two of his red-winged Crimson Hawks strafed the Clan lines; Chynna and Avery, in a *Corsair* and *Slayer* respectively. He'd given his air company carte blanche to operate, and to coordinate with the Hounds when possible. It seemed most of them were still flying, and why not? In a year behind Clan lines, none had been shot down. Jason smiled with pride.

"What are you doing up here, Captain?"

Jason looked to his left and right, where a pair of *Lucifer*s had taken position on his wings. "Hosni, what's the situation up here?"

"The allies have air superiority, for the moment. We're hitting targets of opportunity while Kell's pilots cover the gropos."

"Any casualties?"

"Lancaster put down with a hole through his wing. Landing gear was out, so he had to belly flop and won't be joining us for a bit. Can't raise Washington. We don't know what happened to her."

"Keep your eyes open. If she's down, we may have to wait until this is over to find out." A couple long-range missiles pinged his LAM. "We're attracting too much attention. I think I see our next playmates. Be ready for a Bump 'n Grind."

He pulled away and returned to his ground forces. Grange had busied them with taking potshots at a frustrated pack of Elementals. Once their short-range missiles were gone, the little Toads were only dangerous if you let them catch you. Dewey Mancini was especially dedicated to popping them, pulse lasers blazing from the *Peregrine* he'd liberated from a Ghost Bear garrison on Trondheim to replace his family *Jenner,* torn apart by Elementals just like these.

Jason ground to a halt in a clearing a few hundred meters away. "Let the Hounds handle those Toads. We're about to have bigger problems."

Amid the sea of black came a Star of spotted Smoke Jaguar 'Mechs. These were assault-class machines, huge and powerful, the most dangerous BattleMechs in existence, and they were barreling toward his unit as fast as their thick, stumpy legs would carry them. Every one of his 'Mechs could outdistance them, but one didn't become a legend by running.

"Hawks, to me! Bump 'n Grind on those Jags!"

His MechWarriors responded. With Sonja gone they were short one 'Mech, but they'd practiced for that, too. Grange's Pursuit Lance and Jason's Command Lance turned to the left and right as if fleeing, while the Striker Lance held firm. The intent was for the enemy to focus on them and ignore the flankers, but these Jags had paid attention to their tactical briefings, and kept their fire on the fast 'Mechs.

"They ain't going for it, Cap'n," Grange drawled as he threw twenty Clan LRMs back at their manufacturers.

"Keep moving. I'll draw their fire." Jason converted to AirMech mode, and every Jaguar turned on him. He didn't know why, but god, they *hated* his 'Mech. It didn't matter; they all missed as he zoomed over their heads. Now the Pursuit and Command Lances could get into position. The Jags wasted their ammo on him and soon were surrounded, with strong Hawks in front and fast Hawks behind.

"Now take it to them." Jason converted back to 'Mech mode and scoured the lead Jaguar *Masakari* with laser fire. A PPC hit he took to the shoulder tore off most of his armor and ignited a forest of red lights on his console, but his people were able to advance to punching distance virtually unmolested. One peculiarity among the Clans was their disdain for physical combat. It was such a taboo that they instinctively backpedaled their machines when an opponent got too close, to the point where they would bump butts with their Starmates.

"Just the way we like 'em, Captain," Hosni said as his red-winged *Lucifer* lined up to strafe. "Inbound in five!"

Jason counted three. "Hawks, pull out!" He hit his jump jets and roared backward, heedless of where he landed. The other Crescent Hawks jumped, ran, or rolled clear of the tightly packed Jaguar Star as Hosni hit them with a barrage of missiles and laser fire. Seconds later, Darian's *Lucifer* did the same, followed by Avery Karlson's *Slayer* from the opposite vector. His nose-mounted Clan Ultra-autocannon roared like damnation, shearing the head clean off a Jaguar *Gladiator*.

The ground Hawks didn't give the remaining Jaguars a chance to breathe, but laid into them until the last 'Mech fell. It had been eleven on five, with air support, but still Jason lost five of his own. He counted it a victory well won.

A face appeared in his cockpit, and Jason recoiled. An Elemental, hateful eyes glaring through his cracked visor, and he had friends. Four more had latched themselves onto the *Phoenix Hawk* like leeches. *Good luck to them.*

With the flip of a lever, Jason converted to AirMech mode and grinned at the shock he saw on his visitor's face. A long jump and a sudden impact, and the Elementals lay scattered across the Kado-Guchi Valley like carelessly tossed dice. Jason raked them with his lasers, though it was little more than an insult against their tough hides, then jumped away and left them shaking their armored fists. Distracted by the Jags, he'd allowed those Elementals to close. That was a lapse he couldn't afford. His mind was unfocused, distracted by the shadow haunting Black Luthien. The one casting that shadow was near; he could taste it in the back of his throat.

"Jason," called Morgan Kell over their private frequency. "What's your status?"

"The Crescent Hawks are still flying, Colonel. Half of us, at least."

"I need you to reinforce the city defenses. Take a breather from shooting for a while and hold some ground."

Jason called up his company status and tried to keep the desperation out of his voice. "Yes, sir, but I won't be holding much with six damaged 'Mechs."

"I can send you an ad hoc lance of orphans." Orphans, meaning MechWarriors who had lost their commander and lacked the initiative to act on their own. At least they would bring him to almost a full company.

"I'll look after them, sir. Where are we headed?"

"Cover the left flank of the reserve guards. They have the line. Just make sure nothing tries to skirt them."

"Who is the reserve guard, so I can tell them not to shoot at us?"

"Contact *Sho-sa* Shin Yodama. He's in charge of the Dragon's Claws."

The Dragon's Claws. *His* bodyguard. The most loyal sons of the Combine, sworn to protect its lord. Soldiers of a fading code, as old and feeble as they were in their ancient family machines, men with high honor, slow reflexes, and a driving need to die gloriously. Old men, full of old pride and old hatred, and at their head the most hated of all.

Morgan expected an answer, an affirmation or acknowledgment of his orders, but Jason could not find his voice. He reminded himself that the Nova Cats were the enemy today. *I am not a wolf.*

"Jason," Morgan said softly, evenly. "The Nova Cats are going to break through. If they reach the city they'll dig in and make us root them out street by street. Those may be Combine civilians in there, but they're still civilians, and they have not earned the horrors of war. That price must be paid by men in uniform. Men like you and me."

There was a truth in those words that Jason had accepted the minute he'd enrolled as a MechWarrior, one that had been drilled into him at the Citadel on Pacifica all those years ago. Those were good years, running with the children of Lyran nobility and learning to pilot a BattleMech from his famous father, the great Jeremiah Youngblood.

House Kurita had ruined those times when they'd raided Pacifica and razed the Citadel. The burning towers, the screaming, helpless citizens... they would never leave his memory, but they were memories, and today he must shield the living from that fate.

Because he was not as hotheaded as his father, and because he held a deep respect for Morgan Kell, Jason assented. In short order the Hawks redeployed, a klick and a half from a collection of shiny gold 'Mechs, and a *Phoenix Hawk* quite unlike his own in its junkyard camo.

Sho-sa Yodama welcomed them professionally, without the jibes common between regulars and mercenaries. After two decades of the Combine's "Death to Mercenaries" policy, it was a pleasant surprise. Still, Jason averted his eyes after the initial glance, focusing forward. *That* was where the enemy was.

A few tense hours dragged by. A Kell Hounds ammo truck came to refresh their bins, and two of his people rushed down to a field gantry to have some armor plates hastily welded on, but mostly it was a wait in which Jason dared not relax. His Hawks filled the comm with chatter, jibing each other and reliving the morning's deeds, comparing them to battles long past. Jason let them talk; rather than distract him, he found their voices soothing. It was the missing voices that scraped his raw nerves. He'd seen Clark and Kurst eject, and was sure Dewey had vacated his fallen *Peregrine,* but of Drumm he knew not. The Jaguars had smashed her *Griffin.* Had she been smashed, too? Jason tried to rub the pain over his eye, but his neurohelmet prevented him. *I am a MechWarrior. I can be a human being later.*

His four Kell Hounds orphans rendezvoused early, none of them faring much better than his Hawks. Since then he'd picked up an armless Dragoons *Hermes II* whose pilot utterly refused to vacate the field, and a battered Genyosha *Panther* who'd said nothing besides "I will stand with you." That put him back to twelve 'Mechs, but not a united company. He had a playbook of lance-scale tactics stored on his computer. He selected a few and sent them to his new crew, but maintained realistic expectations of how much they would absorb, or even look at. His cohesive strength consisted of himself and five damaged Hawks; the rest he'd just have to try to keep alive long enough to use them.

Darian radioed him with more bad news: Hosni had been shot down, his *Lucifer* crashing in a fireball in the Waseda Hills. The Crimson Hawks were down by half, all on the ground for refueling and repairs. They'd lasted over a decade as a unit, six pilots of unrivaled skill and camaraderie, and he'd led them here. For what? *For what reason, Jason?* He put Darian in command—she was more than ready for it—and ordered her to stay down unless the Clans won the field.

"Captain Youngblood, sir?" It was one of his orphans, a man named Brant.

"What is it, Sergeant?"

"Can I ask you a question, sir?"

"Make it quick."

"Why are you here, sir?"

"Morgan Kell ordered me to reinforce the city defenses."

"No sir, I mean..." Brant paused, perhaps knowing he shouldn't press, but not yet having reached an age where his mouth kept up with his brain. "I mean, why did you come to Luthien, sir? We all know how you feel about the Combine—"

"That will do."

Brant fell silent. The shoulders of his *Commando* slumped as if in shame, and Jason felt a pang in his heart. There had been no *Commando* in the Crescent Hawks for a decade, not since Rex. *Rex.* His father's best friend, and in truth Jason's as well. Rex would have asked the same question, "Why are you here, Jason?" but Rex would have known the answer. It was why he had left the Crescent Hawks.

"When you're a mercenary, war is a business," said the Rex in Jason's memory. *"It's a business, and if you want to succeed, then you need to treat it professionally. Letting it get personal has destroyed great men, and those who followed them. What the Kuritans did to your father was evil, but we avenged him when we rescued him. It's time to let it lie."* But Jason couldn't, and Rex couldn't understand, so he had left, and their last words had been of anger.

"Don't be a rabid wolf, Jason. When you hate, no amount of death is enough."

"Just one more, Rex," Jason said, unheard by anyone except the LAM that had served him, and his father before him. "There was only ever one more death."

A *Spider* wearing the red of the Sword of Light rocketed over a rise and skidded to a halt just in front of Jason's 'Mech. "Who are you?"

"Captain Youngblood of the Crescent Hawks."

The *Spider* executed a slight bow. "*Gun-sho* Takata, of the Ivory Dragon. The Nova Cats are surrounded. They are trying to break through to the city. They are coming! They are coming now!"

"How many?"

"All of them." Takata's awed whisper silenced all the comm chatter. This was it, the moment of do or die that defined every battle. Most warriors never emerged from such a moment, dying frozen by indecision or fear. Jason Youngblood had dictated his battlefields for the last year, feinting and fading, striking only when the advantage was his, but now war came to him on its terms, and he had to find a way to survive. To victory.

"Fall in, *Gun-sho*. You're a Crescent Hawk now." Jason stepped to the fore of his people and converted to AirMech mode. "I want every eye on that rise. Any Cat comes over it, you send them back or you send them to hell. Weapons free. Fight like your children are watching."

The Cats' line of advance veered right of the Hawks' position, headed directly for the reserve unit. The Dragon's Claws had pushed the Nova Cats away from the city at first, but now the Clanners had identified them as the weakest link in the chain of allied forces. The Crescent Hawks rushed to close the gap as black Clan 'Mechs mingled with golden defenders in a crash that shook the Kado-Guchi Valley.

A *Grendel* suddenly filled Jason's viewport, running in front of him and stopping like a dazed animal caught in the glow of oncoming headlights. Jason could do no more than wince and brace himself as he collided with it at near maximum velocity. His harness crushed the breath from his lungs as his LAM tumbled end over end. He had a sudden image of Pacifica, of seeing the LAM for the first time, hidden in the Star League cache his father had discovered. How proud he'd been to find it.

"Cap'n! Captain! Don't be dead, you owe me fifty C-bills! I'll take it out of salvage of this damn crazy 'Mech, I swear!"

"Grange," Jason spat blood onto the faceplate of his neurohelmet. "Keep the company moving. I'll catch up."

"You ain't dead?"

"I'm considering it. Get going."

"Sir."

Jason watched his company rush off on his sparking secondary monitor. Somehow he managed to rise. His wireframe glowed red; no part of his LAM was undamaged. His left arm lay on the ground a hundred meters away, and the corresponding wing had been smashed. He was stuck in AirMech mode now. At least the damage was confined to that side, leaving his large laser intact. He could still shoot. Just to be sure, he blasted the wreckage of the *Grendel* that had done this. It lay unmoving and sheared nearly in half, but sometimes pettiness had its place.

His jump jets still worked. Heedless of anything but the melee ahead, he rocketed on. He was on his own, but not alone. Cats ran in every corner of his viewscreen. A *Black Hawk* crashed to the ground, on fire from inferno missiles, a crowd of dying Elementals blazed their last shots from atop a wrecked *Vulture,* a *Daishi* fell to the ground, its head a smoking crater, and there, above that *Daishi* was the true Great Death.

The Dragon.

Gold, like his bodyguards, the twisting serpent of House Kurita wound around his shoulders. *His.* The man and the machine were one. Both of them were the Dragon, the beating heart of the Combine, right here in front of him. Jason remembered his father as he'd found him on Dieron, a broken wreck of a man where once had been the dashing, smiling pride of the Lyran Commonwealth Armed Forces.

Would Takashi remember? Would Takashi know who stood before him? Who was Jason Youngblood when Morgan Kell was on the field, when Jaime Wolf prowled Luthien in his *Archer*?

Takashi turned to him. Time was a sludge, sliding by at a pace measured in heartbeats. The battle didn't matter anymore. The Cats, the Jaguars, the errant PPC bolt lazily gliding past his head, none of it mattered. Jeremiah's face gazing up at his son without a hint of recognition mattered, as did the man who had ordered the torture. Was it Takashi himself?

Rex was in his ear, with words that mattered not. Twenty years of anger wouldn't listen. Jason felt his hands tighten, not on his weapons, but on his conn. The mobility that was a LAM's true weapon could crush any enemy, even a dragon. And then...

...then...

The Dragon...*bowed* to him. It wasn't much, just a simple lean of its torso, but it was unmistakable. The pilot of that 'Mech knew who he was, and acknowledged him.

In his time-dilated state, mountains of meaning crashed down on him. With that act, Takashi Kurita told him more than a thousand years of talks, and Jason Youngblood, for one of the only times in his life, was humbled.

I am not a wolf.

His anger vanished in a rush as time returned to its natural flow. The PPC bolt fizzed past his head, on its way to cripple a fleeing Clan 'Mech. The Dragon stood tall before him. Without being able to explain why, but only knowing inside that it was right, Jason returned his bow.

His LAM was an ugly, ungainly mash of BattleMech and aerofighter, but from it Jason drew grace. His nose dipped to the ground, and as it touched the soil of Luthien, he felt the blood feud he had held for so long drain away, and the shadow lift from his soul. There was a new enemy now, not one who threatened from behind his walls, but one who overran all boundaries to conquer, to assimilate. The Dragon threatened life, the Clans threatened existence. There was a new enemy, thus there must be new allies to oppose them.

A laser rocked him back to the present. Jason returned fire, as did the Dragon at his side. The Nova Cats would be stopped, right here on the line Takashi Kurita had drawn, and his allies would stand with him.

I am not a wolf.

I am the Crescent Hawk.

ARC-ROYAL
FEDERATED COMMONWEALTH
21 NOVEMBER 3052

"You know, I don't think I've ever seen you take that off."

Jason looked up into the mirror, where behind him Morgan Kell had entered his room. He rubbed a thumb over the Bushido Blade he'd been pinning to his dress uniform. "It feels good there, like an old friend."

Morgan smiled. "I had to spend a decade in a monastery to learn that lesson."

"Wisdom well-earned." Jason ran a hand through his still mostly black hair. It wouldn't be tamed, ever. "I think this parade will test Melissa's patience more than the medals I wear."

"One day you'll tell me how you know my cousin so well."

"One day you'll tell me how you do that thing with your 'Mech."

"*Touché*." Morgan took a seat, crossing one long leg over the other to wipe something from his shiny dress boot. "How are the repairs coming?"

"They're...they're not." A cloud that Jason had been holding at bay suddenly fell over him, a damp, dark shroud whispering one word: *Dispossessed.* His hands fell from the sash he'd been fastening. "The conversion gear is totally shot, and I can't find parts for less than the cost of a duchy. I'd hoped I could leverage my new standing with Takashi Kurita for something from LexaTech, but with Irece in Nova Cat hands..." He shrugged. "She's one of the last *Phoenix Hawk* LAMs in the Inner Sphere, and it's looking more and more like she'll never fly again. Maybe never even walk." Jason had known this for months, but actually saying the words was like draining all the life out of the room. That 'Mech had been his father's. Now it may as well be buried with him.

"Come on." Morgan stood and threw an arm around Jason's shoulders. "Nothing cheers a man up like a good walk in the 'Mech bay."

A few moments later they were strolling through a place they had no business being in their clean and pressed dress uniforms, but it felt so much more like home that Jason didn't care. Morgan was right. He couldn't help feeling comforted by the sounds and smells, by the rowdy shouts of techs scraping every last bit of dirt from the Kell Hounds machines in preparation for the Archon's parade.

"It's not too late," Morgan said as they walked past his *Archer*. "We can rebuild the Crescent Hawks any time you're ready. Half my Hounds would desert me for your colors if you just said the word."

A ponderous silence fell, which Morgan was kind enough not to break. That monastery had taught him patience, and when to use it. Jason considered it for a long time as they passed row after row of freshly repaired Kell Hounds BattleMechs. Every path of thought led to one conclusion: it wouldn't be the same. His Crescent Hawks were a family he'd lived with for two decades. Many of them had been with him since the beginning, had followed him behind Clan lines for a year of hard living in three *Leopard*-class DropShips, never setting foot on a world where they weren't in danger. Many of those wonderful, strong people hadn't come home from Luthien, and most of who did had taken their hard-earned retirement. Currently, the Crescent Hawks consisted of Jason Youngblood, three seasoned aerojocks, and one stubborn Outbacker without a 'Mech. One did not recruit a new family.

Lost in thought, Jason suddenly realized he was walking alone. Morgan had stopped to stand at the feet of the last BattleMech in line, where he was smiling proudly. "I know it's not quite the same, but I hope it can cheer you up a little."

Jason gazed up at a site familiar, but different. It wore his colors, blue and gray, with his screaming hawk's head on its shin, but it lacked the scrapes and odd bulges, the tells of hidden conversion gear. It was a *Phoenix Hawk,* but not a LAM.

"It's a PHX-3S, fresh from Coventry Metal Works," Morgan said. "Not even I've ever piloted a brand-new 'Mech before. I took the liberty of having them imprint the neurohelmet with your pattern."

"You're making it hard to say no." Jason couldn't help the smile spreading across his face.

Morgan shrugged. "The 'Mech is yours, whatever you choose to do. Consider it a thank you, for everything."

A swell of pride and gratitude put a tear in the eye of the famed Crescent Hawk. Few men would make such a gesture; few men deserved such loyalty. "Tell you what. Let's make it official. Put it in Kell Hounds red and black, and I'll take it."

Morgan smiled, big and broad, and held out his hand. "As Phelan would say, bargained well and done!"

Jason clasped his hand, and for the first time since Luthien, his smile was true. "Just let me keep the Hawk's head."

"Done. Now let's go get a drink."

"And I want to step back from active duty for a while."

"Now you're pushing it."

"I'll be an instructor. I rather like teaching. And I could stand to spend some more time with my son Jeremiah."

"As a father, I can go along with that."

Arms around each other, hearts light, they headed out to greet the Archon.

MISSING DUKE SPURS DEMONSTRATION

PATRICK WYNNE

—*Bueller Times*, December 3094

The streets of Bueller are quiet tonight just hours after unanswered questions regarding Duke Tancred Sandoval's continuing absence from the Draconis March capital sparked a large demonstration before the ducal palace. The missing duke's whereabouts have become cause for concern in recent days since he departed Robinson. Field Marshal Jerome Sandoval, Duke Tancred's cousin and de facto administrator of the Draconis March while Tancred is on New Avalon, made a brief appearance before the crowds assembled in Bueller's central square earlier today to calm the gathered protestors.

"Duke Tancred is currently engaged in important diplomatic efforts in the wake of the Benet disaster," the field marshal assured the crowd of over two thousand. "For security reasons, his itinerary is classified, but I can tell you that as ever his first priority is the safety and well-being of the Draconis March. Much as he has for the past five months, he is seeking a solution for the Benet refugees that will be agreeable to all sides."

However, Sandoval's words placated few among the crowd. Yevgeny Pestov, a veteran of the Clan wars and the Jihad, still had questions after the field marshal's address: "What exactly does 'important diplomatic efforts' mean, anyway? And agreeable to all sides? Does that include the Dracs or the Snow Ravens? The duke already tried to give away Benet to his Drac friends. How many more of our worlds will he sell out?"

These concerns were echoed by protester after protester throughout the day, with many stating their belief that the Benet disaster was a smokescreen to allow the Draconis Combine to annex the system without conflict.

Maryann Lucero, an administrative assistant at the Robinson Exchequer, expressed her doubt regarding the official story. "I heard that the whole 'Death Cloud' thing was faked. People have lived on Benet for centuries, but suddenly there's this urgent problem and everyone has to leave? That's fishy as hell. Nope, it's obvious that Duke Tancred and the First Princess are trying to suck up to their buddy Devlin Stone by giving away more Fed worlds in the name of his so-called peace. Well, that's no peace I want a part of, I'll tell you that for free."

Some among the crowd did express concern for the missing duke. "I can't believe after everything Tancred has done for us, nobody is out there looking for him," lamented Felix Jura, who claims to have been on the last rescue ship off of Benet. "Thousands of us owe our lives to the duke, and if he's in trouble, then someone should do something to help him."

Mr. Jura was present as a representative of the Benet Survivors Assistance League, which seeks donations to fund a search mission for the missing duke. This group's presence was the cause of some tension early in the evening when harassment by anti-Combine protestors led to an intervention by Bueller Civil Patrol officers. The BSAL fundraisers were escorted to safety before the situation escalated out of hand.

IF AULD ACQUAINTANCE BE FORGOT...
(A KELL HOUNDS STORY)

MICHAEL A. STACKPOLE

PART 1 (OF 4)

I

TYROL HOUSE HOTEL, RAVENSBURG
CENTRAL RIVER DISTRICT
ZAVIJAVA
LYRAN COMMONWEALTH
24 DECEMBER 3010

"Veronica?" Morgan Kell, standing in the foyer of the Archon's Suite, could see no sign of his companion. Yet on the table to the left, dinner steamed on plates and bubbles rose in champagne. Over on the right sat a large box, wrapped in crisp green-and-red foil paper, bound with a big gold ribbon and bow.

He hesitated and listened for the sound of water running in the bathroom, or other sounds of habitation, but heard nothing. He descended the three steps to the main floor and set a bag down that contained a trio of presents for Veronica. He'd not been in the suite before, but the bedroom obviously lay through the half-closed doorway to the left. He walked over to it and peeked in, thinking perhaps she'd lain down for a moment and fallen asleep.

Again, no trace. The master bath proved empty when he turned the lights on. The bed hadn't been slept in. But, curiously, the sliding door to the rooftop patio wasn't locked, and the anti-theft bar leaned against the wall.

Morgan snaked a hand around to the small of his back and drew a compact needler pistol. He worked the slide, shaving a cluster of ballistic polymer needles into the firing chamber, and snapped the safety off. He shot his jacket's left sleeve over his hand, sliding the door open and hoping he wasn't smearing any fingerprints. The night's cold air rushed in, and he stepped out into the darkness.

Nothing.

Panic rose, but he forced it away. There could have been a million reasons why Veronica had left the suite. Perhaps she'd gone down a level in the elevator, searching for ice from a machine. They could have passed in elevator cars as he rose and she descended. And while he knew something that simple was likely the most logical explanation, the feeling in his bones told him it wasn't the truth.

He returned to the suite, gun still at the ready. Steam still rose from the dinner, but the food wasn't piping hot. The champagne flutes had no condensation on them. The ice in the champagne bucket had melted a bit, and the candles had burned down somewhat. He blew them out, knowing he could obtain identical candles, light them, and measure the time it took for them to melt down to that point. That way he'd know how long it had been between her lighting them and his entering the suite.

He crossed to the room's communicator and called down to the kitchen. "This is Colonel Kell, in the Archon's Suite. When did you deliver the meal?"

"Is everything to your liking?"

"Yes, quite."

"Did we forget something? We can get that right up to you."

"Actually, can you send up two more candles, identical to the ones here? And please send up the same server. I want to make sure the gratuity was adequate."

"Yes, Colonel, right away."

Morgan glanced at his chronometer. *1945 hours.* His left hand became a fist. A couple of knuckles cracked, then he forced his hand open. *It is probably nothing…*

He opened the door in response to a knock. A petite woman in a white blouse over a black skirt smiled. She extended the candles to him. "As you requested, Colonel."

"Come in, just for a moment." Morgan smiled, returning the gun unseen to its holster. "Could I see the receipt for dinner?"

The woman blinked, but produced a noteputer from the small of her back. "Yes, right here. I delivered at 1925." She swung the screen around so he could read it right side up.

"And did you light the candles?"

"No, sir. I left the food under the cloches, and Mrs. Kell said she'd light the candles."

Morgan nodded, noting that Veronica Matova had signed the charge slip as "*V. Kell.*" She'd also tipped well, 317 kroner—half the price of the meal. This brought him a moment of joy, since either the Federated Suns or the Lyran Commonwealth would be covering the bill.

"I did open the champagne, though, and poured."

"Good, thank you. Can you make another charge slip so I can add to the gratuity?"

The woman smiled, complied, and Morgan doubled the tip Veronica had left. "That's very generous, sir."

"Thank you for the extraordinary service."

"You're welcome, sir. Merry Christmas."

"Yes, and you too."

He closed the door behind her, pulled out his communicator and placed a call. It rang twice, then connected. "Quintus, I have a situation."

"Yes, Colonel?"

"Veronica is gone."

"Gone, gone... So, sorry, when was she last seen?"

"Half an hour ago." Morgan looked around the room. "Quintus, she signed a receipt as V. Kell. And when she received dinner delivery, she tipped 317 kroner."

"Your Nagelring dorm room number in your last year there."

"Yeah."

"So she knew she was being watched."

"No doubt. No trace of her in the room, no signs of struggle, nothing out of the ordinary."

"Right, good. Touch nothing, I'll have my liaison get a team over there immediately. We'll find her, Morgan."

"Thanks, Quintus."

A forensics team from the Central River District's Criminal Investigation Division arrived a little after 8 and pored over the entire room. They literally vacuumed up every eyelash and hair they could find, and took Veronica's hairbrush for harvesting DNA exemplars. They pulled fingerprints off the windows and doorknobs, and again off the cloches that had covered the meals. They bagged up the candles—both the used ones and new—and took notes of Morgan's timing so they could perform the experiment he'd intended to do.

Quintus Allard arrived shortly after the team began their operation. Smaller than Morgan, with brown hair and a very serious expression, he pulled the MechWarrior out of the room and into the corridor. "Let them do their work. They'll have results soon. You and I and *our friend* have other things to do."

"Isn't he already off-world?"

"Turned his ship around. He lands in another two hours." The Federated Suns intelligence officer summoned the elevator. He and Morgan descended to the lobby, then approached the desk.

The woman who had given Morgan his keycard smiled as she glanced up. "Colonel Kell, is everything okay?"

Quintus produced credentials from an inside jacket pocket. "Quintus Allard, with the Commonwealth Criminal Prosecution Unit. I need to see your head of security."

Blood drained from the woman's face. "Yes, sir, right away." She turned and slipped through a door behind her into the office.

Morgan looked over at his companion. "Commonwealth Criminal Prosecution Unit? Is that a thing?"

Quintus shook his head. "Most folks aren't aware of politics beyond their workplace, or institutions outside their district—maybe their planet. Mock up some docs that look good, and they'll believe it."

A heavy-set woman with blond hair pulled up into a tight bun came out from the office. "Arlene Puscht. How can I help you?"

"Please God that you can." Morgan sighed loudly. "My companion is missing from the Archon's Suite. She was taken against her will. With your help, we hope to find out exactly where she's gone.

II

TYROL HOUSE HOTEL, RAVENSBURG
CENTRAL RIVER DISTRICT
ZAVIJAVA
LYRAN COMMONWEALTH
24 DECEMBER 3010

Morgan and Quintus stood in the hotel's darkened security office with Arlene Puscht, staring at a holotable playback system. It showed a man of medium build, with a large-brimmed hat and trench coat emerging from the elevator on the penthouse level. He knocked at the door and spoke to Veronica through the narrow opening. He showed her some sort of identification, then she opened the door to him.

Morgan glanced at the hotel's security chief. "None of the footage of this man shows his face. Shouldn't we be able to slice the holographic data and piece that together?"

The woman hung her head. "Colonel, we use cameras for security purposes, to look for trouble, not to spy on guests. We have a clientele which—"

"No, save it." Morgan shook his head. "Some of your clients are in business, and if the footage could reveal someone they were meeting, a merger might be put off." *Or a divorce initiated.*

Quintus slid his finger along a strip on the table, running the image back five seconds. "Wouldn't have mattered, Morgan, unless they were running ultra-high-end, multi-spectrum cameras. See the halo effect there, where we just catch a glimpse of his earlobe?"

"Yeah."

"He covered his face and exposed flesh with a cosmetic containing micro-flakes that absorb, diffuse and reflect the laser energy used in a standard hotel holo-camera set up. Even if we got a full shot, his face would look like a glowing mask cut from corrugated cardboard. It's meant to thwart facial-recognition software, and decrypting a clean shot would take days, even with the multi-spectral data."

Morgan scratched at the back of his neck. "That sounds like spycraft. Who would have access to that stuff?"

"I'd love to tell you it was restricted, but college students came up with it to avoid being tracked while at underground parties, and every resistance movement in the Inner Sphere has sacks of the stuff. But it usually looks like pancake makeup, so for Veronica to have opened the door, it must have been fairly refined, otherwise the guy would've looked like a clown."

The MechWarrior frowned. "She invites him in, but realizes something is wrong. Then the food arrives, so she has to play it cool. Guy threatens to kill her and the server. This is why she signs the bill as my wife and tips three-seventeen kroner, to let us know there was a problem. Server goes. She has time to take the cloches off the food and light the candles. Why did he give her that time?"

"Waiting on a ride, I would imagine." Quintus glanced at the security chief. "What have you got for cameras outside, monitoring traffic?"

"Views of all four sides."

"Covering ground level, yes? Nothing from above?"

The woman shook her head.

Morgan closed his eyes, remembering the unlocked door to the rooftop patio. "Aircar comes in, she's snatched right off the roof."

Arlene gasped. "That's not...that would be *illegal*. The constabulary would have stopped them."

Quintus snorted. "And on Christmas Eve, how many people do you think they're stopping who run an aircar over the roof to convince their kids that Santa's coming for them? If one of your guests wanted to do that, would they seriously stop them?"

"But, Quintus, the constabulary would have the transponder data for the aircars making the flights, right?"

"Sure, but if I'm running the op, we make the snatch, drop to ground. Abandon the vehicle and pick up another one. We run to a stop-signal, move her to another vehicle, and drive the new car all over the place before dropping it and moving to yet another car. They can do that all night, and unless there's great holo of the places they make the switch, we can't even be sure the switched person isn't a decoy."

A cold hand closed around Morgan's heart and squeezed. He swung a chair around and sat. "Why, Quintus? Why would they take her?"

"Ransom. To get at you. You've got a few enemies, as I recall."

Up until that second Morgan had always believed in the truth of the saying *a man is known by the nature of his enemies*. He had plenty, and some of them *very* powerful. In the last two months alone he'd destroyed the career of Galatea's military governor, General Volmer, and bankrupted that world's underworld kingpin, Haskell Blizzard. Then he and his brother had crushed a rebellion by the leader of the Church of Jesus Christ Majificent. While the Church had passed to more stable leadership, the previous leader had established the Petrine Order—a splinter sect with fervent believers given to terrorist activities against enemies of the Church. On Zavijava he'd been instrumental in stopping raiders from looting the planet, winning him no friends among that crew or the Free Worlds League.

And before that, he'd helped Katrina Steiner avoid the assassins her predecessor, former Archon Alessandro Steiner, had sent after her. She'd returned triumphant and deposed him, and like most Steiners, Alessandro had little use for forgiveness and never forgot a slight. *And he might have access to current or ex-Loki agents, who could easily pull off this sort of kidnapping operation.*

Morgan stared down at his empty hands, wanting to do something—*anything*. "Should I make a list? I mean, Quintus, what do I do here? All the training I've had, doing well at the Nagelring, everything, and none of it pertains to this. What do I do?"

"You leave the investigating to us, the folks who have the training for it. We'll find her, and we'll find the people who took her." Quintus nodded solemnly. "And that's when we turn things over to the MechWarriors, so you can do what you're trained to do."

"Okay, I'm in." Morgan's head came up. "But no 'Mechs. We find these people, and my bare hands will do just fine."

III

LOCATION UNKNOWN, RAVENSBURG
CENTRAL RIVER DISTRICT
ZAVIJAVA
LYRAN COMMONWEALTH
25 DECEMBER 3010

Even before she became fully awake, Veronica Matova knew something was wrong. Her right shoulder and hip ached because she'd slept on her side, which she never did. Cold had seeped up from the floor, and she'd not slept on concrete in many a year. The fingers of her left hand brushed over the cold surface, and she could feel the greasy grime on her skin.

And then there is the stinging pain in my neck.

Normally she awoke quickly, even on those warm and languorous mornings when she woke up next to Morgan. It would take her a moment to realize where she was, then she'd roll up on to her side, snuggle a bit closer and kiss his shoulder or the back of his neck. Most times he didn't even notice. Others he grunted or almost purred. And on the special times he'd roll over himself, so they lay belly to belly, trading kisses and caresses and body heat.

The muzziness, along with the cottonmouth, reminded her of her last waking moments. All day, she'd had a sense that she was being watched. As beautiful as she was, she'd been used to being the center of attention in most places she went. On a backwater like Zavijava, her looks made her both exotic and exquisite, so she was bound to be noticed.

But this had been different. There had been a predatory quality to the surveillance. Try as she might, she'd been unable to see who was following her. Whoever it was had skills, or employed a skilled team that switched off so she wouldn't notice them. She'd picked up on the sense of being watched in the pedestrian shopping district in Ravensburg, right after she'd bought Morgan's gift. Thinking back though, she couldn't be certain they'd not been with her before that.

Still, try as she might, she had no hard evidence she was being followed—and she knew all the tricks to spot pursuit, and how to avoid being spotted. She often used variations of them to snap quick pictures of friends and clients—the former for fun, and the latter for use later, if the circumstances demanded. Despite not having any tangible evidence, she trusted her feelings enough that when she returned to Tyrol House and called down to the kitchen to order dinner, she identified herself to both the desk clerk and the kitchen staff as Mrs. Kell.

While she waited for the food, there'd come the knock at the door. A fairly nondescript man had shown her Lyran Intelligence Corps credentials. He told her they'd had a credible threat against her life, and he needed to look around and secure the suite. She'd admitted him, then he'd immediately drawn a needler pistol and directed her to the bedroom.

Then room service had knocked on the door. The man retreated to the bedroom. "Do anything stupid, and you will watch the server die before I kill you."

Veronica had played it cool, but again signed the receipt as V. Kell. She'd also tipped 317 kroner, a number significant to Morgan. She knew he'd pick up those clues. Once the server left, the man reappeared from the bedroom and pulled the cloches from the meals to inspect them. He mocked her choices, then lit the candles to "set the mood" and ordered her out through the bedroom and onto the roof. An aircar was waiting for them there, and once inside...

She reached her hand up to touch her neck. They'd injected her with something to put her out. *But for how long?*

Somewhere close by, a lock clicked. Veronica resisted the urge to sit up. Instead she barely cracked her eyes open and remained slumped on the floor. She found herself in a dim and dingy room, with bare joists above and wiring and pipes easily visible. Chain-link fencing blocked off a corner of what she took to be a basement. Heavy chains and a combination lock secured a door made of fencing and wood framing.

A skinny man came stomping down some makeshift stairs. He wore nondescript clothes and soiled gardening gloves. More importantly, he wore a balaclava, obscuring his identity.

Relief washed over Veronica. If she couldn't identify her kidnapper, chances that she'd be freed if ransom were paid increased. A victim who *could* identify the kidnapper was a threat, and often ended up dead.

The man stopped before the cage and kicked the wire a couple of times. "Wake up."

Veronica groaned and rolled over onto her back. "Where am I?"

"Don't you worry about that." The man hefted a paper bag with a restaurant's logo splashed brightly on the side. "I brought you some food."

This is not the man who kidnapped me. "I need water."

"Got that, too." He reached back and pulled a small plastic bottle from his back pocket. "Just scoot on back and I'll slip it into there for you."

Veronica slid back, bumping into an empty plastic bucket. She came up on an elbow and rubbed her hand against her neck. "The man who took me, what did he shoot me up with?"

Her captor fiddled with the lock. "What difference does it make?"

"A lot." She sat up and spitted him with a steady stare. "I'm pregnant."

"Um, ah..." The chain dangled for a moment, and he hung the lock on the fencing. "I don't know nothing about that. I'm just here to feed you and stuff." He opened the door enough to roll the bottle of water to her, then tossed the bag in as well.

It landed with a plop and tipped over.

A single French fry popped free.

"I can't eat this."

The man pointed a finger at her. "You'll eat it, or you don't get nothing at all."

"But—"

"Lady, I'm just here to see to it you don't starve or get away. And I don't want to be here no more than you do." He shook his head. "You pissed off some mean people. I don't do for you, they *are* going to do for me and my family, got it?"

"But maybe a salad or something?" Veronica caressed her stomach. "For the baby?"

The man stared at her, then triple-looped the chain through the fencing before snapping the lock shut again. "You just don't cause no trouble, and everything will turn out fine. Don't make me hurt you."

"No, sir. Thank you, sir." Veronica pressed the bottle against her neck. "More water, if you can, I am very thirsty."

His eyes became slits, then he nodded. "You be good, and I'll see."

"God bless you. May angels keep you safe." Veronica smiled. *May Lucifer keep you safe in the bowels of hell. Because when I get out of here, that's where you're bound.*

IV

TYROL HOUSE HOTEL, RAVENSBURG
CENTRAL RIVER DISTRICT
ZAVIJAVA
LYRAN COMMONWEALTH
25 DECEMBER 3010

Morgan sat in the suite's living room, the champagne flat, the food stone-cold, all the ice melted and condensation long since evaporated. The forensics team had left a while ago—he had no idea how long, and couldn't summon the energy to look at his chronometer. He'd thanked them as they left and had been awaiting their reports, but then he sat down and made a mistake.

He opened the present Veronica had gotten him.

The big box held a variety of things, and most brought a smile to his face. Pursuant to a conversation where he'd admitted that most men were clueless about underwear because their mothers or wives usually did the buying, or the service issued their clothes, she'd picked out briefs in a variety of colors, and had added socks to match. She'd also gotten him a very thick bath sheet, having endured his complaint that few hotels and zero fire bases ever had good towels. In and of themselves those gifts were not much, but they showed she'd listened to him and remembered.

And then, nestled within the folds of the towel, he found a flat box. Inside it lay a two-panel silver frame, hinged in the middle. He opened it and found two static holographic images frozen there. On the left, a picture of himself and Patrick, him in his Tenth Skye Rangers uniform, and Patrick in his Nagelring uniform. *Definitely his graduation*. Both of them smiling, eyes bright and grins wide.

Facing it was an image he'd not seen before, but he knew where it had been taken. On Galatea, Patrick had fought against Titan Volmer in an underground 'Mech battle. He'd won, and with his victory they'd broken the power of Haskell Blizzard. Doing that meant their dream of building a mercenary regiment was that much closer to coming true. The image showed two brothers, together, incredibly happy.

Morgan hadn't seen Veronica take the picture. She'd not showed it to him either. She'd managed to capture the two of them, their love for each other, displayed so brightly in a moment when they'd both let their guards down. Just as did the Nagelring picture. How she'd found the Nagelring picture he had no clue, but she'd seen in it what she'd seen in the shot she'd taken.

He couldn't have thanked her enough for the images. *And now I really can't.* He felt as if he'd been hollowed out, and that the knife used in the job had been rusty and dull.

The door lock clicked, and before he could turn his head, a tall man with a long face and long nose strode through the door. "We'll find her, Morgan."

"Ian." Morgan stood and offered the First Prince of the Federated Suns his hand. "You needn't have come back. You surely have more important things to be doing."

"No, my friend, I don't. It's not going to hurt to let Hanse run things for a little while longer, and I consider Veronica as much of a friend as I do you." Ian shook his hand and clapped him on the shoulder. "Part of me fears that because we were all seen together, one of my enemies has taken her."

Quintus Allard entered the suite, and behind him came a trim woman with light-brown hair and dark eyes. "This is Agent Sonya Hallestrom. She is my LIC counterpart here in Ravensburg. She's allowing His Highness and me to sit in on briefings as a courtesy."

"Good, thank you."

All four of them took seats and the woman consulted her noteputer. "Prelim DNA results are negative for anyone but staff, Ms. Matova, and one other person who left a hair on the curtain going out onto the balcony. We might find something more out there after sunup, but with the wind, I am not hopeful."

Morgan nodded. "Anything on the sample you did get?"

Agent Hallestrom frowned. "Local criminal databases came up empty, but we have a hit on someone who has left samples in other places in the Commonwealth and the Federated Suns. It is a person of interest in a couple of deaths which appear to be accidental but had political angles that make us think not. Now, given Ms. Matova's record as a sex worker, is it possible that she could have been blackmailing someone who would hire a mechanic to deal with her?"

"No, I don't think so." Morgan frowned. "I don't believe so."

Ian snorted. "Highly unlikely since we were here incognito, and only for a short time. Someone would have had to spot her here, and the mechanic would have to be here and willing to accept the job. That's a curious set of circumstances, isn't it?"

"Yes, Highness, though having a list of her enemies would be useful as a supplement to Colonel Kell's list."

Morgan sat back. *Did I make this about me when it may just have been about Veronica?* He dismissed the notion that she practiced blackmail, but had to acknowledge that a former client might be fearful about information that she could have obtained somehow. *When she vanished from Galatea, could that have caused someone to panic and send agents to look for her?*

He glanced up. "I don't know of any enemies she might have. She revealed nothing about her business to me."

Hallestrom nodded. "I'll reach out to LIC on Galatea. They'll have a list. I do have to ask you, Colonel, is it possible she just walked away? People in her position, they often shy away from emotional entanglements. Could her connection with you have been overwhelming?"

"Could have been. Isn't that true for everyone, though?" Morgan laid his hand on the closed frame. "If that's what she had been thinking, she wouldn't have identified herself as my wife. She wouldn't have tipped 317 kroner. If she wanted to run away, she wouldn't have left clues that would make me want to pursue her, right?"

Ian leaned toward the LIC agent. "I've known the woman for the past two weeks. She wasn't a flighty girl to vanish when the fairy tale gets serious, otherwise she'd have taken off the second the Ion Knights started shooting things up. Were she a gold digger, she'd still be here because last month, on Galatea, Morgan and his brother made her over a million C-bills, and there's no reason to think that would have stopped."

Morgan sighed. "She bet on my brother in a fixed 'Mech battle, and he won despite the fix being in."

Agent Hallestrom made a note. "Okay, so she didn't do a runner and she's not blackmailing anyone. That helps. Now, I have my people and the local constabulary shaking every tree they can to learn where she's gone. These people are good but, as you can imagine, things are a bit chaotic here after the Ion Knights. My people are stretched to the limit. We're doing our best. We will find her, it's really just a question of man-hours."

"I understand, Agent Hallestrom." Morgan nodded solemnly. "If it is a matter of man-hours, I think I know a way to help."

V

CONSTELLATION GRAND RESTAURANT, RAVENSBURG
CENTRAL RIVER DISTRICT
ZAVIJAVA
LYRAN COMMONWEALTH
25 DECEMBER 3010

Morgan Kell brushed a few flakes from the light dusting of snow off his shoulders and smiled at the maître d'. "I've come to see Count Reynald. I believe he is expecting me."

The young man nodded, then waved another staff member over to take Morgan's hat, coat, and gloves. "This way, please."

He led Morgan through the center of the main dining room. The restaurant's red carpet and dark, walnut-paneled walls combined with the heavy, rough-hewn tables and chairs to create an air of medieval power. Off to the right, a fire burned in a massive stone hearth, both increasing the sense of antiquity and providing a fair amount of warmth. Old portraits and even older armor and swords—some which Morgan suspected were genuine antiques—decorated the walls. The red velvet upholstery was a shade darker than the carpet, and just shy of the hue of dried blood.

They traveled down a short corridor, bypassing another dining room to the right, and into a third room. Halfway into it they descended some stairs and proceeded to a booth at the back of the room which, if Morgan had measured the twists and turns correctly, put them beneath the restaurant's foyer.

Count Emerson Reynald stood at a rectangular table and offered Morgan his hand. "This is a very pleasant surprise, Morgan. I trust you and your brother are well."

"Yes, thank you for asking."

"And your Uncle Seamus?"

Morgan smiled. "Alive and kicking, though *who* he's kicking I have no idea. At least, that's the last I've heard."

"Splendid." The count only came up to Morgan's shoulder and had shaved his head since last Morgan had seen him, but still had that aquiline nose and steady gray-eyed stare. He turned to the maître d'. "Thank you, Andrew. We'll be drinking the Tyrone Rain, the twenty-five year. Use your key, bring the bottle and two glasses. No ice, we'll drink it neat."

"As you wish, my lord."

The count waved Morgan to the chair at his right hand. That put Morgan with his back to the restaurant's foundation, setting him a bit more at ease. "It is good to see you, and to learn you're here on

Zavijava. I would be false if I didn't say I was disappointed that I'd not heard from you earlier."

"I'm sorry, Emerson, I would have trusted you, but it wasn't my security alone that mattered."

"I've heard a rumor that we have a visitor from afar."

"Yes."

"Will you bring him round?"

"I'll see if I can arrange that. And I have a regiment burning in now. They land in a couple of days. I'll make it a standing order that they eat in one of your establishments."

"More trouble with the Ion Knights?"

Morgan shook his head. "No, that's wrapped up, for the most part. They're burning toward their JumpShip, along with the Sixth Marik Militia. We want to get the troops down and reassure folks here that the Archon has not forgotten them. But the reason I reached out to you is a problem of a different nature."

The count accepted his glass of whiskey from Andrew and held it aloft. "To friends and coconspirators."

Morgan touched his cut-crystal glass to his compatriot's, then drank. The whiskey had hints of coffee and chocolate swirling through its core flavor, but the key note was in how smooth it was. *As smooth as kissing Veronica.*

The MechWarrior stared into the glass. "I came here with a friend. Veronica Matova, from Galatea."

"Should I know the name?"

"Probably not. I met her there when Patrick and I were recruiting for our unit. She was—still is, I'm sure—the world's highest-paid courtesan. We became friends first, and then lovers. Less than twenty-four hours ago, she was abducted from the Archon's Suite at Tyrol House."

Emerson frowned. "Go on."

"LIC and local constabulary are looking for her. I've made a few enemies, and it looks like the snatch was a professional job. They're looking at all the local actors but…"

"You can't be certain it wasn't Loki, operating for Alessandro." The whiskey glass rang as the count tapped a finger against it. "This would be a matter for *us*."

"If you have heard anything."

"Yes, of course."

To guard against a state tyrant taking over the Lyran Commonwealth, and using LIC and Loki to destroy opposition, concerned Lyran citizens had created a secret society known as Heimdall. Like its namesake, the organization had eyes and ears everywhere, waiting and watching, tracking operations of dubious repute. Arthur Luvon, the Archon's late husband, had been a member, as were Morgan, Patrick, and the count.

Emerson grinned wryly. "And now I know why you didn't invite Prince Davion to join us."

"He's a good man. I trust him, too. But this is not my secret to share."

"And your friend, she knew nothing of us?"

"She got nothing from me." Morgan toyed with his glass. "It probably isn't Loki, but the professional angle has me concerned. Beyond that, your people are going to be aware of any compromised members of the constabulary, and have a sense of the local underworld."

The count downed his whiskey and refilled his glass from the bottle. "Actually, I've got a better angle on the underworld just dealing with grocery and trash through the restaurants. Most of our people, it might surprise you, are actually quite respectable. But still, we do see a lot, and hear even more. I shall put feelers out."

"Good, thank you."

He poured more amber liquid into Morgan's glass. "Do you want me to feed the information through you, or use my people inside the constabulary?"

"Whatever puts *us* at the least risk." Morgan shook his head. "Am I doing the right thing, Emerson? Or is this a personal problem, and you should just forget I asked?"

"Oh, it *is* a personal problem, Morgan, but it is *our* personal problem. It doesn't matter to me if the state took her, or if the state failed to prevent her being taken, it is a problem *we* shall address."

Morgan nodded solemnly. "Thank you, my friend. I can't tell you how much it means to me."

"I'm not just doing it for you, Morgan." Emerson smiled broadly. "A woman who has you this worked up is a national treasure. I simply have to meet her, so I shall do all that needs to be done."

VI

STELLAR INSURANCE OFFICE (CLOSED FOR REMODELING), RAVENSBURG
CENTRAL RIVER DISTRICT,
ZAVIJAVA
LYRAN COMMONWEALTH
27 DECEMBER 3010

Morgan pulled on gloves as he stared at the holo-display in the shuttered insurance office's back room. In neon-red lines, the computer projected a 3D model of a detached house hidden by a small stand of woods from the strip mall containing the office. The modest two-story structure had a basement; four bedrooms and a bath upstairs; kitchen, dining and living rooms downstairs; and a storage shed at the bottom of the garden near the woods.

A long, wolfish man with an untended beard leaned on the edge of the table. "That's real-time infrared from drones. Got six people up, two down."

A large man of African descent hit a couple keys, and green lines formed a skeleton within the infrared structure. It revealed all the metal and bones in the place. "Everyone is carrying except for person number eight down there in the basement."

Morgan frowned. "Cat, why is she an indistinct blob?"

"Cold down there, so they gave her a thermal blanket. It's trapping heat and reflecting everything else. Good thing is that we got some heat, which means she's alive. And that, right there, the disk, that was brighter before. Soup or oatmeal, something that's cooled off."

"Right, okay."

Cat hit two more keys, then slid his hand over a touch plate. That minimized the building image and dropped it down into the corner nearest Frost. In its place came up images of five people, two women and three men. All of the pictures took the same high-angle approach to the subject, then below an array of smaller pictures formed a foundation. Then the big picture would shrink, and one of the others would take its place.

Agent Hallestrom glanced at her noteputer. "We have images of five of the seven. Two have not come out, so we don't know who they are. Of the ones we have identified, these two are married and do some low-level work for the Barovsky crime family. Hank and Tanya Einhoven. They usually do cleanup work, hiding bodies and such, and have a sideline bootlegging crappy holovids from the Free Worlds League. Watching over a kidnap victim is not outside their remit. Their records have a lot of larceny, some vandalism, and a couple of assaults, but no murder."

Morgan exhaled slowly. "I guess that's good."

The second woman's face flashed up—a wholly unflattering picture with her sporting a black eye and a cut across the bridge of her nose. "Amy Felter. She's Tanya's cousin. She's got a clean jacket, but the constabulary has suspected she's been the driver in a couple of high-end heists. She's got the skills to have gotten the aircar onto the roof and away again. Oddly, she started her career as an ambulance driver, and probably recruited this guy, a paramedic, who would be good to have on hand if they had to sedate Ms. Matova. His name is Percy Blunt, and his only arrests have been for selling stolen meds, which is why he's no longer a paramedic."

"Last guy?"

"Tommy Strand. Street tough. Hangs with the Einhovens, but isn't employed by the Barovsky family."

Morgan nodded. Though Agent Hallestrom didn't know it, Count Reynald had obtained the information through the crime family. The Einhovens had told their contacts that they were involved in something and would be kicking a cut up the line, as they were supposed to do. Emerson had briefed Morgan, then had the information go in through his people in the constabulary and finally on to Agent Hallestrom. They'd both felt confident about bringing her in since they couldn't see any Loki connection to the plot or her.

Once they had the information, they'd located the house and set up drone surveillance. Seconds seemed to pass like hours while they waited to catch glimpses of the kidnappers. The kidnap crew rotated in and out, fetching food and tending to the prisoner. They bought pizza and sandwiches from the shops in the mall, and Hallestrom had managed to pull images from all the security cameras. From those, and drone shots, they'd identified the rest of the kidnappers and constructed dossiers on each.

The kidnappers kept to their routine. Every two hours, someone would head down into the basement and check on Veronica. Every four hours, they'd give her food and water. Food orders alternated between shops and had nothing remarkable about them—save, perhaps, for a lack of sweets and the inclusion of at least one salad.

The only good thing about the delay was that the Kell Hounds had landed, and Morgan had a squad of his best jump infantry to secure the perimeter and conduct the rescue. They decided to go in at night, and since the weather report indicated snow flurries would pick up close to midnight, they pegged the strike at an hour into the storm.

Morgan checked his chronometer. *Two hours.* He glanced over at the other man in the room. "What am I forgetting?"

Prince Ian Davion's eyes tightened. "You're forgetting to give me a gun."

"Your nation would never forgive me, and your brother would never understand."

"Is that so? You think Patrick will understand your going any better than Hanse would my going?"

"No, but they'd both understand our keeping you in reserve in case things go badly."

"Give me a gun and they won't." Ian shook his head. "It's a straightforward operation. You go in a half hour after they've checked on her, so no one should be near her. Sensors haven't detected any sort of communication device on her, so there's no dead-man switch attached to a bomb to kill her if we kill them. I've read the files, and I don't think they're smart enough to have thought that far ahead. Were it my brother, I would be proceeding as you are."

"Except you'd have a gun." Morgan smiled. "I had to say it before you did."

Ian's smile flashed in return for a second. "There is one thing which concerns me. That is, none of these people were bright enough to have arranged the kidnapping. And, Agent Hallestrom, unless you've neglected to keep us informed, there is no indication that these people are connected to the mystery operator who did manage to pull it off."

"No, Highness, there is not."

"Yeah, I'm not liking that either." Morgan rested a hand on the needler pistol at his hip. "So if we get a chance, we keep one alive and see what interesting stories they'll have to tell."

VII

LOCATION UNKNOWN, RAVENSBURG
CENTRAL RIVER DISTRICT
ZAVIJAVA
LYRAN COMMONWEALTH
28 DECEMBER 3010

Veronica huddled beneath her blanket, pulling it tighter around her as the wind howled. Grime caked the basement's windows, but snowflakes fleetingly eclipsed light from the street. They came down thick and, given what she had seen on Tharkad, would blanket the planet with beauty and purity.

The door at the head of the stairs opened, and Slim—as she had taken to calling the first of her captors—descended. Though the balaclava hid his identity, his face broadened with a grin. She caught a glimpse of off-colored teeth through the mask's mouth opening. "How are you doing, Missy?"

"Good." She sat up, holding the blanket close. "I can hear the storm. The floor is getting colder."

"Yeah, maybe I can get you another blanket or something." He paused at the cage door. "You didn't finish that second bowl of oatmeal."

Veronica hung her head, refuting to meet his gaze, then looked up beneath her lashes. "Forgive me. You were so kind. It was so warm. But I just couldn't get through it. I will eat it now, if you insist."

"No, no, that's okay. You know, maybe I can warm it up or something." He jerked a thumb back toward the stairs. "One of the guys is putting together an order for pizza. It'll be warm. Um, what do you want on it, that you can eat, that will be okay for the baby?"

She gasped, then covered her mouth and brushed away a tear. "You are so very kind. Just to ask."

"Look, just because you're here, it doesn't have to be bad, does it?" He laid a hand on the fencing. "Whatever you want, I'll tell 'em it's for me and they'll put it on there, okay?"

"Thank you. Mushrooms and peppers. No onions."

He smiled again. "That's how I like it."

"Really?" Veronica sniffed and forced a little smile. Given what she'd already gotten him to add to the salads he'd brought he, she'd long since guessed at his preferences. "That would be so wonderful, Slim."

He nodded. "I like it when you call me that. Never had a nickname what sounded nice."

"I'm glad."

"Okay, I'll put that order in." He stepped back toward the stairs. "And maybe I can bring you some tea, hot, if that's okay."

"Thank you, Slim."

She watched him go even past the point where his head had disappeared because that's what the woman she was comporting herself to be would do. Veronica held no illusions about her position. She'd been taken by people she didn't know, had been imprisoned and there hadn't been one word about ransom. This meant whoever had her taken either didn't want money from her or was negotiating with others for her return.

Her initial assessment of Slim had been instantaneous, from years of sizing up men and their desires. She'd known from the start that had Slim not had the courage granted to him by wearing the mask, he'd never have spoken to her. He'd been slow to approach, fearful of disturbing her, terrified of disappointing her. Pure beta-male behavior. Even the tone of his voice, softer, with words coming slowly, marked what he was.

This told her exactly how to handle him. Had he spoken of money—and his sort would have if he'd known of any ransom—she would have offered to buy him. She'd have spun a story about how the others didn't respect him and how they were going to cheat him out of his fair share. She would have told him that she *did* respect him and how he treated her, and she'd see to it that he would get what he was owed. And more.

If he would help her.

But this Slim had another vulnerability—one shared with every man who had ever drawn breath. He suffered from White Knight Syndrome. The only way he could imagine a woman like her—any woman, really—expressing any interest in him was if he were to rescue her from distress, thereby earning her gratitude. And she'd certainly been in distress, priming him.

And then I mentioned the baby, and he was hooked.

Morgan Kell might as well have been a different species of creature than Slim. Morgan still fell prey to White Knight Syndrome, but he channeled that into his occupation. Confident in himself and the rightness of his dreams, he and his brother had created the Kell Hounds in the hope of being so good of a unit that no one would dare attack. They wanted to exterminate war by making it too costly to engage in. That was the White Knight Syndrome writ large; grand and bold, just like the men behind the idea.

Morgan had also refrained from judging her for what she did. Sex was her business, but he never pressed. He'd let things develop naturally. He'd let her find her way to him, to whatever was going to happen between them. Had she never become comfortable, had she never taken the leap, he would have still been there. A friend first, and then, when the friendship deepened into an equal companionship, a confidant and lover.

The door to the basement opened again, and heavier feet stomped their way down.

Veronica shrank back against the foundation. She didn't recognize the footfalls, nor the boots. The man had to duck to get his head beneath the ceiling. He wore a tan canvas coat over a blue down vest, both of them open, and a red flannel shirt beneath. Within the vest he carried a pistol in a shoulder rig, and had some other gun slung across his back. Tan canvas pants ended at snow boots, and the way the legs moved Veronica suspected some sort of flannel lining to the pants.

His black balaclava had no mouth.

He walked up to the cage and slammed his hand against it, causing her to start and clutch the blanket more tightly. "So that pizza order, you don't gotta be worrying about it. See, your little friend there, he don't know who you are. Most of them don't, but that's because they're dopes and don't need to know. But I do, Veronica Matova. I know who you are. I know *what* you are."

Veronica sat up straight, her eyes becoming icy slits. "And?"

"And, first, I know you ain't pregnant. Last time your bucket got hauled out, we did a little test."

"How insightful of you."

"Had to. You're getting shipped out tonight." He pointed toward the ceiling. "Zavijava doesn't do so much trade that regular DropShip runs make sense, so we have lots of smaller ships make the run to the recharge point, swapping outgoing cargo for incoming. We've got you slated to make a run. My...ah...one of the girls is going to get you dressed up and ready for the run, and we're knocking you out for the duration. Just so there ain't nothing going to go wrong."

Her nostrils flared defiantly. "What do you want?"

"Just to get you off my hands, lady." He shook his head. "Someone wants you badly, and after tonight, you're his problem, not mine."

VIII

**STELLAR INSURANCE OFFICE (CLOSED FOR REMODELING), RAVENSBURG
CENTRAL RIVER DISTRICT
ZAVIJAVA
LYRAN COMMONWEALTH
28 DECEMBER 3010**

Morgan and the others slipped out of the insurance office's back door and into the howling snow squall. The thermal containment suit—a precautionary measure intended to defeat the infrared sensors they'd seen no sign of on the target house—kept them warm, and effectively made them as invisible in IR as the snow did visually. Their helmets dulled the wind's cry, and data flashed over the inside of the faceplates, including meters to target, ambient temperature, wind speed and direction.

Prince Ian's voice crackled through the radio. "Drone feeds still showing all is normal. One person is in the basement with the package."

"Roger that." Morgan had to smile. While they couldn't let Ian go on the raid, they couldn't deny him a command-and-control role. *He'd have taken over anyway, no matter what we said.* Morgan was happy having him perform overwatch, since he couldn't recall seeing anyone else ever be as cool and aware when a firefight went all to hell.

Frost, all but unseen four steps ahead, led the way into the woods. He'd already scouted it, and laid out a path. Cat Wilson came next, carrying a needler carbine just like Morgan. Behind him came a half-dozen handpicked infantry from the regiment. They all carried needlers, both because of their effectiveness at close range, and the fact that shots wouldn't carry through the building's walls. The last thing any of them wanted was casualties among the residents of the nearby houses.

Under the best possible circumstances, the Ravensburg Constabulary would have gone in and evacuated all the people, but they couldn't risk the kidnappers seeing the houses being cleared out. Moreover they couldn't be certain that the kidnappers didn't have spotters in the other houses just in case. That might have seemed to be overthinking their adversary, but many a battle had turned into tragedy because one side assumed their enemies were flat stupid.

Ian's voice hissed in Morgan's ears. "Stop. An aircar is coming up the street toward the house."

All of them dropped into a crouch and stared toward the house. Through the snow and between houses they caught the faint illumination of a streetlight. Then, from the left, another light grew. Morgan couldn't be certain, but it seemed as if it was slowing down.

Ian's voice became a whisper. "Appears to be a delivery. Giardino's is the sign."

We have their communications tapped. Why didn't we hear the order? Intercepting the order and substituting their own people for the delivery folks would have made things easier. Whoever answered the door would have died immediately, then a flash grenade tossed inside would have stunned the others. *We could have been in and out before the pizza started getting cold.*

The prince's voice remained low. "Not for them. The house across the street. Stand by. I'll give you the clear."

Morgan keyed his mike. "Have the constabulary shut the road down."

"On it." Ian relayed the order to someone else. "Okay, delivery vehicle is moving out. You are clear."

The team worked their way forward. The snow fell fast, and had covered the ground to ten centimeters deep. It muffled their footsteps, but the wind's howl swallowed them, so they didn't worry about detection in that regard.

They filed into the house's backyard. One of the other Kell Hounds jogged forward and slapped a breaching charge around the kitchen door's lock. He pressed a button on the detonator. It blinked bright red, and they all spread back out of line with the backblast area.

The kitchen door evaporated in a fiery flash, converted in a heartbeat into splinters, glass shards, and mangled hardware. Cat darted forward and lobbed a flash grenade in, then ducked back. It flared brightly, and the shockwave thrummed through Morgan's body armor, stopping the butterflies in his stomach for a moment.

Then Frost was in, with Cat hot on his heels. They both went straight into the dining room. Morgan, third in line, cut right through the kitchen, intent on reaching the door to the basement stairs.

One man, very slender, lay on the kitchen floor. The breaching charge had blown through the door and most of the refrigerator. The appliance shrapnel had shredded the man's clothes from knee to shoulder on his left side. He scrambled, but slipped in his own blood, then raised his good hand in surrender.

Morgan yanked the basement door open and, from the side, peeked down the stairs.

A heavy-set man mounted them and snapped a shot off, which tore a chunk out of the door jamb. Splinters clicked against Morgan's helmet.

Morgan dropped to a crouch, then shoved his carbine into the opening and hit the trigger twice. He heard a man yelp. Morgan dashed through the doorway and leaped down the stairs. He landed in the middle, then caught the ceiling with his hand and kept his pistol on the man he'd shot.

The polymer flechettes had laid open the man's right thigh, making a bright red hash of it. The downed man covered the wound with one hand. Blood seeped up through his fingers. He held a pistol in his other hand, and had it pointed toward the huddled figure in the cage.

His words came hissed. "We have a standoff."

More shots from above. Thuds from bodies hitting the floor. A couple of agonized shouts accompanied them, then another concussion grenade went off distantly.

Morgan shook his head. "Your femoral artery is trashed. Your blood pressure is crashing. Ten seconds, you'll be out. Thirty, you'll die unless I put a tourniquet on your leg. Drop your gun and you'll live."

"This ain't so bad."

"You're in shock already, so you can't feel much. You'll feel nothing soon. Five... four..."

The man opened his hand and the pistol clattered on the floor. "You promised."

Morgan descended and cleared the gun. "I also lied. You'll be fine. Just keep your hand pressed to the wound. I'll take care of you once I've got the lady free."

The man's head sank back. "You idiot. That ain't no lady."

Morgan glanced into the cage, and his heart sank.

The man was telling the truth.

IX

RAVENSBURG CONSTABULARY PLAZA, RAVENSBURG
CENTRAL RIVER DISTRICT
ZAVIJAVA
LYRAN COMMONWEALTH
28 DECEMBER 3010

Agent Hallestrom entered the observation room. "I've done all I can with him. It's your turn, Colonel Kell."

Morgan took another look through the mirrored panel at the man seated in the interrogation room. Not quite as tall as Morgan, the slender man looked a wreck. His long blond wig sat on the table beside him, and mascara streaked his cheeks. He'd lost one false eyelash, and the other only half adhered to his eyelid. His bright-red lipstick had smeared all over his chin and along his jawline, and in no way enhanced the two days' growth of beard. And the dress he'd been wearing might have once been fashionable, but the seams had parted, a button or two had disappeared, and the loss of the matching belt just made it a shapeless mass of floral fabric.

Because of Constantine Fisk's involvement with the Ion Knights, Morgan was aware he existed, but new little about him beyond that. Apparently, Fisk had something of a reputation as a holovid actor. Those who loved him really loved him, and the Einhoven gang proved to be some of his biggest fans. They'd stashed carton after carton of bootlegged holovids all over the safe house. Fisk was known for an adventure series of holovids that started with *I, MechWarrior*, but one of his other holovids was titled *Mandy and Mike*, in which he played a man with a split personality—the other personality being female.

He'd led the Ion Knights in their assault on Zavijava. While initially successful, the raid had failed, and Fisk had tried to escape but hadn't been able to reach the DropShip. So he disguised himself and went underground. The Einhoven gang recognized him as a slightly older Mandy and snatched him—certain someone would pay big money for the star's freedom. They'd sent messages to all of the studios but hadn't heard back from any of them.

Ian Davion patted Morgan on the shoulder, and Morgan gave him a nod. He lifted his chin and headed into the interrogation room, glancing at his noteputer. "Good evening Mr. Fisk. Do you know who I am?"

"No, and I don't care. I know my rights. I played a lawyer in a holovid series, so don't think I don't."

Morgan slammed a fist on the table.

The wig bounced high enough that when it landed it slithered off the table. "You have no rights. I am Colonel Morgan Kell, of the Kell Hounds. We are in the employ of the Lyran Commonwealth. We are here to secure Zavijava. Pursuant to Section Thirty of the Lyran Defense Act, I am now this world's military governor. Civil law is suspended. Martial law is in effect. You, sir, have been responsible for an attempted conquest of this world. You and those in your employ have committed war crimes."

The man appeared to have stopped listening halfway through Morgan's angry statement. He sat there, his right fist balled as Morgan's was, just moving it as Morgan moved his.

"What are you doing?"

Fisk held up his other hand. "Nothing. No, sorry. I was supposed to play you in a bioholo about the Archon and you and her husband from when she disappeared. I just wanted to get to feel you--"

Morgan grabbed the man's fist and forced it down onto the table. He leaned on it, keeping it trapped until Fisk stared at him. "Mr. Fisk, I can *legally* have you shot where you sit. Even if it weren't legal, I could shoot you right here, right now, and I guarantee not a one of the Ravensburg Constabulary will come up with a description of the murderer. Your fate is literally in my hands. Cooperate and you will live. Do you feel me now?"

"Yes, very much."

"Good. A friend of mine, Veronica Matova—"

The man's eye lit up. "You know Veronica?"

"How do you know her?"

"*I, MechWarrior*, we shot it on location on Galatea. We had a wrap party—that's where we get together...yeah, doesn't matter. But all the bigwigs were there. Count Somokis, he organized the financing for the film and the Ion Knights, and Veronica organized the, um, companions. I mean, wow, she is so gorgeous. I was thinking I might, but, but, I got warned off because a guy there, Stormy or Winters or..."

"Blizzard. Haskell Blizzard."

"Yes, yes, that's the name. Nice man, had a bit part in the movie. Was a shame to cut it. I guess he considered her his property, so I stayed away. Don't want to piss off the investors."

Morgan released the man's fist. "The people who had you, they never talked about having anyone else in another safe house."

"Did they take Veronica? Was she here?"

Bitterness bubbled up in the back of Morgan's throat. "Thank you, Mr. Fisk."

The actor held a hand up. "I have a question for you, Colonel."

"Yes?"

"Do you think I could play you? I mean, you're younger, but I can play younger, and I'd have to bulk up, but you have this energy and—"

Morgan stalked out of the room and met Ian in the corridor. "I'd have strangled him, Ian, but he got me thinking."

"You should have strangled him anyway."

"The day is young." Morgan sighed. "The man who snatched Veronica had to be in residence on Zavijava. He likely is a freelance operative who lives locally, and someone had a snatch order out on her. He spotted her, decided to take her and whatever money was being offered, even if it might expose his being here. The money must have been enough to buy him another hideaway. Could be Haskell Blizzard did that because he felt she'd betrayed him to me. Could be Alessandro ordered it. Could be this Count Somokis, or someone else like Fisk, who admired her from afar and decided he wanted her."

Ian nodded. "One of the Ion Knights could have decided she was a last bit of plunder to get off-world."

"Worst part about it all is that there's been no ransom demand. Whoever's got her wants her for reasons all their own."

Ian rested his hands on Morgan's shoulders. "Or, Morgan, they're waiting until they see how successful you've been in putting the Kell Hounds together. They could hold her against your undertaking a mission. To get her to safety, your Kell Hounds might have to become the Ion Knights and make life hell on some other backwater world."

Morgan's heart sank. "What do I do, Ian? I mean, I couldn't... But I can't leave Veronica..."

"You'll do what warriors do, Morgan. You'll assess the mission, lock down all the variables, and you'll do what has to be done." The leader of House Davion slowly smiled. "And I'll hope to God it doesn't involve the Federated Suns, because I really don't want to have to kill you."

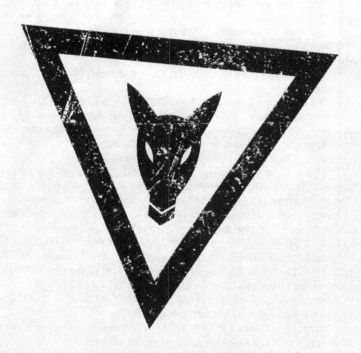

To be continued in *Shrapnel* #2!

UNIT DIGEST:
ERIDANI LIGHT HORSE
11TH RECON BATTALION

MICHAEL CIARAVELLA

Nickname: The Alley Cats
Affiliation: Mercenary
CO: Major Amelia Donovan
Average Experience: Veteran/Reliable
Force Composition: 2 medium 'Mech companies, 1 medium armor company, 1 infantry battalion, aerospace/ DropShip support
Unit Abilities: +1 Initiative bonus when fielding 'Mechs, combat vehicles, and infantry in the same battle. Reduce repair costs by 10 percent.
Parade Scheme: Olive drab

UNIT HISTORY

Despite the Eridani Light Horse being one of the premier mercenary commands in the Inner Sphere, the years following the fall of the Second Star League nearly proved to be the end for the famed mercenary unit. Shattered in the wake of the Word of Blake Jihad, the 151st Striker Regiment was destroyed to the last man on Columbus by a Blakist nuclear bombardment; the Twenty-First Striker and Nineteenth Cavalry regiments was crippled at Fortress Dieron; and the Seventy-First Light Horse forces in the Clan Homeworlds was claimed as *isorla* by Clan Goliath Scorpion, with most of the survivors being killed during the subsequent Society uprising. Many leading military analysts in the Inner Sphere had concluded that the Eridani Light Horse, with no full regiments remaining, had become defunct as a combat command, heralding the end of the fabled mercenary unit whose storied history stretched all the way to the first Star League.

The salvation of the ELH legacy was found in contingency planning left in place by the unit's commander, General Ariana Winston. While history now remembers Task Force Serpent as the bold, vital move needed to maintain the peace in the wake of the diminishing countdown of the Treaty of Tukayyid, it is easy to forget the desperate nature of that mission: an unprecedented deep strike into uncharted territory on a scale that had never before been contemplated. Concerned that the ELH might not return from this epic undertaking, General Winston had left a substantial sum in a series of accounts in the Federated Suns, a nest egg augmented by the contractual payments from their service to Task Force Serpent, protected in case the unthinkable should occur. In addition, the general had left a series of careful instructions in the hands of Colonel Richard Donovan, the most senior ELH commander who did not accompany the unit to Huntress, outlining plans to rebuild should they not return.

Upon hearing of the loss of the final ELH units on the Clan Homeworlds, Colonel Donovan followed General Winston's instructions, but he quickly found himself beset by a threat from an unexpected quarter: legal concerns.

Due to the difficulties in communication with the Clan Homeworlds during the Word of Blake Jihad, the loss of the Eridani Light Horse forces (as well as their commander, Lieutenant General Edwin Amis) could not be officially confirmed. Without confirmation of General Amis's demise (which would have officially placed Donovan in command), the courts would not officially acknowledge his command of the whole ELH. As such, the funds that General Winston had intended as the unit's safety net were held in escrow, inviolable, as the Word of Blake campaign of terror ripped through the Inner Sphere. During that time, several other ELH members and families of the lost soldiers took their own steps to lay claim to the held funds, complicating the legal situation further. While Colonel Donovan retained command of his battalion, the resources he required to rebuild remained permanently out of his reach. Before the courts could confirm the demise of Lieutenant General Amis, Colonel Donovan joined him, leaving the duty of rebuilding the unit to his executive officer, Major Dariah Sayler.

While Colonel Donovan had not left explicit instructions about the disposition of his command, Major Sayler possessed neither the pedigree as a legacy member of the ELH nor the full support of her unit. An effective executive officer but an unpopular leader, she saw her tenure as commander of the Eleventh Recon Battalion beset by challenges to her authority from both within and without. With several of the other ELH survivors refusing to recognize her legitimacy to command and the legal question of the ELH funds still in doubt, Major Sayler decided to move forward without them, focusing on her own unit while retaining the ideals and unit patch of the ELH.

Unlike the unit's previous rebuilding phases, however, this time they were one of many mercenary units attempting to rebuild in the wake of the destruction wrought by the Word of Blake Jihad and the formation of the Republic of the Sphere. Sayler would only find a small measure of relief from the Federated Suns, the long-time supporters of the ELH, where First Prince Harrison Davion, eager to once again boast of the Eridani Light Horse serving his nation, offered the unit a series of lucrative contracts that allowed the Eleventh to maintain its strength. Despite several offers to help them rebuild to multi-regimental strength, Major Sayler cautiously avoided becoming beholden to any single House, all too aware of how easily they could be dragged into the "company store" trap that doomed many mercenary units.

Everything changed, however, when Major Sayler decided to step down from command, five years after taking the position. In her place she promoted her executive officer, Major Amelia Donovan, daughter of Colonel Richard Donovan and a fourth-generation member of the Eridani Light Horse.

With a Donovan returning to command the Eleventh, the movement to rebuild the Eridani Light Horse found new life. While several detractors called Donovan's Alley Cats "the Strays," she took the term as a badge of honor. She is especially fond of quoting the unit's "nine lives" when asked about the viability of the ELH, referencing the many times the unit has been considered destroyed.

Having learned about battalion command at the foot of her father, Major Donovan focused on training, which allowed each member of the Light Horse to become a specialist in their field, and she takes advantage of these specializations to maximize the battalion's versatility. Unlike many of their contemporaries, who were still coping with the changes mandated by the Republic's BattleMech buyback program, the Eleventh relied on combined-arms tactics before the Republic era made it the standard.

Despite mounting evidence that the Eleventh Recon Battalion might be the only true heirs to the Eridani Light Horse legacy, the courts still hold the majority of the ELH war chest in escrow, forcing Donovan to rely on her business acumen as she further rebuilds the ELH. Holding to the legendary reputation and traditions of the original

Star League ensures the Eridani Light Horse is never short of offers, but the veneer of invulnerability that once surrounded them has been dispelled. Major Donovan and her Strays must now prove themselves worthy of their heritage, once again rising from the ashes to make the Eridani Light Horse a name both respected and feared.

COMPOSITION

Going back to their roots as a light reconnaissance formation, the Alley Cats are composed of two companies of BattleMechs and an assorted armor company, as well as a full support staff. Unlike its previous restructurings, however, the Eleventh Recon does not suffer from the technician shortages the unit previously suffered: the battalion's time at the NAIS and the careful focus of two generations of Donovan leaders has ensured that they employ excellent techs to keep in fighting trim.

In addition, the Eleventh maintains a wing of aerospace fighters and attached DropShip support, as well as an infantry battalion, the new Pathfinders, which are trained as elite special operations commandos like their predecessors. This unique mix of forces allows the Eleventh Recon to act as a highly versatile fighting force, able to take on any mission.

TALES FROM THE CRACKED CANOPY: BLIND ARROGANCE

CRAIG A. REED, JR.

At the Cracked Canopy, a MechWarrior bar on the gaming world of Solaris VII, a Memory Wall displays mementos of glorious victories and bitter defeats, of honorable loyalties and venomous betrayals, of lifelong friendships and lost loves. Each enshrined object ensures that the past will not be forgotten and the future is something worth fighting for.

INTERNATIONAL ZONE
SOLARIS CITY, SOLARIS VII
LYRAN COMMONWEALTH
12 JANUARY 3090

The Cracked Canopy is located on the corner of the brand-new Memorial Avenue and Defiance Street. It's easy to find, as it takes up the entire bottom floor of a three-story building and has a *Catapult*'s canopy mounted over the main doors. It's rumored to be from a Wobbie 'Mech, but it's been repainted so many times, there's no way to tell. And yes, it's cracked.

It was mid-afternoon when I walked into the bar. Sedge, the day bartender, was behind the bar, cleaning a glass. "Hey, Leo," he said.

"Sedge," I said, taking off my coat and shaking the rain off it. "How's business been today?"

"Slow," he replied.

"It'll pick up tonight," I said. "Vaughan's facing Dvorak tonight in Ishiyama."

He nodded. "You want me to check the kegs?"

"Yeah," I said, walking behind the bar and pulling out my apron. "We're expecting a delivery from DeBetello's today, so make sure the stock's rotated. Also, tell Mateo to make sure he has everything for a large crowd tonight."

Sedge grinned, making him look younger. "Okay, boss," he said. He pushed through the swinging doors behind the bar, leaving me alone with the empty room.

I'm the Canopy's general manager and head bartender. I run the day-to-day operations, but I don't own the place. The place is owned by one Ms. Silver, a woman I've never met face-to-face. At times, I wonder what she looks like—all I know about her for certain is her silky voice on the phone and her flowing signature on my employment contract.

The front door opened and a stranger walked in. Part of my success is that I can size someone up on sight. He was probably thirty years older than me, with a lined face and salt-and-pepper hair peeking out from under a battered cap. He wore military trousers tucked into boots, a gray tunic under a hard-used leather jacket. Despite his age, he was lean and fit. "You open?"

"Yes, sir," I said. "Drink?"

"Skye Scotch, if you have it."

"Red Isle, MacEwen's, or Thistle's Milk?"

He raised both eyebrows. "What about sake?"

"Six brands, including Black Pearl."

"Plum wines?"

"Three different brands, including Villanueva, but only one from Confederation space. We also had a dozen brands of schnapps, tequilas, and even a few bottles of Dagda Firewater in the back."

He walked to the bar. As he neared, I spotted a few scars on his face and hands, and from the look in his green eyes, he had a few internal scars too. "I'll stick with the Scotch," he said. "Red Isle, straight."

I placed a glass down in front of him, and poured the Scotch. "There you go."

He picked up the glass. "Why don't you have one yourself? I hate to drink alone."

I thought about saying no, but got a glass and poured two fingers for myself. "What do we drink to?"

"Absent friends."

We clinked glasses and drank. Well, I sipped. He tossed the entire contents in one go.

He placed his glass down on the bar and looked around. "What's that wall?" he asked, pointing toward the back of the bar.

I looked at the wall. There were framed photos, patches, armor pieces, and other items, all hanging or sitting on small shelves attached to the wall. Several of the armor pieces displayed insignia from Solaris stables, both current and past. Photos, some MechWarriors, others soldiers, and a good number of civilians were clustered in groups, intermixed with plaques engraved with names engraved. A broken katana hung next to a still-intact claymore, and several religious symbols shared space with a number of unit patches.

"That," I said, "is our Memory Wall. When this place opened, a few customers left items to remember those who had died here or elsewhere in the Jihad. The owner told me that as long as no Word of Blake items were displayed, anyone who wanted to contribute items for the wall could do so."

"Anything?"

"As long as it's inorganic and in the spirit of remembrance, yes."

"What about this?" he asked, pulling a patch from his jacket pocket, and laying it on the counter. It was a red-and-blue five-pointed star, emblazoned with a white *w*, set over a circular red field.

I looked at him. "There's still a lot of places where showing that will get you killed."

"You recognize it then?"

I nodded. "Waco Rangers."

He slowly nodded back. "I was a Ranger," he said, sadness shading his words. "But I left them long before Outreach."

"You want to talk about it?" I asked.

He waved it away. "It's not something I like being reminded of."

"Then why carry the patch?"

He gave me a sad smile. "That's a long story."

"I'll let you in on a secret about that wall," I said, motioning to the Memory Wall. "Every item on that wall comes with a story. I tapped the patch. "This has a story."

He sat there for a few seconds, then nodded. "Pour me another, and I'll tell you about the Waco Rangers—not those who died on Outreach, but the *real* Rangers."

I pour him that drink and he told me about the death of the Waco Rangers.

MANNY'S STORY

Name's Manny Totske. After two tours with the Free Worlds League Military, I struck out on my own in '49. Hired on with the Rangers in early '50, and took the Death Oath like every other member. By '53, I was a lance commander in Romy's Assault Battalion.

I know what everyone thinks of the Rangers these days, and they'll only be remembered for their sneak attack on Outreach, right before the Word of Blake went crazy and started attacking everyone. But when I was with them, they were still a good unit. Rough around the edges, sure, but no different from any good mercenary unit. The Rangers became my family.

Well, until Coventry. That's where the Rangers really died. Outreach was a vengeful ghost, reaching out one last time to fulfill the Oath.

When the Rangers were hired by the Lyran Alliance, Colonel Waco wasn't with us. He was handling the administration back on Outreach. Colonel Wayne "Old Four-Eyes" Rogers was the Rangers' field commander. He was one of Waco's old hands, and steeped in the Death Oath for longer than I'd been alive.

The Rangers-Dragoons feud? I can say it now: it was a joke long past its prime. In the sixty years after Waco created the Death Oath, Wolf's Dragoons and the Rangers rarely clashed. There were a few skirmishes between the two, but no major battles in all that time. We took the Oath seriously, but the Dragoons didn't, and I think that pissed off Colonel Waco more than anything else.

In early '58, the Jade Falcons swarmed across the Alliance borders to blood their new warriors, and they ripped through planet after planet until they hit Coventry. It quickly became a bloody stalemate, and the defenders needed relief quickly. But Archon Katrina had vanished, so it was Mandrinn Tormano Liao who got the ball rolling. Don't know how or why a Liao was advising a Steiner-Davion. I never did understand interstellar politics.

To relieve Coventry, Liao had already hired an Eridani Light Horse regiment, two Wolf's Dragoons regiments, and the Crazy Eights. The Rangers had been hired to guard Tharkad, but the Archon appeared from wherever she was hiding and ordered us to join the Coventry Expeditionary Force. So we went.

From the start, things went wrong. While the Light Horse and Dragoons jumped into battle immediately upon landing, the Rangers and Crazy Eights were held in reserve. Colonel Rogers didn't like that, and he naturally blamed the Dragoons. The Light Horse's General Winston did her best to keep us and the Dragoons from killing each other, but you could have cut the tension with a knife.

After a week of sparring, the CEF brain trust decided on a plan to hit the Falcons at Port St. William. While the Light Horse and Dragoons hit the Birds head-on, we and the Crazy Eights would move through the Dales, and hit the Clanners from behind. Simple and easy, right?

Wrong.

The CEF command attached a company of the Tenth Skye Rangers under the command of Caradoc Trevena. At the time, he was a hauptmann who had survived the Falcon invasion, kept his unit intact, bloodied the Birds' noses a few times, and knew the lay of the land a hell of a lot better than we did. But to Colonel Rogers, Trevena was a two-bit militia 'Mech jockey who couldn't find his ass with a road map and a compass.

I was there in the grand ballroom when Trevena reported to the CEF command staff. It took Old Four-Eyes less than thirty seconds to piss off Trevena. Both the Dragoons colonels jumped in on Trevena's side, and it took General Winston's diplomatic skills to keep the peace. It was an omen, but none of us realized it at the time.

I can still remember that day in the Dales, even after thirty-plus years. I can still see my lancemates' faces and hear their voices. I was in the Maulers—Mace McCarthy's company. Mace was another old-time Ranger, having been born on the Rangers' DropShip a month after the Rangers formed. He hated the Dragoons, and didn't trust them as far as he could throw his *Awesome*.

My lance consisted of my *Marauder*, Ariadne Sherbow's *Griffin*, Parker LaBelle's *Whitworth*, and Hector Shirotan's *Dervish*. Ariadne was my 'Mech sergeant, a tiny woman with a booming voice and a laugh that could cut glass. Parker was a quiet guy, always reading, and never had a bad word about anyone. Hector was a third-generation Ranger, piloting his grandmother's 'Mech.

From the start of the operation, Old Four-Eyes treated the Skye boys like something he'd scraped off the sole of his *BattleMaster*'s foot. He ignored Trevena's suggestions, and when the hauptmann tried reasoning with him, Rogers pointed his PPC at Trevena's *Centurion* and told him to scout ahead. Trevena left, but not before broadcasting to the entire regiment that he was going to punch Rogers out after the battle.

It was midmorning when we crossed Shallot Ford and advanced through the Dales. The Dales are a series of rough, rolling hills with groves of trees and a few creeks scattered across them. It's not the worst territory I've traveled through, but it's not the best either.

McCarthy's company was on the regiment's right flank, and my lance was the edge of the flank. Hector had point, with Parker on the left, and Ariadne on the far right. I walked behind them, my *Marauder* at the base of the diamond. Despite Trevena's people scouting ahead, I couldn't shake the feeling that something was wrong.

"Stay alert, people," I said on the lance frequency.

"You think the Birds are skulking about?" Ariadne said with a laugh.

"I'm not taking any chances," I told her, "and neither should you."

Just then, the command channel came to life. "This is Buckler calling Dagger."

"Dagger here," Rogers said. "Go ahead, Buckler."

"We have enemy contact in sector two-eight-four-three."

I looked at the screen displaying the map of the Dales. Sector 2843 was fifteen kilometers ahead of us, and I saw the land was wooded, broken, and rough—tough for us to move through quickly.

"Hang on, Buckler," Rogers said, "Dagger's on its way." That didn't sit well with Trevena, but the colonel wasn't listening. He ordered us forward, confident that we could roll over any Falcon pickets.

At first, it went well. When we hit sector 2843, a Star of *Baboons* challenged Trevena's scouts and got brushed aside, and we continued on. We emerged onto a large field, bordered on three sides by long rows of trees. The Rangers continued forward without stopping.

We'd reached the middle of the field when the Falcons sprang their ambush.

Several hundred long-range missiles came flying out of the tree line in front of us and slammed into the leading Rangers ranks. Half a dozen Rangers went down in that first barrage, including Old Four-Eyes, and the Rangers fell into disarray. The Falcons quickly followed up with another missile barrage and attacked both flanks.

"Bandits!" Ariadne shouted, spinning and firing her PPC and LRMs at a *Ryoken* who burst out of the trees to our right. A *Black Lanner* and *Black Hawk* also charged out of the trees and cut loose. More Falcons appeared out of the woods, and the fighting got hot and heavy real quick.

"Totske to McCarthy!" I shouted. "Two 'Mech Stars on the flank!"

"Stand your ground!" McCarthy shouted back.

"Pick your targets!" I shouted, bringing both my extended-range PPCs and large pulse laser onto the *Back Hawk*, and fired. One of my particle beams ripped apart a tree behind and to the left of the Falcon, but my second blast struck just below the 'Mech's cockpit and the pulse laser scarred arm armor. The 'Mech staggered but stayed upright.

My *Marauder* shuddered as the *Black Hawk*'s lasers shellacked it. Hector fired a spread of missiles at a *Fenris*, only doing slight damage. Off to my right, I saw a pair of Clanner 'Mechs I didn't recognized trying to outflank us.

"Mace!" I shouted into the radio. "I've got Birds on three sides now!"

"We hold!" McCarthy shouted.

"We can't!" I snarled back, firing at and missing one of the unknown 'Mechs. "We're getting hammered on three sides. We're going to be killed if we don't fall back!"

"And have the Dragoons laugh at us?" McCarthy shot back. "We stand our ground!"

The heat in my cockpit was slowly rising as I fired both my PPCs at a *Ryoken*, scoring with one and missing the with the other. "Totske to lance!" I snapped. "We have to hold!"

"We can't!" Ariadne shouted. Her *Griffin*'s armor had been breached in several places, and heat rose from it in visible waves.

"I know!" I shouted back. "But the orders are to hold!"

"Damn it!" she snarled. "There's too—"

She never finished the sentence. A Gauss round struck her *Griffin* in the side of the head and ripped through the armor as if it was wet paper, and out the other side. The 'Mech toppled like a cut tree.

I spun in the direction of the shot and cut loose with a barrage at one of the unknown 'Mechs, which I learned later was a *Cougar*. The cockpit suddenly felt like I'd stepped into a blast furnace, but I cored that *Cougar*. As it hit the ground, I said, "Parker! Hector! Fall back!"

"Hold your ground, damn it!" McCarthy shouted.

"We're getting slaughtered!" I shouted back. I saw movement behind and to the right of me. A pair of tan-and-olive Rangers 'Mechs, both heavily damaged, were backing away from the fight. "We're beginning to break now! We need to withdraw and do it now!" I fired another volley at the *Black Lanner*, ripping away some armor, but otherwise not hurting it.

An alarm warned me of the incoming missile strike seconds before it slammed into my *Marauder*. The cockpit shook like a rat in a terrier's mouth. I tasted blood; my vision went dim as I gripped the controls and rode it out. When the missiles stopped exploding, I spun to the left and searched for what had hit me.

Smoke and dust was everywhere, reducing our vision to several hundred meters. The field, which had been green and level a few moments ago, was now a sea of craters and broken 'Mechs. The sounds of battles were loud and constant. The hammering of autocannons, multiple explosions, the hiss of missiles—all added macabre melodies to the symphony of battle. I fought in a lot of battles before and after that day, and none of them came close to matching that hell.

Just then, four Clan PPC blasts ripped into Parker's *Whitworth*. The poor guy didn't even have a chance to scream before his ammo detonated and the 'Mech became a fireball.

When that *Masakari* came out of the smoke, I froze. Never saw one of those monsters on the battlefield before that day, and I pray to God I never see another one in person. I've heard a few people call them 'Massacres' because that's what they do—massacre their enemies.

"Hector!" I shouted. "The *Masakari*!"

"Oh my God," Hector whispered. He fired both LRM racks at the advancing monster and hit it with both flights, but he might have as well been throwing water balloons for all the good it did.

"Mace!" I shouted. "We're pulling back!"

"No!" he replied.

"I'm facing three Stars of Clanners, including a *Masakari*!"

"No!" McCarthy shouted. "We—"

There was static, then nothing.

"Mace!" I shouted.

No answer.

"Mace!"

The *Masakari* opened fire, and poor Hector died just like Parker did, in fire and fury. Then, for some reason I don't understand to this day, the *Masakari* turned and moved off into the smoke, as if I wasn't worth killing.

I triggered the company frequency and shouted, "All Maulers, this is Totske. Fall back and regroup! Repeat, fall back and regroup!"

The next fifteen minutes still give me nightmares. Maybe half the regiment was still standing at that point. In McCarthy's company, only four badly mauled 'Mechs answered my call. The Rangers' battle line was falling apart, and they were breaking away and running off in ones and twos.

I formed a small group of Rangers into some sort of order, and we retreated, firing at any Clanner we saw. I lost several Rangers but picked up several others along the way, and we left a few dead Falcons in our wake.

Chaos was everywhere around us. I watched another group of Rangers conducting a fighting retreat, until a heavy Falcon Star appeared out of the smoke, ripped the group apart, and sent the survivors running. Falcon Elementals swarmed over any Ranger too slow or too stubborn to retreat, and Falcon OmniMechs harassed those who ran.

We moved into some woods, picked up a few more Rangers and a couple of the Crazy Eights. Most of their 'Mechs were missing arms or even entire torso sections, while others looked like mechanical skeletons. My own *Marauder* could still move and its weapons worked, but it was one volley away from dying.

My cockpit was an oven, and every breath was like sucking down hot coals. My head pounded, and my eyes felt like someone had rubbed sand in them. But I fought, and those around me fought. The Falcons tried breaking us again and again, but we drove them off every time.

We'd nearly reached Shallot Ford when someone shouted, "Here they come again!"

"Pick your targets," I said.

"I'm redlined," someone else said. "I fire, and Bessie will shut down hard."

"Fire or die!" I snapped.

The first Falcon I saw was a *Mad Cat*. It fired off its LRMs and broke to the right as a *Masakari* appeared and ripped apart a Rangers *Enforcer* with its quartet of PPCs. We fired back, striking the *Masakari* and the trees around it, staggering the monster.

More Falcons appeared on the flanks, and we had to split our fire to keep them back. Thick smoke limited visibility on both sides, but we kept moving toward the ford, firing every time we had a target. Their lights and mediums darted out of the smoke, fired at us, then vanished again.

"They're behind us!" someone shouted.

"Keep on your toes!" I shouted, turning my *Marauder* to face the rear. A battered-looking *Ryoken* appeared to my front left, and I fired. Heat shot through the cockpit when I fired, nearly making me pass out, but the *Ryoken* went down in a heap.

"Rangers *Marauder*, this is Buckler. Keep coming. We'll cover you."

It took several seconds for the words—and who was saying them—to penetrate my foggy brain. For the first time since the start, I felt hope.

"Copy, Buckler," I croaked. "We've got Falcons all around us."

"Understood, *Marauder*," Caradoc Trevena said. "Keep coming."

Suddenly, the woods ahead of me lit up with weapons fire. I froze, wondering if it was a trap, but I then realized the fire was directed elsewhere, along the flanks. "Totske to all Rangers. Break and retreat!"

Trevena's covering fire allowed us to run for it and pass through friendly lines, across the ford and to safety. A few other Rangers had already made it, including Captain Markbright, who took command. We continued retreating, us and the Skye boys covering each other.

The irony of Wolf's Dragoons saving us isn't lost on me. The Dragoons smashed into the Falcons' flank like the Clanners had done with both of ours. The Falcons immediately pulled back and broke contact. And thus, the Battle of the Dales was done...and so were the Rangers.

The butcher's bill for the Rangers were steep. In two hours, the Waco Rangers ceased to be. Out of four 'Mech battalions, only two companies' worth retreated out of the Dales. Of that number, only a third were still combat effective.

The CEF leadership stuck us behind the lines and left us alone. Some of us brooded, while others, like me, tried to put that day out of our minds, usually through drink. Some days I was successful in forgetting, but other days, I failed.

A few more weeks of sporadic fighting followed, neither side having the strength to take out the other. By the end of May, Captain Markbright had reorganized the surviving Rangers into a demi-battalion, and we did a few patrols, skirmished with the Birds several times, but everyone knew we were just going through the motions.

When Prince Victor Steiner-Davion showed up with reinforcements, the Coventry campaign ended. He offered the Falcons *hegira*, an honorable retreat under Clan law, and the Birds took it, freed their POWs, boarded their DropShips, and left.

I was outside CEF headquarters when the released prisoners rolled into the courtyard and climbed out of the trucks. Most were Rangers, and all looked tired, dirty and defeated. I spotted Old Four-Eyes and Mace McCarthy among the prisoners, and neither looked happy.

The colonel's mood got worse when Trevena walked out and marched toward him. "You!" Rogers snarled, taking a step forward. "You—"

Trevena didn't say a word; he just hit Rogers with a right cross that dropped him like a bad habit. Trevena stared at him for a few seconds, glared at the rest of the Rangers, then turned and walked away.

Three days later, I was summoned to the office of newly promoted Major McCarthy. As soon as I walked in, I knew this was going to be trouble. Mace's demeanor had been stuck in fully pissed-off mode since Trevena had belted the colonel, and from his glare, he was going to take it out on me. Old Four-Eyes was loudly blaming the Dragoons for the Dales fiasco, but no one was listening. That just made the colonel madder, and it was flowing downstream.

"Enjoy your vacation?" Mace growled.

"No more than you did," I growled back. I was in no mood to be nice.

"You've been demoted to private," he said without preamble.

That didn't surprise me. "What for?" I asked.

"I'm holding you responsible for your actions out there," he said, rising from the chair behind the desk.

"Which actions?" I replied. "The ones that saved a few Rangers from that disaster?"

"You disobeyed a direct order!" he snarled. "You were told to hold!"

"It was suicidal to hold!" I shot back, putting my hands on the desk and leaning forward until all I could see was his bloodshot blue eyes and he, my anger-filled green ones. "There were three Stars pounding on my lance! I saw Sherbow die from a headshot, then watched a *Masakari* tear both LaBelle and Shirotan apart in less than thirty seconds! I called for a retreat only after you went down, and I tried to save as many of our people as possible! We're damn lucky any of us got out of there!"

"It was the damn Dragoons!" he shouted back. "Those genetic freaks set us up so their fellow Clanners could destroy us!"

"And how did they do that?" I yelled. "Trevena told us there was trouble ahead, but did the colonel or anyone else listen? No!"

"Those scouts couldn't be trusted! They pulled back and let us walk right into that ambush!"

"We never listened to them, and we marched into that ambush all by ourselves!"

"Shut up!" McCarthy spat. "Say one more word, and I swear I will make sure you never pilot a BattleMech ever again."

I decided then that Trevena had the right idea, so I straightened up and hit McCarthy as hard as I could. He fell back into his chair, glassy-eyed and blood dribbling from a cut lip.

I leaned forward again. "Don't bother, you son of a bitch," I snarled. "I quit."

And I left.

Once outside, I took a moment to enjoy the fresh air for the first time in two months.

"Hey look!" someone shouted. "It's one of those Wacko Rangers!"

I turned and saw a pair of Light Horsemen walking toward me. I wondered how they knew I'd been with the Rangers, then I realized I still wore the patch on my jacket.

"Done anything stupid lately?' one of the Eridani boys asked.

I smiled and slowly took out my knife. Both of them froze, but I used the blade to cut the threads around the patch and pulled the patch off the jacket.

"Nope," I said. "In fact, I think I've just regained my sanity." I pocketed the patch. "Can I buy you two a drink to help celebrate my first hour as an ex-Waco Ranger?"

THE PRESENT

Manny looked down at his drink, then at the patch. "I don't know why, but I carried that thing for thirty-two years. Before Coventry, I was proud to be a Waco Ranger. After Coventry, I realized it was never going to be the same."

"What happened after you left the Rangers?" I asked.

"I went to Galatea and spent thirty years with the Tooth of Ymir. I rose to the rank of major, but it wasn't the same." Manny sipped his Scotch. "When Colonel Waco died in that attack on Outreach, it was the last nail in a coffin that had been made on Coventry."

I raised my glass. "May I proposed a toast to the Waco Rangers that died on Coventry?"

He nodded, and we touched glasses, then each took a sip.

"What are your plans?" I asked.

"I'm going home," he replied, then looked in the distance. "A place I haven't thought of in a long time. Probably changed a lot since I was last there, but then again, so have I." He downed the remaining Scotch, then placed the glass on the bar. "Thanks for the drinks and for listening." He snorted in amusement. "Never told anyone the entire story before."

"Maybe it wasn't the right time until now," I replied, picking up his glass. "Stories have a habit of being like that."

He sighed, then looked at the Rangers patch, as if weighing a decision. Then he slowly pushed the patch across to me. "Here," he said. "For the Memory Wall."

"You sure?" I asked.

Manny gave me a tired smile with a glimmer of relief in it. "It's time to let the memories sleep."

"I'll make sure it's given special treatment," I said.

"Thank you."

"You want something to eat?' I asked. "It's on the house. Mateo can make anything you want."

Manny shook his head. "I'm leaving Solaris in three hours, so I need to get back to the spaceport." He pulled out a wallet and dropped a couple of ten-kroner notes on the bar. "That's for the drink and for listening," he said.

I took one note and left the other on the bar. "Listening is free of charge."

He shook his head, turned away, and started for the main doors. "You earned it," he replied. "Bye, Leo. And thanks."

I watched him walk out and disappear into the Solaris afternoon.

Ten seconds later, Sedge reappeared from the back. "All done," he said. He saw the patch lying on the bar top. "Where did that come from?"

"Customer," I replied, putting the Scotch bottle back in its place. "He talked and I listened. Left the patch for the Wall."

"Oh. Sorry I missed it."

I downed the last of my drink and put both glasses in the sink. "It wasn't a happy tale," I said. "Come on, we have to get ready for tonight."

INTERNATIONAL ZONE
SOLARIS CITY, SOLARIS VII
LYRAN COMMONWEALTH
29 JANUARY 3090

It was a rare sunny afternoon when I walked into the Canopy. Sedge was behind the bar, and there were a couple of customers enjoying an early beer.

"Hey, Leo," Sedge called out. He saw the frame under my arm. "What's that?"

"Something for the Wall," I replied, walking toward the bar.

Sedge dug out a self-adhering picture hook from his toolbox, and placed it on the bar. I picked it up as I walked by and continued over to the wall. A minute later, the picture was hung.

The frame held three items in separate panes. In one pane was the Waco Rangers patch Manny had left, looking worn but proud. Next to it, a photo of four MechWarriors took up the left half of the frame. Manny had the same face, only thirty-odd years younger. Ariadne Sherbow was easy to identify, as she was the only woman. She was short and petite, with short blond hair and an animated face. Parker LaBelle was taller than Manny and thin, with a lean face and thinning brown hair. Hector Shirotan was short and chunky, with curly dark hair and a huge grin. They stood together in front of their 'Mechs, at ease with the universe.

"Where'd you get the photo?" Sedge asked.

"Connections," I replied. I glanced at the last pane, above the patch and to the right of the photo. A square section of 'Mech armor the size of my palm occupied the space. On it, engraved in block letters was the following:

WACO RANGERS
3007–3058
BLIND ARROGANCE KILLED US

"Blind Arrogance?" Sedge asked.

"Wayne Waco was blinded by hate," I replied. "He infected his entire regiment with that hate. Wayne Rogers let the hate become arrogance, and led the Rangers into an ambush that destroyed the unit. But the hate continued, and it caused the attack on Outreach."

I stared at the picture for a few seconds. "After thinking about it, I realized Manny was right. The real Waco Rangers died on Coventry, and what happened on Outreach was the last twitch of its corpse."

"That corpse killed a lot of people," Sedge said in a dark tone.

"I know," I replied, turning back toward him. "Back to work. We have to get ready for tonight's crowd."

"MOTHER OF RESISTANCE" DEAD ON VIPAAVA

PATRICK WYNNE

—Dominion Public Report, 3125

Six days ago, Cilla Amdahl, the so-called "Mother of Resistance" and the leader of the Motstånd rebels, was cornered and eliminated by our glorious Alpha Galaxy on Vipaava. Cowardly seeking shelter in the extensive Blue Road cave system, Amdahl attempted to once more escape justice as she had many times in the last five decades. However, Galaxy Commander Dalia Bekker utilized loyal Vipaavans and their knowledge of the cave system to trap Amdahl and her companions in a large gallery that the rebel had used as a base of operations. Although Alpha's 'Mechs were unable to enter the caves, native guides led the way for the Galaxy's battle armor assets. After a brief firefight, Amdahl was captured. Galaxy Commander Bekker then entered the caves and, acting in accordance with the longstanding Insurgent Order 17, summarily executed the "Mother of Resistance" for her crimes.

Amdahl's presence on Vipaava became known to Dominion intelligence through information provided by several Vipaavan sources who risked their lives and livelihoods for the greater good. While the identities of these patriots are classified, we here at the *Dominion Public Report* salute their honor and integrity.

The execution of Cilla Amdahl comes close on the heels of decisive victories against the Motstånd's military forces on Balsta and Predlitz. Demonstrating the success of our unified Dominion, Rasalhague and Taiga Galaxies showed no mercy to the rebels who would tear down what generations of our two peoples have fought and bled to build. There is a particular satisfaction to be had in native Rasalhagians destroying the final vestiges of rebellion within our borders.

The latest uprising, which began seven months ago with assaults on Engadin and Polcenigo, marks the first time that the rebel group has fielded more than a handful of BattleMechs and infantry. The Watch has yet to determine how the rebels managed to raise two regiments of BattleMechs, dubbed the First and Second Snapphanar, without notice, though foreign assistance cannot be ruled out at this time. Due to the age and makes of the 'Mech and armor units, media pundits speculate that they may have originated from materiel surpluses intended for destruction under the Republic's Military Materiel Redemption Program. Diplomatic inquiries have been issued to Terra for confirmation.

With the death of Cilla Amdahl, a threat that has persisted since the early days of the Rasalhague Dominion has finally been vanquished. Amdahl was a founder of Motstånd, and its principle organizer almost from the start. Since escaping justice on Tinaca in 3079, she had been an elusive irritant to civil society for decades, poisoning the minds of several generations of young Rasalhagians with her lies. A once-promising officer in the old KungsArmé, Amdahl's anti-Clan bigotry and inability to face her own inadequacies led to her dismissal from service and nearly fifty years of life as a fugitive terrorist. Our nation can breathe easy knowing that she has finally been brought to justice, and that the soul of the Dominion has been purged of her taint.

CHAOS CAMPAIGN SCENARIO:
TARGET OF OPPORTUNITY

AARON CAHALL

Paladin Sorenson,

I regret to inform you that my primary mission on Wyatt, the protection and retrieval of ComStar Adept Tucker Harwell, has failed.

There it is, in black-and-white. I've never sugarcoated anything for you before, and I'm not going to start now. Nor will I make excuses for my failure. By way of explanation, I can only say that my efforts faced significant opposition from multiple parties, difficulties compounded by the traitorous actions of the late Legate Edward Singh. Adept Harwell's success in restoring the Wyatt HPG almost immediately became the worst-kept secret in the Inner Sphere, a development significant enough to cause Oriente Protectorate forces to jump the border and to prompt ComStar to reveal their own heretofore unknown and highly illegal military assets to reacquire Tucker.

The following brief after-action report and appended battleROM from my 'Mech should provide basic details of my actions on Wyatt. I will report to you directly upon reaching Terra.

Finally, I want to personally commend the Wyatt Militia for their actions in support of my mission. Words fail to describe the sacrifices they made in the name of the Republic, and for Tucker and the hope he represents. The families of those who fell should be given our utmost consideration; those few who survived should—must—be incorporated into VIII Principes Guards as soon as possible.

Knight-Errant Alexi Holt
Outbound from Wyatt
13 June 3135

On the Move

Amid the ongoing communications blackout, it was perhaps unsurprising that any ray of hope would shine like a beacon across the stars. Just such a light flared brightly when ComStar Adept Tucker Harwell restored the Wyatt hyperpulse generator on 5 May 3135. Harwell's use of a simple ComStar mnemonic prayer—and his own unequalled brilliance—to stabilize the HPG's new core and bring the planet back into the interstellar communications grid instantly made him one of the most important and sought-after individuals in the Inner Sphere.

Knight-Errant Alexi Holt, dispatched by Paladin Kelson Sorenson to oversee efforts to repair the world's HPG, assumed responsibility for Harwell's protection until Republic reinforcements arrived to secure the adept and transport him back to Terra. Her mission faced complications from the outset: improbably, just four days after Harwell's accomplishment, the Pouncer Trinary of the Spirit Cats' Purifiers Cluster arrived in-system and burned toward Wyatt. The Cats maintained radio silence on their approach and landed at industrial ruins outside the capital city of Kinross, their agenda a mystery.

Unbeknownst to either the Spirit Cats or the militia, two other rival forces became aware of Harwell's accomplishment within days of the HPG coming back online and moved quickly to try seizing the technician. A small unit of mercenaries—later identified as Chaffee's Cut-Throats, commanded by Captain Rutger Chaffee and under the employ of Jacob Bannson—staged an attack on the Wyatt Militia headquarters on 12 May. Meanwhile, a small Oriente Protectorate detachment called the Eagle's Talons learned of the HPG's reactivation through a well-placed on-world source, and traveled to Wyatt to attempt to claim Harwell.

Knight-Errant Holt ventured forth alone to parlay with the Spirit Cats' commander, Star Captain Cox, and learned that he had received a vision of a "Lightbringer" the same day that the HPG came back online. Finding no answers among the spirits at the ruins, Cox intended to move into Kinross next. Rather than risk a broader conflict, Holt challenged Cox to a combat trial for access to the city. In an intense duel on 16 May, Cox bested Holt.

Last Stands

Abandoning Kinross to the Spirit Cats, Holt and Legate Edward Singh opted to move the Wyatt Militia north along a local highway into a mountainous, heavily forested area. The militia planned to follow the highway to its terminus and bivouac at a wilderness camp in the Crater Lakes region, maintaining proximity to Kinross while awaiting the Republic extraction force coming to retrieve Harwell.

Shortly after the militia's departure, Bannson's mercenaries framed the local defenders for a suicide attack on the Spirit Cats entering

Kinross; the attack enraged Star Captain Cox and spurred the Clanners to pursue Harwell and his protectors into the wilderness. Holt, employing the militia's mobile assets, staged a successful surprise attack on the Cats on 18 May, blunting their advance, and Harwell's own decisive strategic analysis turned aside a desperate attempt by Cox's forces to break through the militia's lines.

The following day, the lead elements of Chaffee's Cut-Throats caught up with the militia. Despite his unit being strung out across the wilderness between Kinross and the militia's position, Chaffee opted to attack. The assault proved disastrous for the mercenaries and Chaffee personally. Led by Holt, the Wyatt Militia drove back the Cut-Throats and took Chaffee captive after downing his *Blade*. Moreover, debris left behind by the militia provided the Spirit Cats with evidence that the Cut-Throats had duped them, and that Holt had honored the terms of their combat trial.

Having suffered more than 50 percent casualties and weary from days of constant engagement, the Wyatt Militia finally reached Crater Lakes on 21 May and prepared their last stand. That same day, Harwell's sister Patricia revealed a traitor in their midst: Singh was in communication with the Oriente force now on-planet, feeding them the militia's location and status. Holt took Singh into custody until the situation at hand was resolved.

On 22 May, the remaining Cut-Throats crashed into the militia lines, but the Wyatt natives' stalwart defense—and a shrewd flanking maneuver by Holt—held off the mercenaries long enough for the Spirit Cats to arrive and shatter Bannson's hirelings. The Cats and remaining militia forces then joined to face the fresh Oriente troops, but were no match for the Protectorate detachment. With the Wyatt Militia on the brink of surrender or destruction, all of the combatants were stunned by the arrival of a *fifth* faction: pristine heavy- and assault-class 'Mechs bearing ComStar livery—a new Com Guards resurrected in violation of agreements with the Republic. Patricia quickly turned Tucker over to ComStar, who departed with the adept to parts unknown.

TOUCHPOINT: POPULAR AS ALL HELL

This scenario can be played as a stand-alone game or incorporated into a longer campaign using *Chaos Campaign* rules (available as a free download from https://store.catalystgamelabs.com/products/battletech-chaos-campaign-succession-wars).

For flexibility of play, this track contains rules for *Total Warfare* (*TW*), with *Alpha Strike Commander's Edition* (*AS* or *ASCE*) rules noted in parentheses, allowing the battle to be played with either rule set.

+++SECURE TRANSMISSION+++

To: Precentor Malcolm Buhl, Crimson Priority
From: Adept Patricia Harwell
Primary asset endangered. Militia encamped at Crater Lakes. Opposition from MERC/BR, SCAT, ORE. Asset retrieval requires immediate action. Deployment of SWORD deemed necessary. Recommend combat drop on this location. Will go to ground pending SWORD arrival.

+++TRANSMISSION ENDS+++

SITUATION

CRATER LAKES, WYATT
PREFECTURE VIII
REPUBLIC OF THE SPHERE
22 MAY 3135

With Chaffee's Cut-Throats in retreat, the Spirit Cats and Wyatt Militia reached a quick accord and turned to face the fresh Oriente Protectorate troops marching up Highway 7. The Eagle's Talons, sensing the defenders' weariness, rushed forward to claim their high value target.

GAME SETUP

Recommended Terrain: Heavy Forest

The Defender arranges two maps with the long edges touching, then selects one side to be their home edge. The Attacker's home edge is opposite. The Defender may deploy their units anywhere on the full mapsheet (*AS:* anywhere on the Defender's half of the play area) containing their home edge; the Attacker may deploy within 10 hexes (*AS:* 20˝) of their home edge.

Attacker

Recommended Forces: Eagle's Talons, Oriente Protectorate

The Attacker consists of a reinforced, mixed company of BattleMechs, vehicles, and battle armor, totaling 125 percent of the Defender's force. No more than 50 percent of the value of the Attacker's force can consist of BattleMechs.

Defender

Recommended Forces: Wyatt Militia; Pouncer Trinary, Purifiers Cluster, Spirit Cats

The Defender consists of a mixed company drawn from survivors of the Wyatt Militia and the Pouncer Trinary. A total of 50 percent of the value of the Defender's force must consist of BattleMechs.

WARCHEST
Track Cost: 300 WP

Optional Bonuses

+300 Long Road (Attacker Only): Assign 25 points of damage in 5-point groups (*AS*: 3 points of damage) to each of the Defender's 'Mechs. Assign 15 points of damage in 5-point groups (*AS*: 2 points of damage) to each of the Defender's vehicles. Reroll any results that would Cripple or Destroy the unit (*AS*: Only apply damage to armor; any remaining damage is lost).

–100 Trailblazers (Defender Only): Up to 50 percent of the Defender's units may use the Off-Map Movement Special Command Ability.

–200 Strung Out (Defender Only): Reduce the value of the Attacker's force to match that of the Defender.

OBJECTIVES

Seize the Asset (Attacker Only). Claim Tucker Harwell (see below) and depart the map from the Attacker's home edge. **[500]**

Valuable Intel (Attacker Only). Exit the map from the Attacker's home edge after the arrival of the Com Guards with at least 50 percent of the Attacker's original value. **[900]**

Hold On (Defender Only). Have control of Tucker Harwell when Com Guards forces arrive. **[400]**

He's With Us (Defender Only). Destroy all Attacking forces, including the Eagle's Talons and Com Guards, and possess control of Tucker Harwell. **[1,000]**

SPECIAL RULES

Tucker Harwell

Place a Mobile HQ unit to represent Tucker Harwell within 10 hexes (*AS*: 20˝) of the Defender's home edge; this unit may not move from its initial location. Any infantry or combat vehicle unit which is not Crippled and spends a full Movement Phase in an adjacent hex (*AS:* within 2˝) is considered to have taken Harwell captive. He may be transferred between friendly units in the same way. If the unit capturing Harwell is Crippled or Destroyed, place a marker in the hex the unit occupied; Harwell may be reacquired by a Defending unit which spends a full Movement Phase in that hex. Harwell may not voluntarily leave the Mobile HQ to transfer to a Defender unit unless first captured by the Attacker and reacquired.

Com Guards Reborn

At the end of Turn 7, a second Attacking force, equal to 75 percent of the starting value of the original Attacker's force, executes a combat drop onto the map. The Com Guards have the same Objectives as the Talons and must attempt to retrieve Harwell and exit the map from the Attacker's home edge.

Forced Withdrawal

Forced Withdrawal (see p. 258, *TW*; p. 126, *ASCE*) is not in effect; the militia have nowhere left to run, and the Talons and Com Guards will not leave without Harwell.

AFTERMATH

The shocking appearance of ComStar military assets threw both sides into chaos. As Tucker Harwell was hustled into a waiting ComStar DropShip, the Protectorate forces pulled back. Their target was gone, but the intel on ComStar's previously unknown combat forces was prize enough. Knight-Errant Holt and the remaining Wyatt Militia could only watch bitterly as Harwell disappeared into the DropShip.

WARS AND RUMORS

KEVIN KILLIANY

URSAMAJORIS BADLANDS
ALCOR
GALATEAN LEAGUE
21 JUNE 3149

Launching from above the *Sagittaire*'s cockpit, Juggernaut Fiona Cooper-Jamison was at apogee in her battlesuit when the Jade Falcon Elemental she was targeting discovered the assault 'Mech had appeared behind them.

The Big Bear Badlands made the Elemental's surprise understandable—a thousand square kilometers of radioactive slag ("extrusive thorianite outflow") spewed eons ago by a long-dead volcano. The hardened lava had cracked and weathered into a maze of ravines awash with radiation strong enough to alert the first orbiting explorers to Alcor's mineral potential. Radiation that had for centuries sickened generations of miners trying to exploit that wealth, and today rendered sensors and radios useless.

But understandable was not forgivable, and being so intent on ambushing Trainne's *Goshawk* that the Falcon had ignored their surroundings was going to prove a fatal error.

Fiona was going to land ugly. Jumping for maximum distance from ten meters above the sloping ground meant she'd be hitting the broken jumble of rubble and fissures at a bad angle—with no time to be choosy about where she landed. She accepted her fate and targeted the Falcon Elemental as she fell, firing her micro pulse laser an instant before impact.

The hit was glancing, the flickering beam doing little damage, but the Falcon, still stunned by the unexpected *Sagittaire*, was caught by surprise. They fired wildly in response—the annular beam of their small laser, pale in the sunlight, hit nothing. The Falcon recovered before Fiona had regained her feet, but hesitated a second time—a common reaction to her highly modified Volk battle armor.

The Falcon aimed as she brought her own weapon to bear, and the two fired as one. Her beam stripped armor from her opponent's launcher while the Falcon's gouged her left shoulder with a near-miss.

Fiona grunted. They'd both followed basic opening tactics, going for the other's missiles, despite the fact she clearly had none—having traded her one-shot SRM 3 for additional armor and the half-dozen Clan power packs that kept her micro pulse laser viable through the longest battle. That change in profile, plus the fact she'd stripped the medium armor of its garish Draconis flourishes, had given the Elemental pause a moment before firing, and they'd still followed basic training.

An assault 'Mech catching the Falcon by surprise began to make sense.

Beyond her opponent, she saw the rest of the Jade Falcon 'Mech-hunting Point rush Trianne. Whether they meant to salvage the ambush or hoped clinging to the *Goshawk* would force the *Sagittaire* to hold fire was immaterial. They should have withdrawn to regroup.

The *Sagittaire* stepped to stand almost directly over them—sending the Falcon Elementals scrambling for cover behind a broken plinth of lava. Even through her armor, Fiona felt the air around her bake as Jerry Jamison vaporized two Elementals, simultaneously hitting both moving targets with an overkill of large-laser fire. Her husband could never resist showing off his marksmanship.

She flared wide, circling the column of stone at distance; her opponent, distracted by the assault 'Mech ignoring them, was slow to react. She used those seconds to target the left knee, shredding its armor with two strikes as quickly as her laser's capacitor could cycle.

The Falcon pivoted to face her—ignoring the damaged joint in their eagerness. Her third burst shattered the over-torqued knee assembly, severing the Elemental's leg and bringing them down. She felt a moment's respect for the fallen warrior when they brought their laser to bear, their last shot burning a scar across her left arm above the battle claw.

Fiona ended her opponent with a burst through his faceplate. "*Solahma that*," she muttered.

She was startled by Jerry's chuckle over their private channel.

It was not certain Fiona would have been relegated to the Steel Wolves' *solahma* Binary if her Star Commander had not led his Nova away from Anastasia Kerensky's heresy. But last week Ahab Wolf—a mere ten years her junior—had attributed her battle armor's design to wisdom gained through "many, many years of combat experience." He'd phrased it as a compliment, but that repeated "many" was suspect.

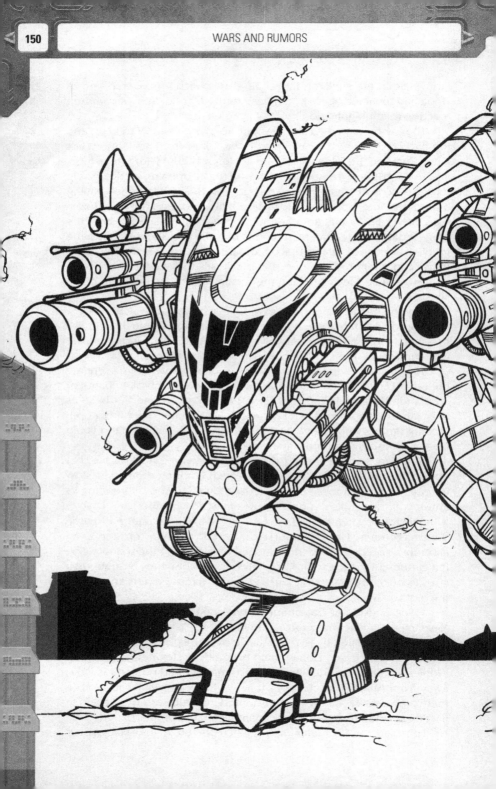

The ground shook as the 95-ton *Sagittaire* strode forward—out of radio range in a dozen steps. Fiona sketched a wave at its back before shadowing Trainne into the knife-slit of a branching ravine.

The Badlands had enabled a Star of Jade Falcon Elemental 'Mech hunters to ambush the *Goshawk* undetected.

She wasn't going to let it happen again.

Tal Sender manually kept the Gauss rifle's reticule floating over the *Stormcrow* as he shifted his *Orion IIC* as far to the right as the narrow ravine allowed. One eye on his three-sixty and the other on the scene before him, he held his finger lightly on the trigger.

Waiting increased the chance of discovery—even sensor-blind, the Jade Falcon had only to look at their own three-sixty display to see the heavy 'Mech less than four hundred meters behind them. But he couldn't risk the shot with Molly Lingstrom's *Sirocco* in his line of fire.

Her quad assault 'Mech was in the a sheer-walled box formed by the juncture of converging ravines. At the moment she was facing a *Hellbringer* half concealed by jagged rocks in the mouth of the far ravine—but the damage to the *Sirocco*'s rear quarter and the *Stormcrow*'s torso told Tal she was already aware of the smaller 'Mech.

His lip curled as the *Stormcrow*'s pilot stepped from cover to savage a rear leg from behind with heavy lasers. Falcon Khan Malvina Hazen had declared mercenaries scum to be exterminated, not enemies to be respected, but no warrior worthy of the name would have obeyed such an order.

In the space of a heartbeat Molly answered the *Stormcrow* with her rear lasers and reduced the *Hellbringer*'s ATM 6 launcher to smoking scrap with her paired Ultra-10s. Molly's combat skills were exceptional—and her *Sirocco* could deal death while taking heavy fire—but trapped as she was by stone walls between enemies without honor, her survival was not certain.

The *Hellbringer* pilot canted the torso left, putting its useless right arm between Molly and vital systems. Angling the left arm across its torso, the Falcon fired their ER large laser into the *Sirocco*'s right leg. The medium laser turret above the knee deformed, the weapon sagging uselessly.

Molly moved to compensate, a sidestep that took her clear of Tal's line of fire. He pressed the trigger.

A silver streak linking the *Orion IIC*'s Gauss rifle and the *Stormcrow*'s left arm glimmered briefly in the sunlight. There was an explosive spray of coolant as the nickel-iron slug tore through at least one of the heavy large laser's dedicated heat sinks.

The Falcon attempted to pivot in place, but unstable footing reduced the crisp maneuver to a shuffle. Tal used the extra seconds to launch his long-range missiles. All twenty cleared their tubes a heartbeat before the *Stormcrow*'s three lasers struck.

The centerline extended-range medium laser scored the armor below Tal's cockpit, but the right arm's paired ER medium and heavy large lasers tore into the *Orion*'s left shoulder. Tal glanced to his 'Mech's wireframe in time to see the LRM 20 launcher flare red and go black.

Surprisingly, six of the missiles in his unguided salvo exploded across his target's legs and torso. Unsurprisingly, eight missiles exploded against both walls of the ravine, two climbed for the sky, and four corkscrewed through the space Molly's *Sirocco* had occupied to blast craters in the far side of the junction.

The *Hellbringer* pilot reacted to Tal's sudden appearance by unleashing an alpha strike against Molly's *Sirocco*. The torso-mounted LB 20-X raked the 'Mech's heavily armored chest while the left arm's ER large and small lasers scoured its head and the two torso-mounted mediums scorched empty air.

Tal had a half-second to wonder why the Falcon hadn't focused on the damaged right foreleg before the *Stormcrow* captured his attention with a single medium-laser hit to the left side of his torso.

The Falcon was targeting his short-range missiles—and worried about heat.

Tal's targeting system was useless—it couldn't read IFF transponders through the hash of signal noise, much less give him a solid lock. But... infrared showed the 'Mech's right half was an angry nimbus of reds and yellows. The Falcon had lost too many heat sinks. And probably assumed Tal's launchers packed heat-seeking missiles—the only guidance system unaffected by this radiation.

Tal wished he'd thought of that.

The orange nimbus disappeared as the Falcon took cover behind an outcrop of rock. They leaned out almost immediately to fire a second single beam, gouging armor from the *Orion IIC*'s SRM launcher. With their escape blocked by an assault 'Mech, the Falcon's only viable option was to generate as little heat as possible, keeping Tal at distance while their damaged systems cooled the heavy large laser enough to fire.

Shutting down the useless computer, Tal answered with a single laser shot, creating the impression that only one worked, and stepped left. Twice the pattern repeated—the Falcon stepping from cover to fire a single shot, and Tal answering with one shot and a step left. If the Falcon noticed they had to move a bit farther from cover to target Tal with each shot, there was little that could be done about it.

Beyond the *Stormcrow*, Tal saw the *Hellbringer* falling back before the *Sirocco*. The Falcon MechWarrior was answering Molly's methodical onslaught with increasingly wild salvos while backpedaling down the far ravine.

The fourth time the *Stormcrow* stepped from cover, the pilot hesitated, as though double-checking their aim. Enough warning for

Tal to fire the Gauss rifle and step his *Orion* to the right just as the Falcon's heavy large laser blazed. Tal didn't avoid the shot altogether—the shaft of coherent energy vaporized torso armor and slagged the *Orion*'s SRM 4 launcher.

But the battle was over before Tal triggered his own lasers—the Gauss rifle had blasted the *Stormcrow*'s cockpit to shards.

"What happened out there?" Jerry Jamison asked.

He and his section commanders were in the incongruously cheerful wardroom provided by the Alcor Planetary Militia. The pastel colors and sunshine streaming through the windows did not match their mood.

"We were hit by a raiding party that acted like a disorganized mob," Jerry pressed. "Like a swarm of solo warriors and a few Stars that didn't do more than punch us in the nose and run away. What the hell was that?"

"The Jade Falcons hit the heart of Alcor's mining industry," Aziz Wolf, infantry commander, responded. "Though their intel was seven hundred years out of date."

"But which Jade Falcons?" Don Avison, armor commander and Jerry's XO, gestured with a protein bar. "The pigeon hiding behind a shield says they're Zetas—but I didn't recognize the unit colors."

"First Mixed Cluster," Tal answered. "The youngest and least experienced warriors—those who failed the Eyrie Cluster—and the eldest combat-worthy *solahma*."

"Teenagers and octogenarians," Avison guessed.

"Yes and no," Tal answered. "More probably sexagenarians."

"The idea being the old teach the young how to earn their way out of the First," Jake said.

"Essentially."

"But the First does not conduct probes or raids," Aziz said. "They garrison low-value worlds in the Reach."

"They the ones who checked our travel papers back in the day?" Avison asked. "Never noticed a third of us were Wolves?"

"Yes," Tal confirmed.

"Think they'd notice we're a quarter Wolves now?"

"No need. We're an established command. Our composition is general knowledge."

"And there you go." Avison sat back.

But Fiona caught the major's point. "They were blooding new warriors," she said, "against Wolves *and* Spheroids."

Jerry frowned for a moment, his right thumb and forefinger rotating the onyx-and-tungsten ring on his left hand as he thought. "The Badlands forced limited engagement," he said, "with little risk of inexperienced fighters being overwhelmed. And they're so far from targets of value there's no chance they'd damage anything the Falcons might want later."

"I may have interrupted a *solahma* warrior in a *Stormcrow* instructing an inexperienced *Hellbringer* pilot on how to engage Lingstrom," Tal said. "The *Stormcrow* hung back, occasionally firing from cover while the *Hellbringer* faced the *Sirocco* openly. I initially mistook them for a coward and treated us as such. But when I fired on them, they proved competent and disciplined—if predictable. Conversely, the *Hellbringer* pilot panicked—firing wildly and retreating."

"So we are practice dummies," Aziz said.

"Inglorious," Avison agreed, "but it earns us combat bonuses."

Jerry rapped the table with a knuckle. "Let's be ready to flunk every trainee they send us."

URSAMAJORISAETI DROPPORT
ALCOR, GALATEAN LEAGUE
11 JULY 3149

Jerry Jamison saw technicians walking Major Freya Hauer's *Malice* into the sunlight as Fiona tightened their car's spiral toward the Galatean Defense Force's DropShip. He neither knew nor cared if his wife's unswerving suspicion reflected her character or training—it had saved the Juggernauts on more than one occasion. He wondered what their current employers thought of her circling survey of the perimeter before approaching.

Major Hauer stood by the base of the ramp, watching her 'Mech's plodding descent like a parent ready to catch a child who stumbled. She did not acknowledge their arrival, but the aide at her elbow nodded, letting them know they'd have her attention momentarily.

Jerry ran a practiced eye over the *Malice* as it moved with the exaggerated caution techs always used when they knew the 'Mech's pilot was watching. It seemed every merc outfit that fielded assaults either had a *Malice* or wanted one, but he'd never seen its appeal. True, it was a few kph faster than his 'Mech, but it couldn't jump and didn't have a lot to show for its extra five tons. Compared to his *Sagittaire*'s ER PPC and array of large and medium lasers, he considered the bigger 'Mech's ammo-dependent primary weapons a serious flaw.

Hauer's *Malice* sported several patches of fresh paint, but no evidence of major repairs. She'd seen action, and come off lightly, in the six months the Juggernauts had been on Alcor.

"Colonel," Hauer greeted Jerry once the tech was safely out of her parked 'Mech. She looked up to meet Fiona's eye. "Captain."

Over her shoulder, Jerry saw a second 'Mech began its slow descent down the ramp.

"So this surprise visit is a surprise replacement," Jerry said. "Something up you don't want broadcast?"

"You're not part of the Defense Force," Hauer said. "The Juggernauts are independent contractors."

Jerry nodded, trusting she was framing her point and not worried he'd gone senile.

"And the Juggernauts' standard contract stipulates you will not act against the home planet of any of your people—" Hauer flicked a quick glance at Fiona, "—nor engage an opponent with whom those in your command have served."

Ah.

"You're expecting Wolves."

"We're not," Hauer corrected, "but the Jade Falcons are. I'll spare you the details, but the Wolves have taken Alhena and Chertan from the Remnant."

Jerry nodded. The Galatean League and the Republic Remnant shared a mutual defense treaty, which made it likely the details Hauer was sparing them included the Roughriders' efforts to support the Remnant—and perhaps how her *Malice* had been shot up by Wolves.

"If Alaric is going after Damien Redburn," he said aloud, "he's moving away from us."

"Intel is the Falcons think he's widening the Wolf Empire's corridor to Terra," Hauer said. "They expect the Wolves to come this way."

"No," Fiona interjected. "They *want* the Wolves to come this way."

"Our after action was wrong about the First Mixed Cluster," Jerry followed her thought. "They weren't training or blooding hatchlings—they were telling the world that Turkina and the One-Twenty-Fourth have secretly redeployed, and the First Mixed can't even harass us properly."

"A childish ploy," Fiona said.

"Which no Wolf would buy," Hauer agreed.

Her lack of surprise told Jerry her battalion was here because the Roughriders had already figured that out. *Another detail she spared us.*

"So if the Wolves *do* come, it will be in two waves," Hauer said. "The first to blunder into the trap, and the second to crush the Falcon forces once they're exposed."

"Tactically and strategically," Jerry countered, "there's no reason for them to play the Falcons' game."

"We're not taking that chance." Hauer glanced up at Fiona, then refocused on Jerry. "We don't want to order your people to fight their people. And we're not leaving you anywhere we might have to. The Juggernauts are recalled to Galatea."

"To fold in with the Roughriders?"

"No, for the same reason," Hauer said. "For the duration, the Juggernauts sit tight."

"With pay for the rest of our contract?"

"Half-pay. And first refusal on any future jobs."

"You'll have to do better," Jerry countered. "We have six hundred combat and support personnel to take care of, and a battalion to keep battle ready."

"Half-pay with no rent on your compound for the duration," Hauer said.

"And the contract's free maintenance and repair clause?"

Hauer sighed. "Stays in effect until the contract expires 31 December."

"Done," Jerry nodded.

Hauer returned his nod, then turned a shoulder to look up at his wife—letting Jerry know he was no longer part of the conversation. "What will you do if the Wolves attack Galatea?"

Fiona considered. "All Wolves are our *sibkin*," she acknowledged. "But if Wolves attack our homeworld? Each of us will do as our honor demands."

If Hauer'd expected a solid answer, she was disappointed. She glanced at Jerry, but he shook his head fractionally. He wouldn't get a better one.

JAMISON'S JUGGERNAUTS COMPOUND
GALATEA, GALATEAN LEAGUE
16 AUGUST 3149

The shrill buzz of Jerry's desk comm rescued him from an interminable quarterly consumables inventory. The incoming ID told him the Galatean Mercenary District Constabulary, formerly Shield-something, a merc outfit specializing in security, wanted his attention.

He glanced around the former file room—now divided into a two-desk office he shared with Avison and overflow storage—and confirmed there was no one else to take the call. He keyed the mic.

"Jamison."

"Brisbane," the chief constable answered. "How did the Jugs get on the Solaris VII radar?"

Jerry frowned at the speaker. The ersatz battles on Solaris VII were a mainstay of the Mercenary District's gambling industry, but he'd lost interest the first time he'd experienced real combat. "Come again?"

"A recruiting team from a Solaris stable is at the district gate, asking to see you."

"A Solaris stable?"

"A good one, and one of the big ones." Brisbane mistook Jerry's incredulity for a question. "Not going to spoil the surprise. I'm betting they're here to headhunt some of your best people. You want to see them?"

Not really.

"Yeah," Jerry said aloud. "Send 'em back."

He broke the connection and buzzed Avison. "Round up Fiona, Tal, and Aziz. We've got visitors, and maybe a job."

"Infantry's on the live-fire range," Avison answered. Meaning Aziz was thirty minutes away.

"Call 'em home," Jamison said.

Avison, Tal, and Fiona appeared in time to hear the front gate notify him the Solaris VII delegation had arrived. Jerry instructed the guests be escorted to his office via the scenic route—code for fifteen minute tour of the Juggernauts' more impressive assets.

"A recruiting team from a stable on Solaris VII is here to see us."

"Ah." An outburst by Tal's standards.

More significantly, Fiona appeared bored—telling Jerry she was on high alert.

"Which stable?" Avison asked.

"Brisbane just said they were major and good," Jerry answered. He looked from Fiona to Tal. "But I think you two know."

"We," Tal paused, "*suspect,* but..."

"But we do not believe it is possible," Fiona completed.

Jerry glanced at the clock and figured he had another thirteen minutes. Clearing his monitor, he called up "last activity" on their compound's gate camera. A party of four—an Afro-Terran male of imposing proportions leading two nearly as imposing men and a woman with the compact build of a gymnast.

"Canid Cooperative," Avison identified, "Founded by a Wolf 'Mech jockey—Yulri Wolf. They've got a dozen former Wolves on their roster."

He pointed to the tall Afro-Terran. "That guy's Simien Fox—"

"No," Tal said.

"Canid's *my* stable," Avison defended his assertion. "Simien Fox bankrolled Yulri putting the cooperative together, carried them when they were struggling. Now they're big time, not far behind Overlord, but Fox still owns all their real estate."

Turning back to his computer, Jerry opened the portal to Galatea's public database and entered "*Simien Fox.*" It was a long shot, but if Fox was a big enough player, he might find something...

Variant name of Ethiopian Wolf [canis simensis], the only citation read. *Terran canid of medium stature native to Africa's—*

He slapped the useless machine off and turned to Tal.

"Colonel Jamison?"

Jerry almost snapped at the young trooper standing in the open doorway, but the kid's stressed expression stopped him. He'd clearly done his best to buy his commander time, but been unable to hold Fox back.

Jerry took a breath and composed his professionally pleasant game face. "Show them in, Westcott."

He rose as Simien Fox strode into the office, respect being good for business.

For his part, Fox swept the repurposed room with an authority that bordered on arrogance before meeting Jerry's eye and nodding his own respect.

The two men and the woman who'd followed him silently ranged themselves along the wall near the door. The arrogance of the two young men told Jerry they were former Wolf warriors, but the older woman's appearance arrested him. The cut of her duty uniform made plain her right breast was gone, and while the left side of her face was striking, the right was disfigured, nearly immobile with scar tissue.

Shotgun blast from waist level, Jerry read her wounds. *Bastard shot through her boob on purpose.*

Expecting introductions, Jerry was startled when Fox turned from him to Tal Sender.

"Star Commander, it has been many years."

"Fourteen, Star Captain."

—?!

"And Fiona Cooper." The man's smile was possessive.

"Fiona Cooper-Jamison," she corrected flatly.

The Star Captain, whose name surely wasn't Simien Fox, smiled more broadly and flicked a glance at Jerry. "A second *abtakha*?" he asked. "Ambitious, even for a former *ristar*."

"A choice." Fiona's voice was dangerously calm. "Made when our Clan abandoned us."

The smile vanished. "You were under communications blackout until—"

"*Until*—" Fiona cut across his words, "—Anastasia Kerensky turned her back on us—broke her oath to us—and became saKhan to Khan Alaric Wolf."

The Star Captain's face became a thundercloud.

"Star Captain." Tal bravely threw himself in front of the storm. "You are the first Wolf officer, first Wolf warrior from outside Galatea, to contact us since 23 July 3135."

The man gaped.

Jerry missed the next few exchanges, watching Fiona's face relax from weary to bored. She'd proposed to him—risked leaping into a relationship unlike anything in her world—three days after the rumors that Annie K had become saKhan were confirmed.

"Colonel Jamison?" Grave concern had erased the Wolf Star Captain's fury. "I am Star Captain Dejen Vickers of Clan Wolf. It is imperative that—" He caught himself. "With your permission, I must speak with all Wolves in your command as soon as possible."

Jerry nodded as though all of this was SOP and turned to Tal. "Captain Sender," he bore down on Tal's Juggernaut rank, "notify all Juggernaut Wolves that they may meet with Star Captain Vickers in the gym for a briefing. We'll have the front gate send Aziz and the others when they arrive. Major Avison, relay that and order all non-Wolves to stay clear of the gym."

Don nodded, typing rapidly on his desk comm's keypad.

At Vickers's gesture, Tal led the way out of the office. The two unintroduced men fell in step behind their leader, and Fiona, after giving Jerry a look he couldn't read, followed.

"A friend of mine once warned me that Clanners don't feel things the way we do," the woman who'd remained said. She'd taken up a position equidistant from Jerry and Avison. "I didn't believe him until the Clan man I thought was *it* told me his Alpha needed him—whatever the hell that meant—and left."

"Your point?"

She regarded him for a moment. Her hazel eyes—one with an elfin upward tilt, the other drooping—were unsettling. "You should brace yourself for some bad news."

Jerry broke her gaze to scan her uniform. There was no name or sign of rank—just a unit patch depicting a dark, powerful hound with shining silver eyes.

Canid Cooperative, Avison had said.

"Who are you?"

"She's Jazz du Martre," Avison spoke up before she answered, "champion scrapper—infantry skirmisher. Locked in the Solaris VII title—individual and squad—in '38. Kept 'em both 'til she retired in '44. She runs Canid Cooperative."

"Not any more," Jazz said. "Canid's dissolved."

"Crap!" Avison turned to Jerry. "I'm going to lose my butt."

Jazz glanced at Avison's lower half. "That would be a shame."

"Do you have anything useful to say?" Jerry demanded.

"You've been working for Annie K."

"What?"

"We all have." She shrugged. "The saKhan does Clan traditions her way."

"Explain."

"Quick question first," she said. "Bear with me."

"Go on."

"When the disgruntled former Steel Wolves joined your command, did they sell you on the idea of cross-training everyone on everyone else's job?" she asked. "Restructuring so you could adapt to setbacks that would stop anyone else?"

Avison met Jerry's glance with a cocked eyebrow.

"From the top."

"Under Clan law, the Clan that owns Terra rules the other Clans—"

"That sounds more like mythology."

"They take it seriously," Jazz assured him. "Annie came damn close once, but things happened. That lesson taught her that she needed a bigger army, and that Spheroids fight like hell when we want to. So in '35, she taught the Steel Wolves warriors to do everyone else's job, then—"

"She broke the Steel Wolves," Jerry said.

"—she sent teams hunting for crack units to build into her new army."

"We thought she'd screwed herself," Avison said. "But that breakup was giving cover for her scout teams."

Like Tal Sender's Nova, offering us exactly what the Juggernauts needed most.

"Most of the Clanners who left wanted her dead," Jazz clarified. "But, yeah, her people were all in the mix."

"That was in '35," Jerry pointed out. "In '46 she folded and became Khan Alaric's right hand. Why raise her army now?"

"In '35 there were factions and splinters all through the Clans— Kerensky just needed an army big enough to take out a Republic on its heels and fight off fragments of other Clans. Now the Jade Falcons are united under a madwoman—"

"Malvina Hazen," Avison supplied.

"—who's turned them rabid. They're destroying worlds, not just taking them. It's just a question of *when* she turns them on Terra and that whole Boss Clan thing goes into effect. All of the Wolves—except the In-Exile gang—are solid behind Alaric and his Wolf Empire as the only thing that can stop her."

"You seem to know a lot about Clan activity."

"Colonel, I know nothing about Clanners, active or otherwise," Jazz answered. "But I do know how to summarize a briefing."

"Fair enough."

"Upshot is the whole Sphere's a few years from all-out war between the Falcons and the Wolves," she said. "It's a sure bet the winner of *that* match will take Terra and rule all the Clans. How bad that is for everyone else depends on who wins."

Jerry considered the options. He didn't know the spinward Inner Sphere, but the Republic was on life support, the Free Worlds League was a basket case, and the Lyrans... *Crap.*

"So Kerensky's mobilizing her army to back Alaric."

"Pretty much."

"Okay," Avison drew the word out. "I get that a bunch of cross-trained commands could mesh pretty much seamlessly. But I don't get why she expected them to fight for her."

"She'd make them Wolves."

"That's ridiculous."

"That's Clan traditions Annie's way," Jazz corrected. "Outsiders need to spend years as bondsmen, servants proving they deserve it, before a Clan lets them in. That *ab*-jerkoff thing."

"*Abtakha*," Avison supplied.

Jazz shrugged. "Kerensky's twist is to count our time working *with* her people as time working *for* Clan Wolf. Fox Vickers says there's a close-enough clause in the fine print. No way to know that." Her unnerving eyes softened with sympathy. "But I do know what happened to Canid is happening to the Juggernauts."

"What happened to Canid?"

"Background first. In '36 and '37 Canid attracted a lot of disillusioned ex-Wolves—technicians as well as warriors—until they made up nearly half the co-op. We really took off in '38—grew to a major stable in five years. No new Wolves, though, so Canid ended up maybe fifteen percent Wolf." The left side of her mouth grimaced. "Somehow we never noticed that fifteen percent controlled all of our key operations."

Jerry cut his eyes to Avison. His XO nodded, leaned his butt against the edge of his desk, and casually rested his right hand on the comm keypad behind him.

"That hasn't happened here," Jerry pointed out.

"Something's gone seriously sideways," Jazz agreed. "Never seen Fox Vickers that rattled."

"What happened next?"

"Six weeks ago Fox Vickers came out of the closet." Both halves of her mouth formed a grim line. "We were disarmed, immobilized, and cut off from the outside before we knew what was happening."

"But—" Avison stopped himself. "*After* the finals."

"Another month before anyone expects to see us," Jazz confirmed.

The half-second hitch in her swing back to Jerry that told him she'd caught Avison's unusual pose.

"All Canid Cooperative non-Wolves, along with their dependents and families—Clanners having figured that out—were respectfully but irresistibly rounded up by neighborhood Wolves we didn't know existed," she said. "Fox Vickers said most of them were bondsmen—property on the way to being Clanners. However, a chosen few of us had already proven ourselves worthy of the Clan. We'd have to pass some combat trials to become full-on Wolves, but we could become semi-Wolves on the spot by swearing an oath to the Clan."

She held up her hand, showing a thin bracelet of braided cord. "We told him to shove it."

"Thereby proving they were more Wolf than they knew." Star Captain Vickers, whom Jerry would forever think of as Fox Vickers, was standing in the doorway, flanked by his two warriors.

Jerry glanced at the wall chronometer. "Short meeting."

"Star Commander Sender has it in hand," Vickers said as he stepped up to stand possessively beside Jazz. "Now that they know Operation Appleseed is in effect, they need to determine their next step. An internal process." His superior smile returned. "I'm here as a courtesy, to explain your role in the coming transition."

"Waving goodbye."

"Come again?"

"You had assets in place before you moved on Solaris VII," Jerry said. "So there's no doubt you positioned assets in the District before you knocked on our door. But you didn't know the tacsit—which means they haven't been here long, they can't surveil worth squat, and they're not inside this compound."

"Neither are your infantry," Vickers pointed out. "They were contacted when I entered your office." A microscopic frown appeared above the smile. "But you knew that."

"Your impatience to reach Tal Sender suggested a timetable," Jerry confirmed. "But that's not the point."

"What is your point?"

Two minutes before he'd expected her, a corporal in a mechanic's jumpsuit and headset slipped between the warriors at the door. She wordlessly handed Avison his helmet and, following her commander's glance, put Jerry's cooling vest on his desk before exiting at the double.

The bemused Wolves made no effort to stop her.

"Scrambling now is a futile gesture." Vickers sounded amused. "As you deduced, we already surround your compound. And once we make our warriors in the gym aware—"

"*Our* people in the gym know we're scrambled," Jerry said. "They know their 'Mechs and tanks are being prepped and their gear laid out, waiting for them to complete their deliberations."

"You are arming Wolves?"

"No. The Juggernauts are prepping to keep your people honest."

Avison, his mouth and one eye masked by his helmet's hush mic and heads-up, gave Jerry a sign. Jerry nodded—no need to tell Vickers the infantry was in compound.

"The only futile gesture here was you pretending you have any leverage," Jerry said. "You can't cart off a battalion of professional soldiers like you did a stable of entertainers."

"Professional soldiers?" Vickers didn't quite sneer. "Mercenaries— hired guns who sell their services for a paycheck—cannot be compared to true soldiers who fight for honor. Much less Clan warriors."

"Think about that," Jerry said. "I know you positioned Wolf warriors around us before you knocked on our door. But you're in the middle of Galatea's Mercenary District—surrounded by tens of thousands of profit-driven hired guns eager to collect bounties on Clanner scalps."

Vickers glared for a moment, then relaxed. "We obviously had no intention of removing you by force," he said as though clarifying a given. "The gain would not be worth the cost."

Jerry kept a straight face, but Avison snorted.

"But neither can you force Wolf warriors to remain under your command when their Khan summons them." Vickers spread his hands, palms up. "Nor will you turn your weapons on them when they compel you to join them."

"No one will be forced to stay and no one compelled to go," Jerry said. "That's what keeping you honest means."

"That I like."

Jazz smiled—an unsettling mismatch of curves—and turned away to face Vickers's bodyguards at the door. Though the top of her head barely reached their breastbones, she immediately had their full attention.

Jerry made a note to research Solaris VII scrappers.

"Do you not grasp the situation?" Vickers demanded.

"You told Canid we're a few years away from all-out war between the Wolves and Jade Falcons," Jerry answered. "A Jihad-class bloodbath where the actions of one battalion would make no difference at all."

"That is not your decision to make," Vickers said.

Avison pulled his helmet mic away from his mouth. "They're on their way."

Vickers looked to his warriors by the door. One pressed fingers to his ear, then tore his eyes from Jazz long enough to shake his head.

Vickers's anger burned through his pretense of civility. "Blocking our communications is unwise."

Jerry didn't bother responding.

Their tableau held for a full minute before Tal spoke from the corridor.

"Star Captain?"

The men at the door made way for his three section commanders and a woman Jerry had seen in the Hiring Hall. If she commanded the covert Wolves supporting Vickers, some merc outfit was hosting them. *Obviously, that's the only way they could be in the District.*

All noted Jazz's stance and the guards' attention; it worried the newcomer.

"Star Commanders," Vickers greeted Tal and the stranger. He glanced at Avison. "Everything is not yet secure."

"Yes, sir, it is," Tal answered.

Vickers frowned. "Star Commander Faulk?"

"Sir." She paused. "On 11 July, the Galatean League determined the Jade Falcons were attempting to lure the Wolf Empire into striking the Falcon's Reach through Galatea. The Juggernaut Wolves decided that if the Wolf Empire landed on Galatea, each Wolf should respond as their honor demanded—to stand down or defend their adopted homeworld."

"Against their Clan?"

Faulk looked down, but the other three met his gaze without flinching.

"Upon learning Operation Appleseed was underway," Tal continued when Faulk did not, "we chose to make a similar determination."

"What determination?" There was cold anger behind the question.

"Seventy percent of us will accompany you to the Wolf Empire."

"Seventy?" Vickers nearly strangled on his fury. "How many traitors are there?"

"None," Fiona said flatly.

Vickers flicked a glance at her before refocusing on Tal.

"Two MechWarriors, twenty infantry, and one Point each of armor and Elementals will remain with the Juggernauts to defend the region." Tal answered promptly.

"Defend the region?"

"We're what, three years from a bloodbath?" Jerry broke in. "Two? You know better than most a lot of that blood will be shed by civilians on worlds of no use to the Wolves or Falcons. Worlds raped by jackals profiting from the chaos. Worse, if things don't go their way, the Jade Falcons will burn every planet they can reach to ash just to spite the Wolves. There are a lot of those low-value worlds in this region, and the Juggernauts, along with anyone else who joins us, could prevent— or at least limit—their suffering. But to do that, we need to be here."

"And you know better than most," Vickers answered, "that we cannot let Spheroid mercenaries aware of our plans go free."

Jerry knew Vickers didn't mean immediately or on Galatea. At any future time, on any world they worked, the Wolves could eradicate his people.

"Then don't," he said aloud.

Vickers blinked.

"Continue Annie's—the saKhan's—strategy, but make it official," Jerry pressed. "The Juggernauts will pose as independent mercenaries while secretly harassing the Jade Falcons under the direction of Wolf warriors."

The Star Captain considered.

"Insufficient," he said at last. "I appreciate your motives, but the situation is not what it was—conditions are too dire for such a ruse. Your only course is to come with us as bondsmen. Otherwise..."

He let the threat hang.

Jerry frowned into the middle distance, turning his ring as he thought. *Go as bondsmen now or stay to be destroyed–or enslaved?–later?* He stopped twisting his ring.

"What if a leader were a bondsman?" he asked. "Would everyone who served under him be considered bound?"

"It has been done," Vickers said slowly. "You are proposing becoming my bondsman in exchange for, as you put it, defending low-value worlds?"

"Not your bondsman." He held up his left hand.

Fiona broke ranks with the others to stand by him and turned her hand to display her own onyx-encrusted band of tungsten.

Jazz's delighted laugh startled everyone.

It took the Star Captain a moment longer to grasp the significance of the matching wedding rings.

"Well bargained," Vickers said, his solemnity marred by a faint glint of amusement. "I will convey your terms to the saKhan. Until we know her decision, we will, on my authority, proceed as though they are acceptable."

"Done," Jerry agreed.

"Colonel," Tal said formally, "it has been an honor to serve with you."

Aziz beside him nodded once, his eyes bright with unexpressed emotion.

"The honor has been mine," Jerry countered. "Now go see to your people."

After they'd left, he said, "Du Martre, the Juggernauts have a sudden need for an infantry commander, and I hear you're the best."

"Sorry, Colonel," Jazz answered. "I'm staying with my own people. Besides—" she exchanged looks with Vickers, "—there's a Wolf I'm going to neuter."

BATTLETECH ERAS

The *BattleTech* universe is a living, vibrant entity that grows each year as more sourcebooks and fiction are published. A dynamic universe, its setting and characters evolve over time within a highly detailed continuity framework, bringing everything to life in a way a static game universe cannot match.

To help quickly and easily convey the timeline of the universe—and to allow a player to easily "plug in" a given novel or sourcebook—we've divided *BattleTech* into six major eras.

STAR LEAGUE
(Present–2780)

Ian Cameron, ruler of the Terran Hegemony, concludes decades of tireless effort with the creation of the Star League, a political and military alliance between all Great Houses and the Hegemony. Star League armed forces immediately launch the Reunification War, forcing the Periphery realms to join. For the next two centuries, humanity experiences a golden age across the thousand light-years of human-occupied space known as the Inner Sphere. It also sees the creation of the most powerful military in human history.

(This era also covers the centuries before the founding of the Star League in 2571, most notably the Age of War.)

SUCCESSION WARS
(2781–3049)

Every last member of First Lord Richard Cameron's family is killed during a coup launched by Stefan Amaris. Following the thirteen-year war to unseat him, the rulers of each of the five Great Houses disband the Star League. General Aleksandr Kerensky departs with eighty percent of the Star League Defense Force beyond known space and the Inner Sphere collapses into centuries of warfare known as the Succession Wars that will eventually result in a massive loss of technology across most worlds.

CLAN INVASION
(3050-3061)
A mysterious invading force strikes the coreward region of the Inner Sphere. The invaders, called the Clans, are descendants of Kerensky's SLDF troops, forged into a society dedicated to becoming the greatest fighting force in history. With vastly superior technology and warriors, the Clans conquer world after world. Eventually this outside threat will forge a new Star League, something hundreds of years of warfare failed to accomplish. In addition, the Clans will act as a catalyst for a technological renaissance.

CIVIL WAR
(3062-3067)
The Clan threat is eventually lessened with the complete destruction of a Clan. With that massive external threat apparently neutralized, internal conflicts explode around the Inner Sphere. House Liao conquers its former Commonality, the St. Ives Compact; a rebellion of military units belonging to House Kurita sparks a war with their powerful border enemy, Clan Ghost Bear; the fabulously powerful Federated Commonwealth of House Steiner and House Davion collapses into five long years of bitter civil war.

JIHAD
(3067-3080)
Following the Federated Commonwealth Civil War, the leaders of the Great Houses meet and disband the new Star League, declaring it a sham. The pseudo-religious Word of Blake—a splinter group of ComStar, the protectors and controllers of interstellar communication—launch the Jihad: an interstellar war that pits every faction against each other and even against themselves, as weapons of mass destruction are used for the first time in centuries while new and frightening technologies are also unleashed.

DARK AGE
(3081-3150)
Under the guidance of Devlin Stone, the Republic of the Sphere is born at the heart of the Inner Sphere following the Jihad. One of the more extensive periods of peace begins to break out as the 32nd century dawns. The factions, to one degree or another, embrace disarmament, and the massive armies of the Succession Wars begin to fade. However, in 3132 eighty percent of interstellar communications collapses, throwing the universe into chaos. Wars erupt almost immediately, and the factions begin rebuilding their armies.

SUBMISSION GUIDELINES

Shrapnel is the market for official short fiction set in the *BattleTech* universe.

WHAT WE WANT

We are looking for stories of **3,000–7,000 words** that are character-oriented, meaning the characters, rather than the technology, provide the main focus of the action. Stories can be set in any established *BattleTech* era, and although we prefer stories where BattleMechs are featured, this is by no means a mandatory element.

WHAT WE DON'T WANT

The following items are generally grounds for immediate disqualification:

- Stories not set in the *BattleTech* universe. There are other markets for these stories.

- Stories centering solely on romance, supernatural, fantasy, or horror elements. If your story isn't primarily military sci-fi, then it's probably not for us.

- Stories containing gratuitous sex, gore, or profanity. Keep it PG-13, and you should be fine.

- Stories under 3,000 words or over 7,000 words. We don't publish flash fiction, and although we do publish works longer than 7,000 words, these are reserved for established *BattleTech* authors.

- Vanity stories, which include personal units, author-as-character inserts, or tabletop game sessions retold in narrative form.

- Publicly available *BattleTech* fan-fiction. If your story has been posted in a forum or other public venue, then we will not accept it.

MANUSCRIPT FORMAT
- .rtf, .doc, .docx formats ONLY
- 12-point Times New Roman, Cambria, or Palatino fonts ONLY
- 1" (2.54 cm) margins all around
- Double-spaced lines
- DO NOT put an extra space between each paragraph
- Filename: "Submission Title by Jane Q. Writer"

PAYMENT & RIGHTS

We pay $0.05 per word after publication. By submitting to *Shrapnel*, you acknowledge that your work is set in an owned universe and that you retain no rights to any of the characters, settings, or "ideas" detailed in your story. We purchase **all rights** to every published story; those rights are automatically transferred to The Topps Company, Inc.

SUBMISSIONS PORTAL

To send us a submission, visit our submissions portal here:
https://pulsepublishingsubmissions.moksha.io/publication/shrapnel-the-battletech-magazine-fiction

LOOKING FOR MORE HARD HITTING BATTLETECH FICTION?

WE'LL GET YOU RIGHT BACK INTO THE BATTLE!

Catalyst Game Labs brings you the very best in *BattleTech* fiction, available at most ebook retailers, including Amazon, Apple Books, Kobo, Barnes & Noble, and more!

NOVELS

1. *Decision at Thunder Rift* by William H. Keith Jr.
2. *Mercenary's Star* by William H. Keith Jr.
3. *The Price of Glory* by William H. Keith, Jr.
4. *Warrior: En Garde* by Michael A. Stackpole
5. *Warrior: Riposte* by Michael A. Stackpole
6. *Warrior: Coupé* by Michael A. Stackpole
7. *Wolves on the Border* by Robert N. Charrette
8. *Heir to the Dragon* by Robert N. Charrette
9. *Lethal Heritage* (The Blood of Kerensky, Volume 1) by Michael A. Stackpole
10. *Blood Legacy* (The Blood of Kerensky, Volume 2) by Michael A. Stackpole
11. *Lost Destiny* (The Blood of Kerensky, Volume 3) by Michael A. Stackpole
12. *Way of the Clans* (Legend of the Jade Phoenix, Volume 1) by Robert Thurston
13. *Bloodname* (Legend of the Jade Phoenix, Volume 2) by Robert Thurston
14. *Falcon Guard* (Legend of the Jade Phoenix, Volume 3) by Robert Thurston
15. *Wolf Pack* by Robert N. Charrette
16. *Main Event* by James D. Long
17. *Natural Selection* by Michael A. Stackpole
18. *Assumption of Risk* by Michael A. Stackpole
19. *Blood of Heroes* by Andrew Keith
20. *Close Quarters* by Victor Milán
21. *Far Country* by Peter L. Rice
22. *D.R.T.* by James D. Long
23. *Tactics of Duty* by William H. Keith
24. *Bred for War* by Michael A. Stackpole
25. *I Am Jade Falcon* by Robert Thurston
26. *Highlander Gambit* by Blaine Lee Pardoe
27. *Hearts of Chaos* by Victor Milán
28. *Operation Excalibur* by William H. Keith
29. *Malicious Intent* by Michael A. Stackpole
30. *Black Dragon* by Victor Milán
31. *Impetus of War* by Blaine Lee Pardoe
32. *Double-Blind* by Loren L. Coleman

33. *Binding Force* by Loren L. Coleman
34. *Exodus Road* (Twilight of the Clans, Volume 1) by Blaine Lee Pardoe
35. *Grave Covenant* ((Twilight of the Clans, Volume 2) by Michael A. Stackpole
36. *The Hunters* (Twilight of the Clans, Volume 3) by Thomas S. Gressman
37. *Freebirth* (Twilight of the Clans, Volume 4) by Robert Thurston
38. *Sword and Fire* (Twilight of the Clans, Volume 5) by Thomas S. Gressman
39. *Shadows of War* (Twilight of the Clans, Volume 6) by Thomas S. Gressman
40. *Prince of Havoc* (Twilight of the Clans, Volume 7) by Michael A. Stackpole
41. *Falcon Rising* (Twilight of the Clans, Volume 8) by Robert Thurston
42. *Threads of Ambition* (The Capellan Solution, Book 1) by Loren L. Coleman
43. *The Killing Fields* (The Capellan Solution, Book 2) by Loren L. Coleman
44. *Dagger Point* by Thomas S. Gressman
45. *Ghost of Winter* by Stephen Kenson
46. *Roar of Honor* by Blaine Lee Pardoe
47. *By Blood Betrayed* by Blaine Lee Pardoe and Mel Odom
48. *Illusions of Victory* by Loren L. Coleman
49. *Flashpoint* by Loren L. Coleman
50. *Measure of a Hero* by Blaine Lee Pardoe
51. *Path of Glory* by Randall N. Bills
52. *Test of Vengeance* by Bryan Nystul
53. *Patriots and Tyrants* by Loren L. Coleman
54. *Call of Duty* by Blaine Lee Pardoe
55. *Initiation to War* by Robert N. Charrette
56. *The Dying Time* by Thomas S. Gressman
57. *Storms of Fate* by Loren L. Coleman
58. *Imminent Crisis* by Randall N. Bills
59. *Operation Audacity* by Blaine Lee Pardoe
60. *Endgame* by Loren L. Coleman
61. *A Bonfire of Worlds* by Steven Mohan, Jr.
62. *Isle of the Blessed* by Steven Mohan, Jr.
63. *Embers of War* by Jason Schmetzer
64. *Betrayal of Ideals* by Blaine Lee Pardoe
65. *Forever Faithful* by Blaine Lee Pardoe
66. *Kell Hounds Ascendant* by Michael A. Stackpole
67. *Redemption Rift* by Jason Schmetzer

YOUNG ADULT NOVELS

1. *The Nellus Academy Incident* by Jennifer Brozek
2. *Iron Dawn (Rogue Academy, Book 1)* by Jennifer Brozek

OMNIBUSES

1. *The Gray Death Legion Trilogy* by William H. Keith, Jr.

NOVELLAS/SHORT STORIES

1. *Lion's Roar* by Steven Mohan, Jr.
2. *Sniper* by Jason Schmetzer
3. *Eclipse* by Jason Schmetzer
4. *Hector* by Jason Schmetzer
5. *The Frost Advances (Operation Ice Storm, Part 1)* by Jason Schmetzer
6. *The Winds of Spring (Operation Ice Storm, Part 2)* by Jason Schmetzer
7. *Instrument of Destruction (Ghost Bear's Lament, Part 1)* by Steven Mohan, Jr.
8. *The Fading Call of Glory (Ghost Bear's Lament, Part 2)* by Steven Mohan, Jr.
9. *Vengeance* by Jason Schmetzer
10. *A Splinter of Hope* by Philip A. Lee
11. *The Anvil* by Blaine Lee Pardoe
12. *A Splinter of Hope/The Anvil* (omnibus)
13. *Not the Way the Smart Money Bets (Kell Hounds Ascendant #1)* by Michael A. Stackpole
14. *A Tiny Spot of Rebellion (Kell Hounds Ascendant #2)* by Michael A. Stackpole
15. *A Clever Bit of Fiction (Kell Hounds Ascendant #3)* by Michael A. Stackpole
16. *Break-Away (Proliferation Cycle #1)* by Ilsa J. Bick
17. *Prometheus Unbound (Proliferation Cycle #2)* by Herbert A. Beas II
18. *Nothing Ventured (Proliferation Cycle #3)* by Christoffer Trossen
19. *Fall Down Seven Times, Get Up Eight (Proliferation Cycle #4)* by Randall N. Bills
20. *A Dish Served Cold (Proliferation Cycle #5)* by Chris Hartford and Jason M. Hardy
21. *The Spider Dances (Proliferation Cycle #6)* by Jason Schmetzer

ANTHOLOGIES

1. *The Corps (BattleCorps Anthology, Volume 1)* edited by Loren. L. Coleman
2. *First Strike (BattleCorps Anthology, Volume 2)* edited by Loren L. Coleman
3. *Weapons Free (BattleCorps Anthology, Volume 3)* edited by Jason Schmetzer
4. *Onslaught: Tales from the Clan Invasion* edited by Jason Schmetzer
5. *Edge of the Storm* by Jason Schmetzer
6. *Fire for Effect (BattleCorps Anthology, Volume 4)* edited by Jason Schmetzer
7. *Chaos Born (Chaos Irregulars, Book 1)* by Kevin Killiany
8. *Chaos Formed (Chaos Irregulars, Book 2)* by Kevin Killiany
9. *Counterattack (BattleCorps Anthology, Volume 5)* edited by Jason Schmetzer
10. *Front Lines (BattleCorps Anthology Volume 6)* edited by Jason Schmetzer and Philip A. Lee
11. *Legacy* edited by John Helfers and Philip A. Lee
12. *Kill Zone (BattleCorps Anthology Volume 7)* edited by Philip A. Lee
13. *Gray Markets (A BattleCorps Anthology)*, edited by Jason Schmetzer and Philip A. Lee
14. *Slack Tide (A BattleCorps Anthology)*, edited by Jason Schmetzer and Philip A. Lee

Made in the USA
Monee, IL
15 June 2022

98077148R00096